Also by

Tŀ
Fuɪɪ oɪ ɔɪn

For my two ladies, Wiola and Maya.

And in memory of my father, Zsolt Vadaszffy, a true Hungarian gentleman whose world-class fencing skills and personality touched so many, and whose far less adventurous exit from Hungary during the Revolution of 1956 inspired me to create this story.

Author's Note

As you read this story of the past coming back to haunt a person's present, I hope you gain a better understanding of the world of fencing and the events of the Hungarian Revolution of 1956.

I'm particularly indebted to Victor Sebestyen's fantastic book, *Twelve Days* (Phoenix, 2007), which gives a detailed day-by-day account of those days of pain and heartbreak. I recommend it to everyone eager to gain a fuller understanding of the history of Hungary's second great revolution.

Readers who already know about the Hungarian Revolution and those with an understanding of Budapest (in particular the New Public Cemetery) and fencing will likely recognise where I have made changes and steered away from reality for dramatic effect. I hope I'll be forgiven for imposing dramatic licence on the story.

Sins of the Father is also written in memory of former Hungarian Prime Minister Imre Nagy, who tried relentlessly to bring the Revolution to a peaceful conclusion and did so with blind faith in his Russian superiors. He was executed on 16 June 1958 and then reburied with full honours on the same day in 1989.

As seen on this book's cover, the Hungarian flag is a horizontal tricolour of red, white and green. It has been used as it is known today, a tricolour with no coat of arms, since 1 October 1957. From mid-1948, the Russian symbol, the red star, began appearing on buildings throughout the country and an addition was made to the national flag. The emblem designed by the nineteenth-century revolutionary hero, Lajos Kossuth, was changed to a Soviet-style hammer and sickle. On Tuesday 23 October 1956, amid a march to the Technological University, someone in the crowd created one of the most powerful symbols of the Revolution: by cutting out the hammer and sickle from the centre of the flag, a new flag, with 'a hole in its heart', as Victor Sebestyen describes it, was created. This, we have tried to highlight through the inclusion of the flag with a hole in its heart on the book cover.

Karl Vadaszffy, April 2014, Hertfordshire

Glossary of Fencing Terms Used in this Novel

Balestra: a forward jump, typically followed by an attack such as a lunge or fleche.

Counter-attack: an attack made in response to an opponent's attack, to take the right-of-way.

Croisé: an action in which the opponent's blade is forced into the high or low line on the same side.

En garde: the stance that fencers assume when preparing to fence.

Fleche: an attack in which the aggressor leaps off his leading foot, attempts to make a hit and then passes the opponent at a run.

Froissement: an attack that displaces the opponent's blade by using a strong grazing action.

Lunge: an attack made by extending the rear leg and landing on the bent front leg.

Octave: a type of parry, the blade down and to the outside, the wrist supinated.

Parry: a block of an attack, made with the forte of one's own blade.

Piste: the strip on which a fencing bout is fought, it is approximately 2m wide and 14m long.

Plastron: a partial jacket worn under the main jacket on the weapon-arm side of the body for extra protection.

Quarte: a type of parry, the blade up and to the inside, the wrist supinated.

Quinte: a type of parry, the blade up and to the inside, the wrist pronated.

Riposte: a hit made immediately after a parry.

Salle: a fencing hall or club.

Sixte: a type of parry, the blade up and to the outside, the wrist supinated.

Fight duels on all occasions, the more so because duels are forbidden and consequently it takes twice as much courage to fight them.

Alexandre Dumas

And each man stands with his face in the light Of his own drawn sword, ready to do what a hero can.

Elizabeth Barrett Browning

A sword never kills anybody; it is a tool in the killer's hand.

Lucius Annaeus Seneca

Fencing is like a physical game of chess.

Zsolt Vadaszffy, under-18 European Champion, Hungarian National Foil Champion, three-time Eastern Section (UK) Foil Champion, three-time Hertfordshire (UK) Epée Champion, five-time British Professional Epée Champion, and under-20 British Olympic Foil team coach.

Prologue

It's Wednesday evening. I know where she goes on Wednesday evenings. Every Monday, too.

I've been watching her for the past month, tracking her every move, working out her pattern of movement and behaviour. I have to get this right, can afford no errors, as once I start there's no going back. Nothing can stop me.

No one can stop what is about to begin.

Once what I've done becomes clear, one of them will try to stop me. He will fight valiantly, no doubt, but to no avail, for I have planned this to the smallest detail, for no one will see it coming, nor will they understand where it is going.

She emerges from the building just after half-past nine, stepping into the light of the darkness. My heart skips a beat. Finally, the moment has arrived.

This is the start. This is what I've been preparing to do for so long now.

The road is well illuminated. She walks along the path, pulling her bag along on its wheels, heading for the underground station. She passes the pub that sits at the end of the road – not going in tonight, which means things will happen sooner rather than later – and waits for the traffic light to turn red.

I come to a halt right next to her. She's never seen me before, so what's the harm now, especially at this late stage? I'm so close I could touch her. I want to but don't. I don't look directly at her but turn my eyes so that I can see the front part of her face. She's none the wiser of my presence, of who I am, of what I intend to do. She looks content, probably thinking about the evening's successes. She could be whistling a happy tune, ignorant of what's to come.

The light turns green for pedestrians, so we both cross the road. I'm tempted to walk side by side with her all the way to the station, to reach out and hook my arm in hers, to skip happily, eagerly, but she can't become suspicious. So I stride ahead of her, merely a stranger, just another body in the street, rushing through a London street, knowing exactly where she's heading to.

I'm soon out of view and reach the curved steps that lead down to the underground station. I descend, passing the odd red tiles, and move quickly to the entry barrier. I already have a ticket, insert it into the machine and head straight to the platform. *Her* platform.

She reaches the platform only a few minutes after me. I can see her, despite the masses of people who fill the space between us. I've taken a seat on a green steel bench towards the far end of the platform. I watch as she slowly walks along it towards where I'm sitting, sifting her way through the crowd, steering the awkwardly sized bag. She stops about fifteen yards away from me. Now, just a handful of people are between where she stands and where I sit.

I don't need to get on the same carriage as her, so when the train arrives, only about two minutes later, I casually board and sit down. I know when she's getting off, after all.

I cross my legs and pretend to read a newspaper that I find lying on the seat next to me. That seat is quickly filled by the large bulk of a person who may be male, may be female, and smells insanely bad. I do all I can to ignore the odour and allow my thoughts to replay what I've been planning for the past month. I visualise what I'm going to do, how it's going to happen, step by step, moment by moment, blow by blow.

As we move away from the centre of London, the carriage becomes emptier and fewer people embark. The colossus, my neighbour, gets off. A couple remain sitting opposite me with their tongues down one another's throats. An elderly Chinese woman remains sitting three seats to my left. Four scruffy teenagers enter and stand in the centre of the carriage. They make noises, guffawing apparently at nothing, shaking their heads along to whatever's blasting through their headphones, scratching, sniffing, spitting. Irritating me. I look closely at them, eye them carefully, wish for them to make eye contact. All piercings and dyed black hair and fake nails and fake fucking eyelashes. One of the boys has got so much chewing gum in his mouth he looks like he's sucking on a tennis ball. I want to make him swallow it, choke on it.

No, I need to avoid them and remain focused. I turn to my right, try to see through the carriage that separates her from me, and smile. When I visualise her and what's to come – not just tonight but in the coming days – excitement starts to fill me, so much that I have to sit on my hands to prevent myself from grabbing hold of one of the scruffy shits nearby and smashing his head through a window for the sheer delight I'll get from exerting myself.

Calmly. Soon.

The train journey lasts thirty minutes. I don't get off

3

straightaway, give her time to pass my carriage on her way out of the station and then step onto the platform as the doors are about to close. She's making her way up the staircase towards the exit as I emerge and then I begin my slow walk after her.

When I leave the underground station, she's on the other side of the road and trotting now as rain spits on our faces. I place my hands in my coat pockets, lift up my hood and follow, cautiously this time and at a reasonable distance.

The high street for a hundred yards. I'm careful to keep close to the main road, as far from the row of shops and security cameras that adorn their doorways. Then a right turn as the area becomes residential. Houses, a road, a central reservation that's filled with bushes, a road on the other side and more houses beyond it. Fifty yards along and she crosses over. A right turn into a smaller residential street. A left turn followed by another right where the road opens up into a foyer-like car park. Beyond it, some grass and then Chistle Gardens, an old mansion house, now apartments.

She's already inside the building when Chistle Gardens comes into my view. I stand before it, ignoring the rain, looking at the building, imagining what's inside waiting for me. Imagining her and what it will feel like.

It will be my first time. But it won't be my last.

I step back and retreat to the car I parked earlier in a nearby street. From its boot, I retrieve a pair of leather gloves, which I put on, my tools and a box about shoulder width in length and half that size in height. It fits firmly, securely, in my grasp, central to my body, like a battering ram held out in front of me.

I walk slowly, very slowly, towards Chistle Gardens and walk around the building, following a pathway to the back entrance where I know I'll find the door that's used by residents to access a large shared recreational space. Locks aren't a challenge for me – growing up, I mastered how to find my way in and out of places that strangers weren't welcome – so using a lockpick and torque wrench, I get the door open and am inside in around three minutes.

It's not my first time outside the building and it's not my first time inside either. I know the quickest way to her apartment door.

Apartment 3c.

Once there, I knock. I'm sure she looked through the spy hole, so, with the hood still on to cover my hair and the box lifted to conceal the lower part of my face, in the most pleasant tone I can muster I say, 'Package dropped off for you earlier.'

I hear a chain rattle and a lock unlock. When she pulls the door back and shows her face, I lower the box a fraction, give her a quick wide grin and then, with all the force I can generate, I use the box, which I've weighed down with hardback books, as a battering ram, hitting it hard against the door and her body, and charge forwards. The door collides with a doorstop, reverberating too loudly, and she falls back to the carpet. I slam the door shut, drop the box and grab her by the hair as she half crawls, half runs deeper into the hallway, trying desperately to get away from my reach. I twist her round with ease and place an arm around her neck, my other arm holding on to the arm that she's desperately trying to strike me with over her shoulder. I push her, face-first, against the front door. As I press her body against it, I lock the door and then I drag her deeper into the hallway. She reaches out to the wall, her fingernails scraping along it as I drag her.

As we're halfway down the corridor, I strike her on the base of the skull, disorientating her, and pull her into the living room. I throw her towards an armchair. She collides with the back of it, tipping it over, and falls down. I step towards her and, as she tries to stand, I kick her in the face, sending her falling behind the sofa. Then I crouch down and I hit her again in the face, and then again.

When I see she's not going to get up, I go back to the box that I dropped near the front door. I remove a glove, lift the tape that holds the lid shut and see what will be my calling card. What I must use. Both the act and the message are important.

I put the glove back on, lift my offering out of the box and return to find her stirring. I crush my foot on her sternum, one quick, hard blow, and then I place it between both hands, lift it high into the air, look at it for a long moment, thinking about the havoc it will wreak, the surprise it will garner and the clues it will offer. Then, using all the force in my body, I bring it crashing down upon her, again and again and again.

This is the moment, the moment when we will begin the journey of vengeance, and the endgame will only be arrived at when I say that moment has come.

I know when that moment will be. I already know everything.

Part One: En Garde

England

Chapter One

'En garde.'

The words echo. All that fills the air is silent anticipation, but the words manage to echo in my mind. They always do. I hear nothing else. Utter concentration, complete focus.

En garde. *In other words, get ready.*

En garde. *Speaking to me, urging me: prepare yourself.*

En garde. *It's so simple: remain calm, deep breaths. In through the nose, out of the mouth.*

We face each other, ten feet apart. We raise our blades, bring them swiping down against the still air, a salute, a symbol of respect. The most important thing to remember about fencing is that it's a sport in which respect for the opponent is at the core.

Masks on, the view now through tiny black crisscrossed wires, like steel gauze consuming the front of the head. It's the only material protection between the blade and the face. The only other protection – the most important – is the competitor's skill in defending himself.

Deep breaths, bend the knees and crouch down, low, to stretch the hamstrings, then leap up and back onto the feet. Small jumps from side to side, press the nimble button. A stretch of the shoulders.

Three steps forwards as the official, or president, calls, 'Ready.'

My opponent steps a bit closer. We're eight feet apart now. He's tall, much bigger than me, but I've got speed, the kind he's never seen before. And did I mention confidence?

We move, in tandem, into the en garde position: feet

shoulder width apart, front foot facing forwards, back foot at ninety degrees, creating a reverse L position for the right-handed. Knees bent, low, weight centred. Left arm – the back arm – up in the air, with elbow slightly bent to help keep balance, while the leading arm, my right, semi-extends as if pointing a gun, elbow slightly bent and tucked in. Like a Nike tick.

We're ready.

'Allez.' The call to fence.

As expected, the bigger man, over-confident because of his superior size, comes charging towards me. I'm ready for him, of course, jump back as he lunges towards me, block the blade with a short, sharp movement to the left – a simple parry quarte, the blade's tip pointed towards the outside edge of the top of his leading shoulder – and then riposte, a direct hit.

First point, that easy.

I hear him swear. The mask might be able to cover the eyes, it might be able to hide visible signs of anger, but it doesn't shield sound and all the telling things revealed by it. I can tell that although we've only just begun, I've pissed him off already. Perfect. Now he'll come at me twice as hard; he won't be able to keep his anger at bay, and I know that the more I defend and strike back, the more frustration he'll feel. More frustration means more fury and force, which inevitably leads to more mistakes. It's typical of the big guys: miss once, then give it more power, push harder. But, sorry, you'll miss again if you do that.

No matter how much force he applies to each attack, he won't be fast enough.

We return to our en garde positions.

'Ready,' the president calls.

Knees bent, arms in position. Blade only partially

extended. Weight slightly forwards this time, totally concealed of course, preparing to pounce.

'Allez.'

I hold back, wait for his initial move. His engine is on full. He powers at me, a human barricade on the move.

When he gets close, a side step combined with a fleche – a short, sharp burst of movement forwards, like a mini-sprint that covers only a couple of metres – surprises him, and I've hit and gone past him before he can so much as blink.

This time, he shouts, cursing himself loudly. I laugh to myself. I feel like saying to him, 'You're all too predictable, calm down', but I don't. Because winners don't give advice.

I need to win. I have to win every fight.

For five further points, he tries the same thing: quick and heavy, plodding attacks . And I pick him off every time. He hasn't even connected with my blade yet.

On the sixth point, finally, he's learned his lesson, seen sense. He stays back when we hear the call of 'Allez.'

So, now, it's my turn to be proactive. I take a small step forwards. He takes a large step back. I repeat, exaggerating my movements, toying with him. He responds in the same way to each of my advances. But then I go for it, and now he's not expecting it. Four quick steps, all small, always small, a balestra (a short, sharp jump forwards) as I feint sixte – to just below the shoulder on my right side – and then I sneak around his blade with a disengage, connecting with the right side of his chest.

Seven-love. We'll be at fifteen in no time.

Each time he attacks, I defend or counter-attack. When he stays back, I thank him for the invitation and move in without hesitation. He doesn't see where I place the blade until he peers down at it connecting with the jacket he's wearing for protection.

And then we're at fourteen-love. On 'Allez', he comes forwards. I step back as he inches towards me, still eager to get closer despite the drumming he's receiving. I maintain the ideal distance between us: eight feet. And even though he's advancing on me, there's a touch of resistance in his step, he's unable to conceal it; his body language is defeatist, he's scared. Plus, I've got the score margin on my side, so I decide to end it with the kind of hit that will get everyone on their feet.

He's slowly pushing me towards the back of the piste. I won't go off the end – would forfeit a point if I did – but I'll make him think he might be able to push me off. Right at the last moment, with only centimetres to spare, I freeze. My sudden lack of movement in retreat surprises him. It's only for an instant, but it's enough.

He realises what he's done, that he's left himself with no choice but to go for it now, so he lunges at me – his arm extends fully, his leading leg rises and he pushes off his back leg. He aims to hit me low, somewhere above the groin, and his front foot crashes down on the floor.

And this is when I do it.

I jump backwards, a small leap to create only centimetres between my body and his fully extended arm and blade. In that position, he's stuck, immobile, with nowhere to go. As I'm in the air, I raise my hand and wrist so that they're at a right angle to the rest of my arm. I extend my arm up and forwards and flick my wrist. The tip of my blade goes over his shoulder and lands on his upper back before my feet land on the ground, off the end of the piste. But I've hit him before I leave the piste, so it doesn't matter.

It's spectacular, over in only a second, but it receives rapturous applause from the couple of hundred people who are looking on. I've not noticed them till now, finally out of the zone, the match over.

I snatch off my mask, raise my arms in the air, absorb the ovation, the lauding faces that are everywhere.

He removes his mask. I can see embarrassment in his eyes; he knows I was showing off on that last point and he was helpless to do anything about it.

We shake hands, his eyes aimed at the ground. I feel smug. I look round to see my brother and father. I notice my brother, in the distance, walking out of the gymnasium. My father is standing near the end of my side of the piste. He's clapping his hands, has a warm smile on his face.

As I turn back to look at my defeated opponent, everything turns blue. My hand is still holding his. I shrink. My shoulders hunch forwards, I start coughing and my stomach aches. I feel like I'm bleeding inside.

With my head pointed at the ground, I realise that the gymnasium floor is no longer under my feet. The applause has died away. My father has disappeared. The spectators, too. I crumble onto cold tarmac, rubble all around me, his hand still in mine. It's freezing – the hand and the air. As I exhale, steam surrounds me. My body's shaking. I look down at the hand that's in my grasp. It's been severed from the body it belongs to.

And then the body is attached to it. A young man, his neck flooded with blood. A gurgling sound – he's drowning – and, in only seconds, lifeless eyes.

And then he dissolves into nothingness. In his place, a different face appears. It looks shocked, betrayed. And then he dissolves, and there's a third face. Her face. I'm holding it, my palms on her cheeks. So beautiful. It's her head and then it's attached to her body, which appears on the ground to the *side of me.*

I look to my left. There's blood everywhere, all over her clothes, all over the ground.

I look down at her face. She's mouthing words to me, but I can't make out what she's saying. I want to speak to her, comfort her, but my mouth is tied shut.

I close my eyes tightly, wish the moment away. But it's still here. She's still here.

She's not going to survive.

I open my eyes. A woman's lifeless body lies in front of me, her head in my lap. I scream but can't make a sound.

*

Shuddering. It was so cold, the lungs stung. Desperate gasps for air were painful.

József Varga opened his eyes. His body was covered in sweat, a stinging heat emanated from him and he was breathing heavily, but he was shivering. He'd been sleeping through the dream, enduring it, for almost fifty years, but the effect it had on him had never let up; it was still so powerful that it crushed him, made his chest shrink.

He sat up slowly. Despite the excellent level of fitness he possessed, his sixty-six-year-old body needed more time than it used to for the completion of menial tasks, for movements that for so many years his sprightly physique had managed with ease.

He sat on his side of the bed, his arms pushing down into the mattress. *Relax*, he encouraged himself in thought. *Relax. In through the nose, out of the mouth.* It was a technique that still worked a treat. He just needed some time to feel its effects.

He wiped the sweat from his forehead and looked over at the dressing table. Everything was still set out as before, when Maureen was here. Her hairbrush, her jewellery box, her hairdryer. And in the centre of the table, in a frame, their wedding photo. The year was 1969. Black and white, showing signs of age. She in his arms, clinging on as if she never wanted to let go.

But she let go. Two years, it had been. Two years since he'd watched cancer eat away at her cells, overpower her, drag her from him. Two years apart after thirty-seven years together. The worst two years of his life.

He smiled as his eyes met his wife's, but it lasted only a moment. Re-adopting the cool and composed Hungarian persona, he shook his head to knock away the emotion of the dream and the memory of his wife's illness, and he stood up and went into the bathroom to prepare for the day ahead. He put on the shower to allow time for the water to warm up while he emptied his bladder.

Stinging. No doubt he'd held the urine in there for too long again. A lingering pain, it would be with him for the next hour at least.

After showering, József glided over his face with a Phillips electric shaver. He was careful, despite being in his seventh decade, to take pride in his appearance, even though he might not see anyone he knew till the evening when he went to teach.

A man of great pride, another Hungarian trait he'd never leave behind.

He coached fencing, was still fit and able. It's a skill that never leaves an individual, not one as blessed in ability as József. Yes, he was physically less able than in his younger years, unable to move as quickly as before, the aches and pains failing to disappear after forty-eight hours' rest, but the speed and accuracy of his hand movements were as impressive as they'd ever been. *You never lose the eye for it*, he'd told countless students, who were always amazed by his skills and activeness in what for most people are the years of retirement. *As long as I can see, no one will be able to find a way around my hand.*

Indeed, when his son was a child, he'd spent many a moment amusing young Michael and his friends, holding a pen and telling them to take it from him. József's arm wouldn't move; just his fingers and wrist as he went from quarte to sixte, from the left to the right, avoiding the young boys' clasping fingers no matter how hard they tried to take the pen away from him. No one had ever succeeded.

Fencing is in my blood, he regularly said to his students to conclude a conversation that had become stale, it had occurred so frequently. He'd repeated the response so many times, but it still got a chuckle from his audience, ever expectant, ever waiting, ever keen. *They'll be prising the foil from my corpse before I give it up.*

That always resulted in a laugh, but as he got older the realisation that life was ticking away left a bitter and unpleasant taste. He didn't openly show his feelings about mortality, of course; that would be to express too much, to demonstrate frailty, something he wasn't capable of – no, something he wasn't willing to allow to happen. More of the Hungarian in him.

Shaved, Aramis aftershave patted onto his cheeks and neck, and dressed, József made his way downstairs. There was certainly a stiffness to his movements, he couldn't deny it, but he wouldn't let that stop him. With each step, the pain still lingered in his groin. Nothing unusual, though. It didn't concern him. Besides: *It'll go soon*, he thought.

The daily newspaper was on the hallway floor, so he picked it up and went into the kitchen, flicking on the kettle switch when he reached it. As it came to the boil, he put two slices of bread into the toaster. When they were ready, he applied to them a thin layer of butter, aware of the need to keep his cholesterol levels low, filled his mug with coffee, and went into the dining room. He sat down, placed the newspaper on the table in front of him, the mug on a coaster, and began eating the toast as he read the front page.

The toast finished and the coffee halfway there, he heard today's post land in the hallway. He didn't go for it immediately. First, he finished drinking his coffee and worked his way through the rest of the day's news stories. He'd save the sports pages for lunchtime.

József went into the hallway and picked up the post. Four letters, some leaflets advertising conservatories and window cleaners, and a medium-sized brown padded envelope. *Postmark: Budapest.* Strange, unusual. He wasn't expecting anything from the few friends he had who still resided in Hungary. The majority of the family he'd had there had died, except István and his brother, and he wasn't really in touch with his sibling; an occasional Christmas telephone conversation hardly counted.

Capital letters written in black ink, no return address.

József took the post into the lounge. He sat on the settee and placed the post on the coffee table, except for the brown envelope, which he kept in his hands. He

17

turned it over and tore open the sealed end.

He placed a hand inside it. Cold. Sharp. Gritty.

He clasped what it contained, removed it. A piece of metal. Part of a blade. A foil, in fact, he recognised instantly, the smallest of fencing's three weapons. It was the tip end, about four inches in length, and it had been snapped from the main body of the foil. In the middle of the blade was a piece of paper. The blade had pierced through the paper.

József lifted the paper over the end of the blade and saw there was some writing on it. He looked around the room for his reading glasses, saw them on the mantelpiece. He placed the blade on the coffee table and took the paper with him as he retrieved his glasses. He opened the case, removed them, snapped the case shut. The glasses on, he looked down at the piece of paper. His eyes squinted, despite the use of glasses.

Confusing.

It ends only with you.

The words didn't mean anything to him. But the blade had pierced the paper in the centre of the circle in the middle letter of *you*. The *O*. Bizarre. What could it mean? Was it a threat of some kind?

Over the years, he'd upset a lot of people. You don't become an internationally successful athlete without crushing a lot of people's dreams along the way. And the kind of commitment that's needed, many people see it as selfishness. It wasn't only competitors he'd upset along the way; some of those close to him had been hurt, too.

It ends only with you.

It? What could that be?

József exhaled through his nose. He had no idea.

His head remained lowered towards the sheet, but his eyes travelled towards the blade that sat on the coffee table.

Blades break in fights all the time. They break in training, too. And when they snap, they become sharp. Famously, once a competitor was killed when a blade snapped. His opponent lunged at him, the blade connected with the mask, bent and snapped. The momentum drove the snapped blade through the mask and impaled the fencer's face. He died instantly.

Such danger, and so close.

Chapter Two

'Leaving early today?' Detective Constable Sally Davison asks.

'Training tonight,' Michael says.

'Oh, yes,' she beams. 'The swashbuckling adventurer.'

'If you want to call it that, then yes, got it in one.'

'I've heard people talking about it,' she says casually, sitting next to Michael on the bench in the staff changing room, while he puts on his trainers. He's wearing his black-and-white custom-made Salle Worth tracksuit. The club's logo is on the back of the jacket: the shape of a fencer extending a blade, knees bent, in red. 'Tell me about it.'

Michael stops and makes eye contact with her. He's noted her good looks before: green eyes, smooth skin, shoulder-length brown hair, slim figure, shapely in what he thinks are the right places. 'Well, what do you want to know?'

'What do you do?'

'I coach,' Michael says nonchalantly. He's found that acting coolly always impresses women more than bragging. 'But I still fight. I can hold my own after all this time. Can still frustrate the teenagers who are desperate to beat their maestro.'

'Maestro?'

'Yeah, it's like a title. You'd say master in English. Kind of like sensei in karate. It's a sign of respect for achievements in competition and skill.'

'So what have you won?'

'I was British Foil team champion twice. And epée once.'

'What's the difference?'

'Foil's the smallest blade. The target's the lamé, which is the electric jacket you wear. The target doesn't include the arms or the hands, the legs or the mask. Epée's the biggest blade, heavier. The guard – that's the circular bit of metal that encloses the grip and keeps your hand protected – that's larger because the hand is a target in epée, as is the whole body, from mask to foot.'

'How long have you been fencing?'

Michael thinks deeply, or at least pretends to, like he's never been asked before. 'Since I was ten, so that's… twenty-two years.'

Sally gets up and swipes her arms from side to side, her hair swaying in opposite directions. Wild, exaggerated movements. 'So how's my technique?'

Michael recognises his opportunity. The invitation – or he thinks it is.

Smiling and laughing, he gets up and walks behind her. Slowly. Wants to see if she is actually inviting him in. 'Here,' he says, taking her by the wrist with his right hand and pressing onto her left hip with his left hand. 'Hold your hand like this and bend your knees.' He applies downwards pressure onto her hip. 'Bend,' in a whisper. Her breathing deepens. She bends her knees, and her backside presses into him. He inhales, likes how she smells.

'So none of that swiping stuff then?'

'No. That's sabre you're thinking of, only it's not done wildly like that anyway. Movies. They distort everything. See, everything in fencing is about *small* movements,

21

especially with the hands. Like this.' He wiggles her hand around. 'Loosen. Relax. It's all in the fingers, minimal wrist.' And he demonstrates with his own wrist and fingers how to move a weapon.

'No pirate stuff then?'

'Not quite, no. I'm afraid not. No swinging from ropes either.'

'So what's sabre?'

'You have a large guard because, again, the hand's a target. And the rest of the target is everything above the waist, the mask included. The hits are done differently and the en garde position – that's the stance you use to balance – is slightly different, too.'

She touches his shoulder and keeps her hand there. Michael smiles into her eyes.

'Do you use a sabre?'

'No, I focused on the other two. Not many people can manage one weapon, let alone two.' He hesitates. 'My father's one of the rare exceptions.'

'Your father?'

'Yeah. He's a Maître d'Armes.' There's an attempt at dismissiveness in his tone, although he knows when he explains it it'll impress her, and at the moment that's important. But only at the moment.

'What's that mean?'

He sits back down and ties his trainer laces. 'Master of all *three* weapons. Master of Arms. The ultimate fencing master.' He gazes up at her and, with a wink, says, 'Me, I can only kill you with two blades.'

She sniggers and sits next to him again.

He sees an entry. Michael makes it clear he's thinking, then he says, 'Look, training finishes at ten. How about meeting for a drink afterwards?'

*

Michael arrives at St James's School for the evening's training a little before 6PM. After parking his car, a two-year-old Renault Megane, he pops into the newsagent across the road, buys an isotonic drink, and takes it into the school's gymnasium. Here he goes to a coffee machine and purchases a cup.

The mandatory warm-up session is due to start at half-past six, with combat beginning an hour later. He always makes sure there's time for a coffee before club begins.

Michael's warm-up is a gruelling challenge for everyone who attends, whether they are new to the club or old-timers: forty-five minutes of bashing each of the major muscle groups. It's adapted from his father's warm-up, itself a thing renowned in the fencing world.

Adapted is perhaps a loose term; it's almost a carbon copy. Jogging, mixed with interval sprinting, moves into in-motion stretches, static stretches, arm work, leg work, ground work, races, then finally lunge practice, with other footwork skills mixed in.

The club fills up slowly, but by half-past six over forty people have arrived, almost at capacity for the venue.

Michael's father's club, Salle Victory, on the other side of town, draws almost double that number nightly, a record for London, in fact a record for the UK, but Michael's is a healthy and growing club nonetheless. He doesn't have his father's reputation, not yet, but he's doing well in the capital's fencing establishment.

23

As people arrive, they greet their maestro, who sits in a corner of the gym. There isn't a moment when Michael is alone. Women are particularly drawn to him, women of all ages. He exudes a coolness, a confidence, and they've seen his skills, observed him as he's given lessons, watched him closely when he's taken to the piste. He impresses them, and he barely has to try.

At six thirty-five, after finishing the last mouthful of coffee, Michael blows his whistle to signal the start of the warm-up. It doesn't take long before a lot of faces look strained, but it's a test of fitness that, over time, increases the condition of the participants to brand-new levels, and then they're thankful.

The jogging begins before Michael even gets up from his seat. He smirks when he sees some of the men struggling, and winks at one of the young blondes as she saunters past.

He's slept with several of the women here and many who are no longer members. He didn't have to try hard to get their attention; he's not bad looking and his success and skills create an allure. It's not every day that someone meets a fencer of great ability.

Twenty-five minutes later, the footwork part of the warm-up begins. Michael stands in the middle of the gym, the fencers lined up on two opposite sides, half in front and half behind him, in the en garde stance. He maintains a grounded stance. One step forwards from him, they move backwards. One step backwards, they move forwards. The speed and number of steps quickly increase and the movements intensify. Left arm raised and it's a lunge. Right arm and it's a balestra lunge. Steps and lunges mixed together, the speed varying.

It doesn't take long for several of the fencers to start making mistakes, stepping forwards when they should have stepped backwards or vice versa. Even quicker come the laughs of embarrassment when they realise their stepping skills are lacking.

Then Michael makes it more complicated. A blow of the whistle means jump back, jump forwards, lunge. And the stepping becomes even faster. More and more fencers falter. The fitness of others fails them as they have to lunge, recover, step forwards, step backwards, lunge, recover, balestra lunge, recover. The sequence of moves pounds the knees, sucks the oxygen from the lungs, pushes balance over the edge.

And, suddenly, when the fencers least expect it, instead of telling them to recover from the lunge, Michael yells 'Fleche', and a short, sharp burst of energy, from an already stretched forward position, is required. The fleche, an attack in which the aggressor leaps off his leading foot, attempts to make a hit and then passes his opponent at a run, takes the fencers to the other side of the gym so that the lines swap sides.

A countdown of twenty-five lunges comes next, to conclude the warm-up. Simply five sets of five lunges in a row, counted down by Michael, the lunge held, the arm remaining extended, until Michael calls for recovery. Sometimes the countdown remains at a constant speed. Sometimes it speeds up. Sometimes Michael slows it down, teasingly, devastating the people before him, their desperation for it to end too obvious, perhaps an entertainment for him.

He still remembers being in their shoes.

At twenty-one, the lunge is held, the arm extended.

Michael stands still. He does nothing. As arms become heavy and fencers look like they'll succumb, have to give up and recover, Michael calls, 'Hold it', and observes faces even more strained than they were when the jogging was taking place. But they have to hold their extended arms still, keep their legs bent. It's like torture, sports' equivalent to waterboarding.

He sees signs of exhaustion, but he won't let them give in, pushes them, constantly challenges, gets angry if necessary, for that's how to demand perfection. And that is what was demanded of him. It's the expectation of perfection, he believes, that makes the best be the best, that separates champions from wannabes and almost-weres.

When he's toyed with them enough, Michael shouts 'Twenty', which commences each fencer's movements from one side of the gym to the other, one balestra lunge after another, until they reach the other side. It takes about ten to cover the distance.

Then, when on the other side of the gym, only a moment is given for everyone to catch their breath, to get ready for the next five lunges, which will, of course, be far more than five.

Twenty-five lunges? By the time Michael has finished with this exercise, they'll have done seventy. Another gift from his father: always demand more.

The next five lunges completed, Michael calls for a sequence of moves. 'Step forwards. Step back. Two steps forwards. Two steps back. Three steps forwards. Three steps back. Three steps forwards. Balesta lunge. Recover. Two steps back. Balestra lunge. Recover. Jump back. Two steps forwards. Balestra lunge. Recover. Balestra lunge.

Jump back. Lunge. Jump back. Lunge. Recover. Balestra lunge. Fleche!'

And the fencers are back in position, ready for the next five lunges, most bent double, gasping for air.

Similar delay tactics, which carefully ensure fencers are practising moves they'll need to use in only a split second's notice in a match situation, are employed by Michael until he reaches the countdown to the final five lunges.

Of course, five still won't be enough. When they get to the final lunge, Michael lifts the whistle to his lips. 'The last lunge,' he says, scripted, to the exhausted men and women, '*has* to be the fastest.' And before anyone has the time to prepare, he blows the whistle. Only a few react. 'Not fast enough!' he calls out. 'Again: one. Get ready.'

This time all the fencers are ready, poised to take off, their knees bent deep, their faces stained with concentration. Despite their exhausted bodies desperate for the torment to stop, their minds fight on. That's half the battle with fencing.

'Use your mind,' Michael's father would tell him time and again when he was a child. 'Remember, fencing is like a physical game of chess. Your body has to respond to your brain, which has to think carefully. The decision has to be the right one and you have almost no time to think.'

So the fencers are poised.

So what?

Michael waits. He doesn't blow the whistle. He builds the sense of anticipation. Looks like he's about to blow the whistle. Teases them. It's little more than a moment before one of the fencers giggles. That makes another one laugh. Then another.

And that's when their concentration is broken. And that's the moment Michael's been waiting for. He blows the whistle. Half the participants don't move.

'Come on!' he calls. 'You've got to be ready for anything.'

This goes on for a few more minutes, before Michael announces that the perfect final lunge has been executed. 'Good stuff,' he says. 'Now, let's get the gear out.'

Michael watches as exhausted fencers glug water and isotonic drinks, sit down, some stretched out flat. A few chew vigorously on bananas. It's a challenging sport, most unlike any other sport that people who take it up have encountered before. But it's one they quickly fall in love with.

The difference between Michael and these people is that he was born into fencing. It's in his blood. His father made him pick up his first blade at age ten, a year younger that he had himself held the steel, when at the age of eleven he'd convinced his parents in Hungary to permit him to start fencing; the young József had watched his brother, Ákos, two years his senior, start and wanted desperately to best him on the piste.

It took József only two years to do just that. And then, by the age of sixteen, he had become Hungarian Foil Champion, beating men, in some cases eight years older than he had been.

So, for Michael, it had never been a choice. The blade had been thrust into his hand at ten, training three times a week had become a routine and he was pushed into believing he could achieve extraordinary things in the mask, with the blade in his hand.

And he did. Two British team foil championship titles and one in épée proved that, but it had taken him nine years what it had taken his father five years to achieve with regard to a national title. And it had only ever been in a team situation; he hadn't achieved in singles competition even a fraction of what his father had.

He had never managed to match his father's achievements: champion in two weapons and one of the most respected men in fencing in the country, renowned also in his homeland for the achievements of his youth.

When Michael reached twenty-one, he realised he wouldn't make the Olympics, which was the only thing that had kept him going. It was something his father hadn't been able to do – not because of talent and results but because of opportunity.

The relentless training sessions, which had increased from three to five times a week when he was fifteen, had become a thing he repulsed. He pushed on, hopeful to fulfil the Olympic dream, to win the one title that really meant something to him, the one success his father had never managed to have.

But he failed. He wasn't talented enough; good as he was, he wasn't exceptional.

His father, Olympic in standard from a very young age, didn't make it to the Olympics for one unavoidable reason: the Hungarian Revolution of 1956, which resulted in him fleeing the country and eventually settling in the UK. Time was lost as he tried to find work and a way to finance the opportunity to fence in a nation that was new to him and whose language he had to learn.

He offered free lessons in London, but he couldn't train the six days a week he'd become accustomed to while in Hungary; clubs just didn't run that often here.

And then, when he could afford to train, when he showed he was better than everyone he encountered, he decided against going to the Olympics for Great Britain because he, a Hungarian, felt awkward about taking the place of a Brit on the British team. What right, he always asked, did he have to do this, to come in late and crush someone else's dream?

He always finished conversations about his one-time Olympic hopes by saying that even if he had gone he wouldn't have managed to win – that he was good but not *that* good. No one who heard him say this believed a word of it.

Hearing this always made Michael sneer. He knew false modesty when he saw it.

And when Michael couldn't get the individual ranking required to win a place at the Olympics – he could manage as part of a team but saw limited glory in that – he was crushed. He'd almost given up fencing for good when this happened in his early twenties.

But he couldn't deny the feeling of pleasure – a kind of ecstasy – he experienced when physically, psychologically and mentally taking down an opponent.

Coaching seemed like the next logical step when he reached age twenty-eight, even though he was still able to compete. He knew there'd come a day when he'd start to lose more frequently, something no fencer enjoys, especially one so competitive, and he knew the state of coaching in the UK was desperate; only a handful of coaches were the real deal, his father one of them, so he decided to join them. Competing, therefore, became merely for exercise.

Many in the fencing world expected him to join his father's club, Salle Victory, as a junior coach, one day to take over the reins from the great one. But that didn't happen; it wasn't even something he discussed with his father.

Instead, he did the opposite and set up on his own, with Salle Worth, which came with the message that it was *worth* coming to him to learn how to be one of the best. His father saw it as healthy competitiveness – you don't get as far as him without relishing challenges – but Michael found the more energy he put into the club, the more he wanted to lure his father's best fencers towards his own offering.

He's failed, of course – fencers are, in general, incredibly loyal to their coaches – and his club continues to lag well behind his father's not only in numbers, but in successes and high-quality competitors who attend.

Yes, he has a few good fencers, but no one yet who's at the level required to lift trophies. He sees serious talent in one or two of the youngsters, teens he's personally training. But they're still some years off their greatest achievements, and that only with unrelenting commitment, which as a teenager isn't easy to maintain.

Members of the club bring out the electric boxes, spools and ground cables to set up the makeshift pistes that are used to host bouts for the evening. They're set up across the width of the gym. A spool on either side, near the walls, marks the ends of the piste. Ground leads connect each spool to the electric box. The fencers connect, with body wires threaded through their jacket sleeves, to the spools. The body wire plugs into the foil, or épée, or on rare occasions sabre, where the guard meets the grip. This is how a hit to an opponent's electric jacket, or off-target areas including the floor, result in the electric box lighting up. Green and red for a hit, a point scored as a result. A white light for an off target, no point awarded.

Rachel Bradshaw, who acts as the club secretary, collects members' fees for the evening and compiles the list of fencers who want lessons from Michael. She sits on a stool near the entrance, her hair tied back. She's not very tall and she's got a nice figure, well toned from fencing, badminton and volleyball, all of which she takes part in every week.

Michael, who's been attracted to her since they first met around six months ago and flirts with her every time he sees her, winks at her when she tells him who's paid for lessons tonight. He's biding his time with her; he wants to enjoy her physically, has imagined doing so many times, but because she handles the club admin and helps with the finances, he's hesitant. He doesn't want to lose her. His hesitation won't last, though; eventually, he won't be able to control himself.

He offers fifteen- or thirty-minute lessons. He keeps strictly to the times to enable himself to get through what is always an exhaustive list. Different from his father there, who never looks at his watch while he teaches and gives each student far more time than they pay for.

Michael teaches along one end of the hall, using the basketball court tramlines as a footwork guide for his students. Footwork is one of the most important aspects of a fencer's arsenal, so they have a lesson in a straight line and are expected to keep their feet – the whole of the front foot and the heel of the back foot – perfectly on the line. If either comes off, Michael notices, and all action halts until the footwork is sorted. It's a habit he's been taught by his father.

In fact, so important is footwork to his father that earlier in his coaching career he didn't allow a student taking up fencing to hold a weapon for at least six months. During this time, they'd work only on footwork. 'You can't attack or defend if you don't move properly,' he'd say, and it's exactly what he said to young Michael when, at the age of ten, he desperately wanted to get hold of a sword and whack someone with it.

Michael, his father made sure, didn't hold a weapon for a year. Which is why Michael's footwork is perfect.

Michael gives seven lessons over the next two hours. In between lessons, he watches the fights that keep flowing. Yes, he sees some talent. He stands here, nodding his head, pleased. Something will come of all this effort one day.

At the end of the night, Michael goes downstairs and into the changing rooms. A quick shower and then he changes into the clothes he popped home to collect while on his way here. A black shirt and navy blue jeans. Black shoes. He gels his hair neatly into place.

He's going to meet Sally in the pub across the road in ten minutes. Usually, he spends the hour or so following an evening of training in a pub with the club's members – another pub a few minutes' walk from the school. They are a social bunch, fencers, and Michael enjoys his group's company. But for tonight he has different ideas altogether.

As he's approaching the main exit, he encounters Rachel. Her hair is loose and she's looking particularly inviting; there's something about the way a polo shirt clings to a woman's body, especially a taut one, that Michael takes pleasure in. He holds the door open for her and they emerge into the street. A few streetlamps provide mild illumination. The air is breezy.

'Good night?' he asks.

'Lost just one bout.'

He inhales through his teeth, makes a pained expression. 'Next time they better watch out.'

'You got that right.' She laughs. A pause, then, 'Drink?'

'I'd love nothing more, but…' He hesitates, but it's feigned. Inspiring jealousy, he thinks, might be the key here. 'I've got a date.' He says each word slowly.

'Oh,' she replies, smiling. 'Enjoy.'

'I will.' And a wink. 'But next time. Definitely next time.'

'Definitely.'

They go their separate ways. After placing his fencing bag in the boot of his car, Michael walks to the pub.

Sally hasn't arrived yet, so he orders a Jack Daniel's and coke for himself and a glass of white wine with which to welcome her. He chooses a booth towards the side of the pub, which comprises two large rooms separated by a narrow corridor where the toilets are located. There's one bar and that's in the other room. Michael anticipates that this part of the pub will be quieter: only a pool table and a couple of fruit machines nearby. Some of the tables and booths have couples sitting at them. Others are empty. It's a Wednesday night, after all.

Sally arrives within five minutes. She walks in and tucks some of her hair behind her left ear. She has on a stunning one-piece red dress, which hugs her figure perfectly, black shoes, red lipstick, and she carries a small shiny black purse-cum-handbag.

Michael rises. 'You look beautiful,' he says, stepping forwards to kiss her on the cheek as she reaches the table.

She smiles. 'Thanks. You don't look bad yourself.'

'This is nothing. I was going to come in in my fencing garb. That would have looked sharp. You'd have loved it.'

'I'd love to see that.'

Michael grins. 'Maybe I'll give you a lesson one day.'

'Why not. I'll hold you to that.'

'Please,' and he signals the booth and they sit down. 'Pinot grigio,' he says and indicates the glass with his hand.

'Thank you.' She sips it. 'Mm, good choice.'

Michael looks into Sally's eyes. There's something deep there, something he can't identify, but it draws him in, it calls to him. And her skin, it glows in this dim light.

'So why fencing?' she starts.

'Why fencing? You sure you want to talk about *sport*?'

'I'm interested. Why fencing and not football or something like that? That's what you normally hear men bang on about.'

'True. Could make a hell of a lot more money if I'd picked something like football.'

'Oh, that doesn't matter. They can't kill anyone. Just kick a ball around a bloody big field. And they're all dumb.'

'Good point. So, why fencing?' He inhales deeply. 'I didn't really pick fencing; it kind of picked me. Simple answer, really: my father. He started me off when I was ten. I didn't really have a choice. Classic pushy-parent scenario. He was – *is* – an expert, the best, and he wanted to pass his legacy to me. And it worked, to an extent.

35

You know, I don't remember a time when I haven't held a foil or an epée. Even when I didn't want to. As long as I can remember, in fact. So I started when I was ten, won my first junior tournament at fourteen, my first senior at seventeen, then became British Team Champion at nineteen. Managed to repeat that the year later, also with epée that second time.'

'I've always wanted to be good at something. You know, I mean *really* good. To know that when people saw what I was doing they'd be impressed. That all the effort would be noticeable and really mean something to someone, anyone. It must be a nice feeling, to win a championship, to coach people. To be something special.'

He nods and smiles. 'It's not a bad feeling, that's for sure. But then not everyone can look as amazing as you do in that dress. That's a kind of talent, too.'

'Oh, give up. I try, but I've seen real beauty before. Trust me, some women I've seen are truly stunning.'

'Funny,' Michael says, taking a mouthful of his drink, 'stunning's the word I was thinking when you walked in here.'

Sally looks down at the table. Picks up her drink and drinks. 'Oh, stop,' she says, embarrassed.

'Kiss me.' Said slowly, not as a question, not as a demand. Said simply.

For a moment, she keeps her eyes lowered, then she looks up. 'Kiss you?' she says teasingly. Her teeth gleam as her face breaks into a smile.

Michael nods, doesn't say anything else. He leans forwards, his elbows on the table.

She gazes into his eyes. His features are soft, his light brown hair tidy, stubble just beginning to appear on his face. She can smell his aftershave travel towards her as he moves forwards. There's a sweetness to the scent.

As she approaches him, she closes her eyes. Michael keeps his open. Always does. They kiss. First, one soft, brief pressing together of the lips. Then a separation of only centimetres before their lips connect again, this time deeper, longer. Then their mouths open in unison. He massages her tongue with his. Her hands fall into his.

They drift back into their seats.

'Stunning,' Michael repeats.

*

They'd gone back to Sally's place. Michael always prefers it that way. Easy to make a quick exit if one is necessary. It usually has been.

But he hadn't taken off early this morning. After they'd come here and had sex, they'd talked. It was something he usually steered away from. For years, he'd enjoyed the women he'd impressed on the piste, taught or met during training. Enjoyed them too much, sometimes to his detriment.

One of those women cost him his marriage seven years ago. Left him with a son he rarely saw and an ex-wife who hated him. Hated him even more because he said he wouldn't teach his son fencing, that his son shouldn't take it up, or should at least wait until he could truly decide for himself. Fifteen years old, that was when he said he'd consider it, if Ricky wanted to try. Fifteen was the *right* time.

That gave Julianne more fuel to attack him with; he'd given her plenty in the past and it was his fault that approaching a decade later she was still bitter and trying to find further ammunition. But he hadn't really learned from his mistake.

As he lies in Sally's bed, Michael wonders about what's kept him here this morning, what's different this time. At the station yesterday, when they'd begun speaking and he'd invited her for a drink, he'd wanted to sleep with her, but he hadn't thought about anything beyond that; he'd planned, if that were the right word, to act as he usually did, departing early.

But when, last night, they lay exhausted in each other's arms – the time he usually closed his eyes and fell asleep – Sally had started talking, asking him more questions. About himself, about fencing again, about why he'd become a police officer, about why he coached and didn't compete any more even though he was still able to. She'd been genuinely interested in *him*. And her inquisitiveness had quickly convinced him to ask her questions. And her responses had interested him.

She's one of five siblings and smart. She was at Oxford studying law, hoping for a career in criminal law, but she got bored; suddenly, studying didn't excite her any more and, even though she frustrated and shocked her parents, she withdrew from university towards the end of her second year, instead joining the police force.

Smart and determined, she achieved successive promotions, and then, as detective, she moved to Camden after policing in the suburbs didn't bring with it the excitement she was expecting. But now, having experienced that excitement for too long, she craves smaller-town life again, after all the sickness she's witnessed in the city. She knows she'll remain here for years to come, though. She isn't one to quit the life she chose, regardless of the horrors.

Last night, when she spoke, she lay on her side and looked into Michael's eyes. She was studying him, he could tell. Her eyes, in return, were something he found himself getting lost in. The colours around her pupils twinkled.

'Morning,' she says, bringing into the bedroom a tray on which are mugs filled with coffee and plates piled with toast. 'Hope this is okay?'

Michael sits fully upright. 'More than okay. Thank you.'

She places the tray on the bed and spies his naked chest. It's toned – muscular but not excessively so. 'I had a good time with you last night.'

He won't normally say it, won't normally encourage expectation in a woman, not after his years of marriage and the years of conflict resulting from divorce, but something about her manner coerces it out of him. 'Me too.'

She hands him a mug. 'Help yourself,' she says, indicating the toast, and then she leaves the room, saying, 'Won't be a moment.'

She has on a light beige silk nightgown. Her skin is visible through it. As she walks away, Michael's reminded of the shoulders he massaged last night, of the small of the back he ran his tongue along, of the backside he pressed with his fingers. And her legs – long, tanned and smooth. He remembers running his hands up and down them, and he wants to do it again. Strange – a longing of some kind. An unusual feeling.

His beeper sounds. A signal to call the station urgently;

it wouldn't seek him out otherwise.

'Sally,' he calls, 'I've got to call the office. The phone in here okay to use?'

'Sure,' she calls back. An echo in her voice suggests she's in the bathroom.

He lifts the receiver that's by the other side of the bed and dials. 'Michael Varga here.'

He listens intently. Sally walks back into the room, her hair wrapped in a towel.

Michael doesn't move as he takes note of every word. To conclude the call, he says, 'Thanks.'

'What is it?' Sally asks.

Michael doesn't look at her. His mind is already thinking about what he's going to see in less than half an hour.

'Michael?'

He comes to. 'A body. Female. Suspected murder.'

'Another?'

'No, this is something else. They've called me because…'

He doesn't know how to say it.

'Because?'

Michael shrugs. 'Because of *fencing*.'

Sally is taken aback. 'What's fencing got to do with anything?'

'The victim's been stabbed with a snapped fencing blade.'

Chapter Three

It's raining heavily when Detective Sergeant Michael Varga arrives at Chistle Gardens in Hendon, near the northern tip of London. Twenty-five minutes have passed since he left Sally's home. The Chistle Gardens property is an old mansion house that's been converted into apartments, its occupants not shy of a pound or two.

He ducks into the foyer and, before he runs upstairs, he prepares himself to receive an earful. He takes his mobile phone from his pocket and dials his ex-wife, Julianne.

She answers quickly. 'Michael.'

'Hello Julie. How's Ricky?'

Her voice is curt. The hurt she's experienced because of him is still palpable. 'Well, you'll find out yourself this evening when you pick him up.'

He takes a deep breath. 'Listen, about that. I'll have to work. There's been a –'

'Another floozy at the fencing club?'

'No, listen –'

'Fuck you.' And she hangs up.

Michael sighs. Now he'll have another rung of the ladder to rebuild. It seems like every time they speak, there's something else, something new. Yet he knows it's his own fault. He can't blame her.

Apartment 3c is on the third floor and is situated at the property's far right side, with a view that overlooks the grounds at the rear.

After parking out front, Michael is permitted past the police cordon when he shows his warrant card, entering the building as quickly as he can to escape the rainfall, and he takes the stairs two at a time.

He arrives on the landing and turns right. A uniformed officer stands outside the apartment's front door. When Michael flashes his warrant card, the officer nods and moves aside, holding the door open, a senior officer in his midst.

Michael walks into the apartment and finds himself in a long corridor. On the walls are paintings and a large mirror. On the left-hand side is a bracket of hooks. On them are several coats, appropriate for the weather.

He can hear noises from the room that's directly in front of him about ten metres away, but he refrains from going straight to it. He wants to look around first.

He comes to a door on the right and, after applying a latex glove to his right hand, applies light pressure to push it open. The bathroom, the sink full of water, a cotton pad and a bottle of cream next to it. He dips a naked finger into the water: stone cold.

He leaves the bathroom and enters the room that's a little further down the corridor and on the left. The kitchen. Units on both sides and a small table at the far end. He doesn't spot anything odd on first inspection.

After he exits the kitchen, he's about to enter the room opposite: the bedroom. But he stops; he's noticed something. He looks around and reaches for the light switch. After pressing it, he moves closer to the wall on the other side of the corridor.

A scratch. Over a metre long, in places two, three and four marks. 'Fingers,' Michael says to himself. He steps a few paces to the right, towards the bathroom, and locates where the scratch marks begin. High up – about his shoulder height – and they get lower as they near the bedroom. He traces them with his gloved hand and then goes back into the bathroom.

He removes a Dictaphone from his pocket and presses record. 'So,' he explains, 'you're in the bathroom getting ready for bed, doing your face. You've filled the sink up and you're about to put –' he picks up the bottle, reads the label – '*skin tonic* on your face. You've got a pad out and you're about to pour the liquid on it. You hear a noise, so you put down the bottle and pad and go to see what it is. You step out of the bathroom and into the hallway.'

He leaves the bathroom. 'Is he standing by the front door?' He turns to the left and sees that the lock has been broken. 'If he is, does he grab you as soon as you see him? Or is he standing slightly down the corridor towards the right so that he can be concealed and grab you as soon as you step into the hallway? Either way, he gets hold of you. You fight him and your hand reaches for anything it can get hold of. Maybe you scratch him. You scratch the wall and, as he drags you down the hallway, your hand remains clawing at the wall. You leave scratch marks almost all the way to where the bedroom door is. Does he knock you onto the floor at this point? Or do you run out of wall?'

Michael puts his head into the bedroom. Everything appears to be untouched. *Odd.* So he goes into the room at the end of the corridor.

The lounge. It's a large space. A smashed picture frame is on the floor. A three-seater sofa stands centre, with a coffee table, askew, in front of it. An armchair to the right of the coffee table. Another armchair, this one on the left of the coffee table, has been knocked onto its side. Pillows lie strewn across the floor. To the far left of the room are a dining table and a cabinet full of glasses and pictures. To the right is a unit containing an entertainment system. The television is against the near wall a few metres in front of the coffee table.

Two men are kneeling on the floor behind the sofa. A female is dusting for prints around the dining table. The crime scene investigators.

'Anything?' Michael asks.

From behind the sofa, Steven Donner rises. He smiles. 'Michael,' he says, sounding chirpy. He moves towards Michael, removing a glove, his hand extended. 'Nice to see you. It's been a while.'

'A good few months. Not enough vicious murder in that time, obviously. How are things?'

'Yeah, good, good. Mustn't grumble.' Steven Donner is bald, has a moustache and wears the white garb of a dental professional. 'It's a nasty one, I'm afraid.' He leads Michael to where the body is, concealed behind the sofa.

She lies on her back. She wears a night robe, although it isn't done up, with a bra and knickers underneath. Lacy. She's an attractive woman. A young woman's body, tight, firm, fit. White, cold, empty. Her left leg is tucked beneath her back, which means her body is arced slightly to the left. Her eyes are wide open.

Blood covers much of her chest and stomach. Wedged into the middle of her sternum is a piece of metal. Michael instantly recognises what it is. 'What the…' He crouches down beside the body. 'Just like they said, the end of a foil.'

'Now why didn't I think of that?' Donner asks, sarcastic, a wry smirk on his face. 'Why do you think you got the call?'

'I know. But a snapped foil. Unbelievable.'

'So just how dangerous are these toys you play with in your free time?'

Michael stands up. 'Hardly. They snap when you fight, typically when there's air in the blade. Then you get an unclean break. They can snap from age as well. But only a few people have ever died as a result. A few people have been impaled. But rare. So rare.'

'Well, fuck me.'

'It's not common, Steve. Not common at all. Blades usually just bruise you.'

'It seems that someone is trying to make it more common then.'

'It's an electric blade. The wire's still in it.'

'Electric?'

'Yeah. For years now, fencing's been electric. The blade has a wire in it that runs from the point to the guard. The fencer plugs a body wire into the guard socket, so when a hit is made the tip of the blade, which is like a sensor, sends a signal down the wire of the blade, through the body wire and to the electric box to indicate the hit. The light on the box then comes on. So this was an active weapon, not cheap. We can test it to see what kind of blade it is, find out what sort of money was spent on it. If it's maraging steel, they're expensive, and they don't, on the whole, snap; they're tough and don't lose their malleability. You've got to be aware that the blade will likely hold prints from whoever put the wire in it – it's done manually. And you'll probably have the prints of someone who sells blades on it, not to mention countless customers who looked at it if it was sold in a shop.'

'It'll be dusted when I'm done, along with the body. I doubt we'll get anything useful – you know how careful these people usually are. But she put up one hell of a fight by the looks of things, so I'm hopeful we'll get some skin samples from underneath her nails at the very least.'

Michael nods. 'Let's hope.' He pauses. 'I don't get it, though. There are so many easier ways to kill. The force required to do this must have been immense, especially if she was struggling. What can you tell me about the wound?'

'It wasn't a quick death, that's for sure. The wound's opened up and the blade's angled to the right inside the body. That means that whoever killed her pushed the blade in and then pressed it sideways so that outside the body it was angled towards the skin, like a V-shape if one side of the shape was the skin. Wouldn't have killed her for some time. He, I assume because of the amount of force that would've been required to keep her held down, must have held her on the ground and kept hold of the blade until he watched her expire.'

Michael sighs. 'Any idea yet who she is?'

'Yep. No rummaging, so I'd assume no property's been taken. Doesn't look like a robbery. Her ID's there.' He points to the dining table, which houses several bags containing sealed evidence.

'Fill me in.'

'Nicole Sarsons. Thirty-two years old. ID found in her handbag says she works for a solicitor. Hobbins. Liverpool Street.'

'I guess that's my first stop then. Anything else?'

'Only one more thing, I think. Look here again.' He indicates the body and they crouch down. 'The blade.' He points and runs his finger along the line of the blade, lifts his finger and shows the orange residue. 'It's very rusty. So much so that the wound's got specks of rust in it. I'd hazard a guess that this is an old blade.'

Michael doesn't say anything, just nods.

'Mean anything to you?'

Remaining silent, Michael lifts his hand to his face, raising his eyebrows and slowly moving his head.

'Mike?'

'Yeah, it means something all right. He's not just going shopping to find a murder weapon. It means he's a fencer. Rusted means it's a heavily used blade.'

Chapter Four

József Varga stared at the phone that was in his lap. He sat on the armchair in his lounge, a room of average size and tidily presented. The television sounded in the background, to him nothing more than an incomprehensible buzz.

He picked up the phone and dialled. His distant cousin, István Novák, who still lived in Budapest, answered. They spoke every week, but this week József had called a day earlier than usual. István was the only person in the world, now that Maureen was no longer with him, who József spoke to about private matters.

The blade in the post concerned him – so much so that he wanted to hear István's thoughts. István wasn't privy to József's deepest secrets, but he was a reliable voice that could be turned to when advice was needed or when words needed to be said to someone.

Both voices were deep, softly spoken and slowly spoken. István listened intently, as he always did. József described the envelope, the blade, the note, the troubling tingle in the base of his stomach. He understood that anything he felt was just a hunch about potential turmoil to come, but something unpleasant already seemed real. Therefore, he was nervous. Therefore, he called István for counsel.

József was ten years older than István, godfather to István's first son. When they were children, István looked up to József. István wasn't a fencer – he wasn't an athlete at all – but he was drawn to József's personality, his sense of humour and his winning advice. He seemed to have a solution to any problem. They enjoyed talking, drinking, smoking.

As the years passed, the roles became a bit more equal. István still called József for advice, but the older man turned to the younger just as often. They got on so well, they could have been brothers. It was just a shame that a sea and part of a continent were between them.

They'd kept in touch since József had settled in the UK and István was a frequent visitor during József's formative years here. During the past two decades, however, it was József who did the travelling.

They spoke about why this package might have arrived, who it could have been sent by. And they realised the list could be long. But why? *Why* was something they couldn't figure out.

And then they discussed what it could mean. Why a blade? Why snapped? Why the pierced paper? Whatever conclusions they came to, none was welcoming.

József and István finished the phone call the same way as always: *Speak to you next week.*

Which was when the incomprehensible buzzing of the television came into focus just enough for two of the news reporter's words to attract József's attention… and then his glance… and then his despair.

'… Nicole Sarsons…'

József Varga's eyes fixed on the television. The telephone remained glued to his hand.

49

Chapter Five

Michael leaves Chistle Gardens and drives towards the centre of London. The seven-mile journey from the apartment takes over an hour by car. Traffic's horrendous and, several times, Michael thinks about putting his portable blue light onto the roof and speeding through it, but he resists the temptation.

He arrives in Liverpool Street and parks at a pay meter. He displays a Police sign on the dashboard, avoids the extortionate hourly parking rate.

The rain hasn't subsided over the past hour, so he jogs from the car to the building of Hobbins Solicitors. The ground floor houses the reception area. Michael estimates that there must be at least ten floors above where he stands. It's clear that Nicole Sarsons had worked for a prestigious employer.

The lady behind the counter, a pretty young blonde with glasses, scripted and on cue, says, 'Good morning. Welcome to Hobbins. How can I help you?'

Showing his warrant card, leaning on the counter and flashing a smile, he says, 'I'm Detective Sergeant Michael Varga. I need to speak to the person a Nicole Sarsons works for.'

'One moment.' She opens a directory and shuffles through a few pages. 'That'll be Roger Davis. Let me check if he's available.' She picks up a telephone and dials. 'I have a Detective –' She peers at Michael, the question in her eyes.

'Varga,' a flash in his eyes.

She doesn't respond; is used to being hit on.

'Detective Varga to speak to Mr Davis about Nicole Sarsons.' A lengthy pause. 'Great. Thank you.' She replaces the receiver, then says, 'Take the lift to the fifth floor. There'll be a reception desk in front of you as you exit it. They'll be expecting you.'

Michael thanks her, winks and walks to the lift. As he approaches it, a group of people emerge, so he goes straight inside and presses the button marked the fifth floor.

He appears on the fifth floor in a matter of seconds and in front of him is a desk behind which sits a plump woman, in her thirties and with curly brown hair. 'Detective Varga,' she says, not a question.

'Yes, I'd like to speak to Roger Davis please.'

'Not a problem. He's in a meeting at the moment and has asked if you'd kindly wait.'

'Absolutely.'

She offers Michael a coffee and some croissants. The view of Nicole Sarsons' body has put him off food – it always happens when he views a person whose life has been so violently ended – but he accepts the offer of coffee. He needs a strong one, but has to make himself drink it.

There's a waiting area: three leather sofas and a small table nearby with magazines on top of it. Michael settles with his coffee and picks up a glossy.

He's been waiting for almost half an hour when the receptionist comes over to him. 'Mr Davis is ready to see you now, Detective,' she says, unapologetically.

Michael puts the magazine back on the table and follows her, the coffee cup in his hand. He's led through the office, past numerous desks that form an open-plan space, and they arrive at a room in the corner. Its wall is a sheet of glass. In it are a conference table, a dozen leather swivel chairs and a noticeboard.

Roger Davis is already in the room, standing. The receptionist makes the introductions, then backs off. On her way out, Michael hands his empty coffee cup to her and thanks her.

'Thank you for seeing me,' Michael says.

'Not a problem,' Roger Davis says, and he indicates with his hand that Michael should sit down. They sit opposite one another, at the narrowest part of the table. 'So, my receptionist mentioned this is about Nicole Sarsons. She hasn't reported for work today, so I assume it's got something to do with that.'

'I'm afraid it has. Ms Sarsons is, at the moment, involved in an investigation I'm conducting. I'm afraid I can't go into any particulars, but I can tell you it's serious. What I really need to know right now is some background information about her: anything you know about her family, her friends, her life in general.'

'Well, not much about her personal life.' Roger Davis leans back in his comfy chair. 'She's worked here as one of my legal clerks for, oh, about two years. Came from a regional solicitors in…' He doesn't finish the sentence. 'Somewhere slightly north. I don't remember exactly, but we'll have it on file. I can find out for you.'

'Northampton?' The apartment manager told Michael he'd remembered her saying something about living there before she moved to London.

'That's right, that was the place. She came with a good reference, was very personable at interview. Good

52

skills, too. It turned out I made a wise choice. She's been very reliable and a great asset to the company. Beyond that, though, I'm afraid there's little I can tell you. I didn't know her socially – I never socialise with anyone except the other partners – and I never got to know the finer details about her life, other than she was bored where she'd been before and wanted a challenge in the city. We gave her one here, I can tell you. This is a tough place to work at and survive.'

Michael looks up, his eyebrows raised, his forehead creased. 'And she survived?'

Roger Davis makes eye contact and holds it. 'Yes. Unless, that is, you can tell me otherwise?'

Michael ignores the question. Now isn't the time. First comes the family; out of respect, they have to be the first to know.

Amid the silence, Roger Davis locates a file containing Nicole Sarsons' next of kin details: her mother. Michael's next stop will be to pay her a visit, break the news and ask her to the station to make a formal identification, unnecessary though it may be.

As Roger has claimed he knows nothing more of use, Michael asks, 'What about friends? Any staff here she was particularly close to?'

'Have to check with my PA. I don't know.'

Roger Davis disappears from the office, returning to say, 'Clare Jenkins. She's one of the admin assistants. Apparently they were on good terms. I've asked for her to be sent for. She's a nice girl. Will be helpful, I'm sure.'

Clare Jenkins appears at the conference room door a few minutes later. She's blonde and about thirty, Michael estimates. Still in possession of a good figure, she has dark marks under her eyes, a strained look, one of a parent, perhaps a single parent, struggling to keep up with the demands of everyday life.

Roger Davis remains in the room.

After Michael gives Clare the same introduction he gave Roger Davis, he says, 'I really need to find out about her private life. Were there any boyfriends, friends she saw a lot, hobbies, places you know she went to often?'

'Sure.' A brief pause. 'Me, for one. I'm a good friend. We go out every week. One night a week, my partner looks after the kids. My only reprieve.' She laughs, a shameless laugh, one full of self-mocking, defeat spreading across her face, and she falls back into the chair.

'To do what sort of thing?'

A moment longer, then, 'Anything to get me out of the house. She knows how hard I've been finding things.' She realises she'll have to explain more and adds, 'I came back to work six months ago, only three months after giving birth. Twins. Couldn't afford to stay home for longer.' She wants to say more, likely about pressure from the firm, Michael reckons, but she chooses not to say anything in front of her employer. 'My husband isn't paid enough, so here I am. It's bloody hard. And she's good enough to be the ear I can let some steam off to. So we meet once a week, just for a dinner, or a film, or a few drinks. We don't have a routine or anything, so I can't point you in the direction of her favourite places. She's pretty lonely, men-wise, at least since she split from her fiancée. Three years ago, I think she said it was. I didn't know her then. We became good friends only before I went on maternity leave. We kept in touch during and even more so since I've come back to work.'

Michael makes careful notes as he listens. His tactic is always to say as little as possible when he interviews: *let them speak freely and we may stumble upon exactly what I need to hear.*

'No, no boyfriend. A few friends, but none that I've met before. She's spoken of someone called Holly. And I think Diane. I know nothing more about them than that. Some other friends of hers. Hobbies – well, she's into reading. Spends much of the weekend in the library. I don't know what it's called, though, as I live north of London. She likes music. Has spoken of some concerts she's seen recently. She likes keeping fit. Just over a month ago – five weeks ago, I'd say – she took up exercising and was raving the last couple of times we spoke about the fencing class she was going to.'

Michael's attention piques. 'Fencing?'

'Yeah, that's right. 'A real fat burner,' she called it when she first spoke about it.'

'Do you know where? Somewhere here in London, after work?'

'She's been going every Wednesday. Thursday's the day we usually go out. Her body was exhausting her, she said the last month or so. Somewhere local. She told me the name, but I don't remember it. Some word that I've never heard used before. Might not be an English word.'

'Salle?'

Clare shrugs. 'Don't know. Could have been. I really don't remember. It wasn't a word I've heard before, that's all I'm sure of.' She scratches her cheek. 'Salle. Salle. Yeah, could be, I guess.' She thinks some more, nods her head. 'Could be.'

There are only two in London containing the word

Salle and one is Michael's club. So he only has one other option. 'Salle Victory?' he asks.

'Victory?' Clare clicks her fingers. 'Victory, yes. That's it. Victory, I remember now. Like *winning*. That's what she joked about, when she said she was bloody useless at it.'

Chapter Six

Michael spends the rest of the day routinely. He visits Nicole Sarsons' mother, arriving a while after news of her daughter's death has been broken to her, escorts her to formally identify the body. He asks questions, tries to find out about a boyfriend, any friends that Clare Jenkins hadn't known about. He consoles, prompts, presses.

Some time during the day, his mobile phone rings. It's the office.

'Okay, thanks. If he calls again, tell him I'll be there at nine if I can.'

Michael had hoped the station would be calling with a new lead on the case, but instead is told his father has called him, inviting him for a late supper, that he'd get home early from teaching at Salle Victory.

His father doesn't ring mobile phones, even though Michael has given him the number several times. These calls to the station come occasionally, usually at random, usually for no good reason other than his father becoming bored and wanting an evening's company that will ultimately result in them both drinking a lot of whisky while saying very little and thinking too much.

What's odd, though, Michael thinks, is that his father would be home early from fencing. Still, the investigation would dictate what he could do today; supper might not be possible, however late.

Michael visits the few friends who have been mentioned by Nicole's mother. Asks the same questions, receives the same few responses.

Dead ends. Nothing more.

When he arrives on his father's doorstep at 10PM, he's in little mood for one of their rare father-son dinners. But duty compels him to resist the urge to cancel, to go and see what his father wants, to spend a bit of time with the old man. To say the right things and try to feel adequate enough to be the son of the great József Varga.

The rain hasn't let up, but Michael holds off knocking for a moment and remains on the doorstep. His hair is wet, but he doesn't care. He still has Nicole Sarsons' corpse on his mind, can't seem to shake it off. The blade in her chest. Then her mother's sobs. She was about his father's age and she'd crumbled at the news, physically clinging onto the nearest pillow, a picture of her long-deceased husband on the mantelpiece above the fireplace.

He tries to imagine his father crying, a man from whom emotion has never come freely, and realises he'll never see tears leak down that face. He wasn't even privy to that sight when his mother died. The only memories he has connected with his father contain the fencing piste; Michael on the piste and his father standing at the other end, behind his opponent, in sightline, making enthusiastic signals with his hands, directing his son to do this and that, how to win. At first, these signals made little sense to Michael, were more of a distraction. But, over time, he came to recognise them. Recognised the tips his father was giving him, the valuable advice that worked.

When he had success with them, his father smiled proudly. When he didn't, he saw only hunched shoulders, a shake of the head, a frown, disappointment, something that said, *That should have been easy*.

And it's disappointment that he believes has remained in his father's grasp throughout Michael's fencing career. The simple fact is, as a competitive fencer, Michael never matched up to the special talents of József Varga, nor now as a coach for that matter, however much he tried and tries. And every shake of the head, every frown, every signal to feint to the lowline before going to sixte, has remained with Michael, has forced a bitter taste to bury itself deep in his mouth.

At all competitions, from the first he ever entered to the last, signing in with the name *Varga* caused unwelcome, at times nauseating reactions from tournament organisers: initial gratitude towards Michael for entering; the expectation of an incredible performance, even when he was a novice, inexperienced, not yet good enough; kissing arse about Varga Senior in the hope that messages of adoration and respect would be relayed at home; desperation for József Varga to bequeath them with his presence one day in the future.

His father's reputation, he couldn't escape it.

After losing at a novice competition in his second year of fencing, Michael called his father. Told him he'd failed. He heard his father swallow. No other words. 'My foot,' he said. 'There's something wrong with my heel.' He was told to come back home.

He and his father never spoke about the competition. His father never asked him about his heel and he didn't mention it to his father. It was left to another senior member of the club to get him a heel guard, a piece of thick curved plastic that's placed inside the heel area of the shoe, in which the heel sits. It cushions the blow when the heel collides with the floor.

He's had to use one ever since.

Looking down at his shoes, Michael shakes off the memory. Now he's soaking, despite the small cover above the doorstep. He can't stay out here forever. Plus he's tired.

It's time to get through this and then get home, sleep and be ready for the next day's investigation into the murder of Nicole Sarsons. He takes his eyes off his feet, looks at the house number and brings his fist to the wooden door, despite the key that's sitting in his pocket.

Within seconds, he hears his father's footsteps moving towards the door.

*

The chicken was in the oven. The vegetables were on the stove. József Varga sat in the armchair in his living room. On his lap sat the snapped fencing blade he'd received in the post this morning. His head was bent down, his eyes fixed on the rusted blade.

He'd thought carefully about this evening, about what he believed should happen. He'd gone through his precise words, the conversation he and his son would have. The one he wanted to have. But still he hesitated. He hesitated because, if he spoke up and explained, he'd have to ask for someone else's help. His son's help.

And not only that. What he'd kept to himself for five decades – what he hadn't even told his wife, the woman he'd trusted more than anyone he'd ever known – would have to be revealed. He'd have to say the words. He'd have to open up.

And József Varga didn't open up.

60

How could he reveal the contents of this morning's post to his son without having to explore his own past and tell Michael about how he came to leave Hungary and the things that happened subsequently? Was there any way to figure out who had sent him the blade without doing that?

He held the rusted steel in his hands. On the television, but muted, was the latest news bulletin, which had again repeated initial details about Nicole Sarsons' death.

Nicole Sarsons, a member of his fencing club.

The note that came with the blade may have been a threat. It lay on the coffee table. *It ends only with you.* It didn't scare him; what instead scared him was that someone had died, and that death may have been as a result of him. What scared him even more was that the note implied there'd be more to come.

He put his head on the headrest and closed his eyes. *What am I supposed to do?* he thought.

His thoughts travelled back. 1947. He was ten years old. He saw his brother facing him. He was in goal, his brother standing next to the penalty spot.

Ákos, two years the elder, took a four-step run-up and struck the ball. József spotted his brother's eyes flit to the right corner of the net a fraction of a second before kicking the ball, so he dived and knocked it aside.

There was pain in his brother's eyes. And it was a look that would be shared between them for several years to come, especially when they would compete on the piste.

It was the picture of his brother's face that József was visualising when the knock at the front door stirred him back to reality. His son had arrived.

*

After the front door opened, father and son shook hands. They attempted a hug that comprised reaching towards the other's back, bodies leaning forwards and hands briefly patting the back of the other person, but there was no meaningful contact.

'Drink?' József asked as they entered the kitchen.

'I'll get it.'

'You know where it is.'

Michael opened a cupboard and pulled out a bottle of Scotch whisky. 'Do you want one?'

'Is the Pope Catholic?'

Michael pulled out two glasses from another cupboard and poured. He took some ice cubes from the freezer and dropped them into the glasses. He handed one to his father, lifted his own, and they brought the glasses together.

'Egészségedre,' Michael said, offering a toast in his father's mother tongue, one of the few things he knew how to say in Hungarian beyond swearing.

'Cheers,' his father said in return.

The whisky burnt, but it felt good. In his father's chest, Michael doubted there was a burn; any warm-blooded Hungarian knows how to drink and how to take it.

'Need any help?' Michael asked, nodding towards the oven.

'No, I've got it. The table is ready.'

While József removed the chicken from the oven, carved it and placed the vegetables into bowls, they didn't speak. Michael watched his father work. With precision – every cut, every movement.

Michael helped József carry the food into the dining room. They sat at the table.

'Help yourself,' József said, the same two words with which he began every meal.

Few words were shared between the men while they ate. Afterwards, they moved into the lounge and sat down, József in the armchair and Michael on the sofa.

József sipped his whisky. 'How's work?'

'Not bad. Difficult. You saw the news today?'

His father drained his glass. Then he nodded his head. 'Yes.'

Michael waited. His father didn't continue. 'So you recognised her?'

A long pause.

'Nicole?'

Michael didn't answer.

'Yes.' József sank deeper into his chair and rubbed his face. 'She was a nice girl.'

'How long has she been going to the club?'

'Not long. Maybe two months. She was in the novice group but interested. Some talent, but it was very, very early on, you understand.'

'Is there anyone at the club who's taken an unusual interest in her, or women in general for that matter?'

József offered an inquisitive look. He spoke, as he always did, in soft, quiet tones, with a deep and gravelly voice. 'Michael, you know one of the reasons men take up fencing is because they will meet women. Become good enough and the women will be interested in meeting you.' There was an oppressive silence. 'No, no one out of the ordinary.'

'Another drink?'

'Sure.'

Picking up both glasses, Michael left the room to top them up. József remained in his chair. He ran a hand through his thinning grey hair, took off his glasses and pressed his fingers against where the top of the bridge his nose met the inner edges of his eyes.

Now was the time to mention the blade.

Of course he knew it – but he couldn't find the words. People don't just change overnight, or after an afternoon's thought.

'There you go,' Michael said, returning and putting the glass in front of his father.

József picked up the glass. He sniffed the whisky. 'It's good.'

'Oh, yes,' Michael agreed as he sat down.

'How is the club?'

'So-so. Full, which is the main thing.'

'Anybody to keep an eye on?'

'Nobody you're going to have.' His tone of voice came out all wrong: too abrupt, too much force. He realised instantly, regretted it. 'A couple. One or two young ones that show a lot of promise.'

'Good.' His father nodded in agreement. 'Nurture them, Michael. Make them realise all they can have if they commit themselves.'

'I do.'

As if he wasn't listening, József repeated, 'Nurture them. And then they can achieve *anything*.' He turned to the left to face his son. 'I have booked a Mass for your mother. Four Sundays' time.'

'Good. Thanks.'

'It should be nice. Maybe we can go to the cemetery

together afterwards.'

'Of course.' Michael took a large mouthful of his drink. He looked up at the cabinet on the far side of the room. Several pictures of his parents stared back at him. They were smiling for the camera in all of them. 'The same as every year.'

A matter-of-fact tone: 'It goes so quickly.'

'Very.' His eyes moved from picture to picture. And then he thought about Nicole Sarsons. 'Too bloody quickly.'

'Look, Michael.' József faced his son again.

Now was the time.

Now…

But the words wouldn't come.

'Yes?'

He couldn't speak.

'Yes?'

A pause. Thinking.

'It's gone so quickly. Since your mother…'

'Yes. Yes, it has.'

He wouldn't.

'Too quickly.'

Chapter Seven

József Varga opened his eyes. All was dark. Underneath his back, the spot on which he lay was damp.

As soon as he realised he was awake, he was transported back to dinner with Michael. He wondered why he hadn't opened up and, almost instantly, he came to the answer: he wasn't that kind of person.

When his eyes and head settled, he took his watch from the bedside table and switched on the lamp that sat atop it.

Just after 3AM.

He turned towards the closed bedroom door. He thought he could make out a noise. Some kind of tapping sound.

A faint sound, repetitive, metallic.

He got out of the bed and went to the bedroom door. Opening it, he peered into the hallway.

The sound was clearer from here. Definitely a tapping, like the tin lid on a chocolate box being lifted up and down. It was coming from downstairs.

From the front door.

Then József realised what it was: the letterbox.

He stepped back into his bedroom. Reaching his hand to the wall, he clasped metal. A remnant of his past, from his early years in Hungary.

His grandfather's sabre had been well taken care of. His father, he remembered from his childhood, had polished it religiously. And so too with József, to this day.

Now in the darkness, he removed it from its sheath

and held it out, partially extended.

The uneasy sensation the noise has caused in him disappeared. This sword was part of him, belonged in his hand. With this blade in hand, with his skills, he had nothing to fear of anyone.

He felt the carpet between his toes as started to move slowly down the stairs.

Still more tapping, metal clearly against the letterbox frame.

He was approaching the front door, its brown shape blending into the darkness in the distance. Ten feet from it perhaps. Another step down and even closer. Seven feet away. Three steps to go.

He lay his wrist back, ready to cut at whoever might be on the other side.

His feet made contact with the hallway floor. The tapping stopped, cutting off like a perfectly timed battery-operated toy.

He reached for the front door, turned the key, pressed down the handle and pulled it open. He let the blade exit the house first, then stepped out after it.

No one was there.

He looked at the car in the driveway, the bushes nearby and beyond the property line. No one.

He walked into the street and looked both ways. Not a soul stirring. But he felt like he was being watched. Invisible fingers crept along the sweat on his back. In retaliation, he held the blade high up in the air, like a prize for victory in a competition. 'En garde,' he said quietly. He turned around fully, three hundred and sixty degrees, and let whoever was hiding observe the blade, the flash of metal in the dark night's sky, as he swiped the stainless steel through the air, cut with exaggerated ferocity. 'Allez!' he shouted.

Chapter Eight

When he woke up to daylight, József dressed in his Salle Victory tracksuit, complete with fencing club emblem on the rear of the jacket, went downstairs, put on his coat and left the house.

A tension grated between his shoulders – an area that had been worked on by physios many times over the years, partly because of the strains of fencing for so many years, but also because of the accident. He recognised the warning sign like the back of his hand: he'd need to return to the physio soon.

He drove to the local shops, parked and went into the newsagent. He needed a distraction. After seeing Nicole Sarsons' face on several front pages, he selected a football magazine and went into the nearby café.

After he finished the coffee and magazine, only partially managing to remove Nicole Sarsons from his thoughts, József returned to his car. To home.

Parked, he got out of the car and walked towards the front door. He unlocked it, stepped forwards, froze.

His eyes fixed on what lay in wait for him on the hallway floor.

'No.'

He waited for a moment before he crouched down and picked up the brown padded envelope. *Postmark: Budapest.*

He stepped into the house and closed the door behind him. He turned the package over. It was blank on the back.

With one swipe of the hand, he opened it. He peered inside.

Again.

He pulled out the blade, careful that the piece of paper didn't come loose. A broken blade, about six inches long, rusted, a sharp crooked break at one end, the point at the other. He held it in his right hand and twisted the piece of paper round with his left.

You, it said, and the blade had pierced the paper through the centre of the middle letter. He tore it off and creased it up in his hand.

'Me,' József said to himself. He closed his eyes.

Chapter Nine

Michael spends the morning meeting people whose names were on a short list his father gave him yesterday. Men at the fencing club who had seemed friendly with Nicole Sarsons. Three so far, leading nowhere.

He's sitting in the reception area of Matewood High School, where Ralph Goodge is a history teacher. His is the fourth and final name on the list. He's still in class, should be free in less than ten minutes, the pretty young receptionist told Michael shortly after he arrived.

Michael leafs through a copy of the school prospectus, a pile of which sits on a small table that's in the corner of the area. He's torn away from the images and self-congratulatory spiel by the emergence of the receptionist's voice. 'Mr Goodge is on his way down.' There's a twinkle in her eye.

Michael stands up, walks towards her and smiles. She looks down, but he knows she's aware that he's moving closer.

Just as he's about to speak, his buzzer, which is clipped onto his trousers, vibrates. He peers at it.

He pulls out his mobile phone and dials the office. Detective Constable Millie Turner answers. He pictures her sitting behind her desk. She's a diminutive figure, red haired and big-boot wearing. Her nose is pointed and her eyes are sunken into her forehead.

'What's up?'

'A call's just come through for you,' she says. 'There's been another one, Michael.'

The body lies at the bottom of the staircase of a block of flats in Daywell Rise, Golders Green, London. The victim, a woman likely in her early twenties, her head perched atop the bottom step, her body twisted awkwardly to the side, her right arm underneath her back, her left arm to the side of her body. Blood envelops her torso, but also covers the floor around her body, and splashes of the murky substance have stained the white walls, Pollock-style.

Michael Varga stands over her. He scans her body. He makes eye contact – hers are wide open, a look of awe on her face. Her face speaks to him. He reads the words on it, silent tomes it emitted moments before she expired. *This is death. This is the end. It's over.*

Realisation.

He pities her. Even after years of gazing at lifeless bodies, broken hearts, distraught parents and families, deranged killers, the effects of gangs intent on causing carnage, Michael still has an emotional connection with victims – he's managed to neutralise it, but it's always there.

The snapped blade – the killer's calling card – is wedged into her stomach, but it was plunged in and withdrawn from her body numerous times before it was brought to rest. A frenzied attack, that much is obvious, far more vicious than Nicole Sarsons' murder.

He's getting braver.

Michael estimates that there are more than a dozen stab wounds. The white T-shirt she wears has been infiltrated all over the chest, shoulders and stomach, where the blade perches like a flag marking a conquered spot.

Steven Donner is standing behind Michael, silent, Michael the first to arrive this time. A moment longer and he asks, 'Anything interesting?'

'Only the location, I'd say.' The staircase is accessible to anyone entering the building. It lies beyond a set of double doors at the end of a straight entry corridor. A lift, closer to the main entrance, is available.

'I bet she's blue in the face she didn't use the lift.'

'Classic one, Steve.' Michael kneels over the body. 'Perfectly timed as usual.' With a gloved hand, he peers into her handbag, which remains in the space between her legs. Tissues, mascara, powder, mirror, house keys, car keys, a purse. He withdraws the purse and opens it.

'Bingo,' he says. 'This also wasn't a robbery. Cards and cash are here. Driving licence, too.' He pulls it out. 'Brenda Harrison. Twenty-three years old.'

'So he grabbed her, pulled her in here.'

'Maybe.' Michael rubs his temple, concentrates. He looks her up and down, thinking, trying to spot anything that might lead him to the next step.

On her feet are white trainers. She has on black tracksuit bottoms. On top of the white T-shirt is a tracksuit jacket, black and white, that match the bottoms, only it's been pulled off her shoulders and ended up behind her so that it pincers her upper arms closer together than is natural. There's an Adidas logo on it.

'Sports,' Michael whispers.

'Mm?' Donner says, startled because the lengthy silence has been interrupted unexpectedly. He's not been paying attention.

'Sports,' this time louder. 'She's wearing a sports jacket. Maybe she was on her way home. Maybe she *chose* to take the stairs, not the lift.' He bends down, extracts the car keys from her handbag. He stares at the key for a moment: it's a remote-locking key. 'Maybe he followed her home, attacked her before she got upstairs.'

'But why the difference from last time?'

Before Donner receives an answer, Michael is already on his way out of the building. Donner follows him. As soon as Michael emerges into the daylight, the rain now a light drizzle, he holds the key in the air and presses the remote button.

Out of the half dozen or so cars in the car park, the signal lights of only one vehicle flash, and a beeping sound echoes, joining the patter of the drizzle. Michael runs to the car, peers inside. Seats empty. He opens the boot.

He gazes down at the bag, doesn't move.

Donner, his bald head shiny with sweat and rainwater, appears alongside him, out of breath. 'Michael, what –'

Michael points towards the space in the boot. 'Fucking fencing bag.'

'Fencing? What the fuck. Why?'

'The hell I know, but there's our link. Last night, she'd been exercising. Look at what she's wearing. So she took the stairs because she wanted to keep up whatever exercise she'd started. And, in doing so, she gave him his fucking opportunity.'

Chapter Ten

'Do you know a woman called Brenda Harrison?'

'No.' Michael heard József sigh on the other end of the line. He knew his father wasn't answering the question, was instead reacting. 'Merde.'

'What? What's the matter?'

'Merde... Come here. Come here *right now*.'

'Now?'

'Right now.' Then all urgency left his voice. Resigned: 'I have to show you something.'

After replacing the receiver, József closed his eyes. He saw Brenda Harrison. And, next to her, Nicole Sarsons. And then the brown padded envelopes and the snapped blades.

When he opened his eyes, he saw them in person, in front of him on the coffee table. He cursed again in Hungarian, without a clue about what to do, about how to make this right, about how he could help end it. He was powerless, something he wasn't used to being, something he hadn't felt since the day his wife died, and the only time before that, aside from during childhood, was something he wasn't prepared to discuss.

He walked towards the cabinet in the lounge and made eye contact with a picture of his wife. 'Please, my love. Please. Tell me what I can do. Help me. Give me strength.'

He'd done terrible things, one of which must have caused hurt, excruciating pain, for things to go this far. Something so awful that someone out there didn't care that others would have to suffer to make him suffer.

All a lifetime ago, and now consuming, crucifying his presence.

József Varga fell to his knees before his wife.

Chapter Eleven

Michael leaves the station and drives to his father's house. Traffic is heavy, it's rush hour, so it takes longer than usual. All the way, he tries to imagine what his father wants to say. Will he admit to affairs with the women? He didn't kill them, surely. Does he know who has, why they've done it?

That's stupid. Michael knows how ridiculous all this speculation is. Just why he's let his mind wander, he has no idea. He wipes the thoughts from his head.

This time, when he arrives, he knocks without hesitation.

József opened the door and walked away without a word. Without even acknowledging his son. Michael followed him into the lounge.

'So, what's up?' Michael asked as he entered the room.

József Varga stood at the other side of the room, beyond the coffee table. He was looking at it. Michael noticed and changed his line of vision so that it also fell onto the coffee table.

'What are these?' he said, walking towards what his father was glaring at. He picked them up one at a time. 'What are these?'

'Sit down.' No emotion. József turned around and opened the drinks cabinet. He poured himself a whisky. He poured a second for Michael. Closing the cabinet, he turned around slowly and placed one of the glasses on the coffee table in front of Michael. Then he backed away and sat down in the armchair. He took a long drink, let it warm his insides, and closed his eyes.

Michael waited patiently.

'The shorter piece of blade, it came in the post yesterday. The other one arrived today. Both postmarked Budapest. And with these.' He pulled from his pocket the two pieces of paper, one crumpled. 'These came in the envelopes.' He handed them to Michael. Without giving Michael the time to read and think: 'Somehow I'm connected to these murders. Somebody's after me, telling me what they are doing and that I'm to blame.'

'You? Why you?'

'That's exactly what I've been trying to work out. I don't know. But I am part of somebody's plan.'

'Why didn't you tell me straightaway?'

József looked blankly at Michael.

'At dinner yesterday? It didn't cross your mind to speak up?'

József leaned his head against the armchair's cushioned rest. 'Michael, there are things…'

'Things? What things? How many people have to…' Michael was starting to lose patience with his father, a man he normally tolerated, normally showed respect for, even though the respect didn't always match his thoughts, a man he considered to be smart.

'Things are complicated, Michael.' József took a sip of his drink, urging the alcohol to revitalise him, spur him on. 'It's complicated. When that blade came, I knew it had to be a message. But from whom? I didn't know, and I still don't know. I knew the message was to tell me that Nicole's death was my fault. And then the second one came this morning. A message to tell me now I can blame myself for Brenda as well. All this blame, all because of something in my past…'

József didn't continue.

'Something? What, for fuck's sake?'

József's eyes rose towards Michael's, but he lowered them. Michael didn't usually swear at his father, in his presence even. 'I don't know. But it must be something from the past. In Budapest. The postmarks.'

'But how do you explain them? You can't post something from abroad and guarantee the delivery date through the normal post. You can't post something, kill someone and then know the package you sent is going to arrive just afterwards. That's impossible.'

'Well, that's part of what you need to work out.'

After they had both taken a few sips from their drinks, József continued. There was reluctance in his voice. 'You see, Michael, I've made enemies in my life. That's the natural part of being successful on the piste. Now I suppose one of those enemies has followed me off it.'

'Were you having an affair with either of the women?'

'No.'

'With both?'

'No, Michael. Don't be ridiculous.'

'Then why target them? I don't see.'

'That much I do understand. This person knows me. He knows fencing is *my life*. Destroy my club by killing my fencers, destroy the people I train passionately, then, as the note says, destroy me personally. *It all ends with me.*'

'Then who? If you're so sure, who?'

'That will take some digging.'

'But you must have some ideas. Dig and I'll get you a shovel. Have you ever… ever pushed someone so far that maybe you pushed them over the edge?'

József stared coldly at his son. His breathing was heavier than usual. Still through the nose. He cleared his throat. Finally: 'I was attacked once. You ask me to think back and that's one of two things that keep coming back to me. Somewhere along the line, I pissed someone off so much that they knocked me unconscious.'

'When? Did you ever find out who?'

József shook his head. 'It was a long time ago. I was a teenager. Such a *long time ago*. But it was connected to fencing, that much I do know. You see, I was successful… young. I beat people, lots of people – men even – and some of them didn't like losing to a teenager.

'Within two years, there was no one at my club who could beat me, not my brother, no one. And fencing in Hungary then wasn't anything like fencing in the UK is now. It really meant something. It was *the* national sport.

'After a handful of matches, my brother and I stopped fighting against each other. We stopped talking as well, if I'm honest. Ákos hated losing to his younger brother.'

Michael sat forwards. 'So him. Could it be him?'

József raised an eyebrow. 'My own brother? He's a lot of things, but he's not that. No, it couldn't be him.'

'But –'

'No, Michael,' József said calmly. 'No.'

'So someone else, some other competitor?'

'I won several tournaments by the time I was fourteen and, somehow, my coach managed to enter me into the Hungarian Foil Championships when I was sixteen. The men's championships. No one thought I had a chance.

'When I got to the final, I was facing the favourite. His name was László Polcz. He was twenty years old and made of muscle.

'He took the first five hits in a row. I don't even think I landed an off target. Nothing like that had happened to me since I'd started competing. But I didn't panic.

'On the sixth point, I caught him with a direct counter-attack. It was a simple hit and made me feel alive. And I think its simplicity flustered him. After that, he started to miss, and I started to land hits. I caught up and then I won.

'The whole gymnasium erupted. László looked so embarrassed. Nothing like that had ever happened to him before.

'I won the same title for three years running. The following year, I beat László in the final again, and after that he drifted away. Or he moved away. I don't know. There was talk that he'd turned to drink and drugs.'

'So he sounds like an interesting possibility.'

József snorted a dismissal. 'Last I heard, he was a drunk in a gutter somewhere. He has probably been dead for years.'

'I'll check him out.'

'Polcz was weak. To do this takes someone with courage. What this person's doing isn't easy.'

'What this person's doing is *sick*.'

'I didn't disagree with you, Michael.'

'So if this Polcz character is irrelevant, why mention him to me?'

'Because of what happened next, Michael.'

Michael rested back into his seat. His father looked beyond him, to the curtains.

'That success made me somebody. I became *popular*. Celebrating became a bigger part of my life and, at seventeen, I was drinking quite heavily. I had a lot of women. They loved my success. I was smoking a lot, too. In fact, smoking was such a big part of my life that my coach used it as inspiration to push me harder on the piste. He'd stand at my end of the piste, a lit cigarette in his hand, and I'd be allowed to take a drag between points after each point I won.

'One night, after another tournament victory, I went to a party. As I was leaving with a girl on my arm – I don't even remember her name – I was kissing her and I didn't see anything, didn't hear anything, but something sharp hit the side of my head and I fell to the ground. I awoke the next day in hospital.'

'Where did this happen?'

'In Bródy Sándor Street, just round the side of the Budapest Radio building. It became the scene of a lot of fighting during the Revolution of 1956.'

József let the word *Revolution* linger in the air. To Michael, it seemed as if his father wanted him to enquire more about it. He didn't.

'Did you ever find out who was responsible?'

'I never found out. Oh, I asked around, and I heard names, Polcz's included, but no, I never found out who attacked me. And as I said, it could have been anyone.'

'Then that's a dead end. There's no way to find out. Except that Polcz guy, I'll dig about him.'

'Whatever you decide.'

Michael filled up their glasses and began to drink another whisky. 'You said there were two things.'

'What?'

'*Two* things from your past. Two things that may have inspired revenge in someone.'

'Ah,' said József, and he let out a long sigh. 'Yes. *Two things.*'

He downed the whisky, leaned forwards for the bottle and held it still in one hand, the glass in the other. 'You know, my father and I, we shared a glass of whisky the evening before I left my family home forever. It was Friday October 26th 1956. The Revolution had been going on for four days. I returned from fencing and we shared a toast. *To your future happiness*, he said, amid the turmoil the city was in. The country, actually. To this day, I believe he was reading my mind. I believe he knew that the next day I would leave for good.

'And that's what I did. I kissed my mother and father goodbye, told them I was going out for a packet of cigarettes and never returned home. They didn't even know I'd survived until they heard from me four months later when I'd settled in England.

'I left Budapest with scores of others. Four evenings later, I found myself near the Austrian border and had befriended two others: András and Dávid.

'That night, as we tried to find a border area that wasn't being guarded, we ended up in the middle of a crowd of revolutionaries who had escaped from somewhere. Before we knew it, all hell broke loose. Soviet troops exploded upon us from all sides. People were falling fast. It was only seconds before I was struck on the head.

'I awoke to find myself tied up with about thirty people in an abandoned warehouse. Some were dead, some alive.

'We were kept tied up for two days. There was no way out.

'Then, starved of food, those of us who had survived were led out into a field. I feared we were going to be lined up and executed.

'We were forced onto the ground in small groups. There was some kind of raised concrete platform up ahead. On top of it was a table and on top of the table there was a dead pig.

'A soldier stood over the pig. He pressed the blade of a knife into its abdomen, cut off some skin and threw it to the men on the ground. The soldiers laughed as the men lapped it up like wild dogs.

'Desperate to vomit but unable to, I crawled round the side of the building, leaned against a wooden wall and closed my eyes.

'A soldier found me sitting there. He had in his hand some pig flesh. 'Hungry boy?' he said. 'Eat it.'

'I shook my head, pressed back against the wall.

"Eat it,' he repeated. He stepped over me.

'He clutched my hair, pushed my head back so that my chin was raised and my neck was exposed, and pressed the flesh against my closed mouth.

"Eat,' he roared.

'But he'd left himself exposed. He had a sword in a sheath tucked into the side of his belt. While he was trying to push the flesh into my mouth, I punched him in the stomach, pulled out his blade and lifted it into the air. With a flick of the wrist, I cut into his forehead.

'To this day, I have no remorse. I can't. No human could, after what he, and they, had done to us. What *their kind* was doing to all Hungarians.

'I had to do more to help the others. I peered round the corner of the building. Two soldiers were talking, enjoying the entertainment that they took the men for. They were several metres into the distance, with their backs to me.

'I held the blade in my hand and walked towards them with the steel partially extended. I bent my knees and went into the en garde position. That's when they heard me.

"Allez,' I thundered, cutting the blade from right to left, my whole arm following through. I hit the first guard on the left side of his head and then brought the blade into the other's ribcage.

"Run!' I shouted, spinning towards the men, noticing for the first time that Dávid and András were on the ground. Recognising me, they got up and joined me.

'As we ran towards the side of the building, a soldier was already coming out. He'd unsheathed his blade, but I didn't give him time to attack. With a froissement the speed of which he'd never experienced before, I grazed along the side of his blade, forced it from his hand and landed a direct hit to his chest.

'I didn't see another soldier come at me from the side. He knocked me to the ground. I quickly rose and turned in a fluid motion, extending the blade. It pierced skin, went right through. And that was when I found myself face to face with Dávid. The rock he'd used to prevent the soldier from stabbing me dropped from his hands. For the slightest moment, his eyes and mine locked. His hands reached down to the blade that had entered his stomach. I caught him as he fell and lowered him to the ground. I couldn't speak.

'Before I could fully comprehend what I'd done, András pulled at me, shouting. I had no control over our next movements. To the bushes, over them, to the left and down the path that was behind it. We didn't stop, but I had no idea.

'All I kept thinking was, *Dávid.*'

József stopped speaking and bowed his head.

Michael could make out a slight shine in his father's eyes. 'He died?'

'He must have.'

'And what was his surname?'

'I don't know. We were only together for a couple of days… But I have never forgiven myself.'

'So maybe it's him. Maybe he got away somehow.'

'Michael, I put a blade right through him. We were in the middle of nowhere and he was a prisoner anyway.'

'So a relative of his,' Michael suggested, 'who somehow found out what happened. What about this András? Maybe he told someone. Maybe he knew the family.'

József shook his head. 'András and I remained friends for many years. After Austria, we went to Belgium. From there, we planned to take a boat to Canada. There was the earlier option to go to the UK. I took it, he didn't. He had family in Canada. We kept in touch for years. He died just over five years ago.'

'And you're sure he could be trusted?'

'Like my own family.'

'So we'll explore the Dávid angle,' Michael said. 'I'll try to locate his family. There must be records of everyone who died in the Revolution. It'll be leg work, but there must be a way to get a list of Dávids.'

'Maybe,' József said. 'But a lot of people were never discovered. Thousands were killed, Michael. Thousands. But if that's our only chance… Let us hope.'

There was a pause. József filled his glass and nestled into his armchair. No eye contact now. 'I need your help,

Michael. I have killed and I have never found a way to get over it.' Saying it felt like he'd absorbed a forceful blow.

An even longer pause. The statement was indeed a first. The first time he'd ever asked Michael for help.

'Only you can end this, Michael.'

'I'll try. You have my word.'

'And that is all I ask. No matter what.'

'No matter what.'

József emptied his glass and looked at his watch. 'Would you like to stay?'

'After all this whisky, I've no choice.'

József stood up. 'I'll make up the bed for you.'

'No.' Michael stood up, raising his hand, encouraging his father to sit back down. 'No, I'll do it.'

Chapter Twelve

The following day, no blade arrived. József was relieved. Michael, too. He arranged for two officers to be stationed outside his father's house, hopeful they'd spot the bearer of any future blades, and left for work.

After getting others in his team to start working on the list of Dávids who had died during the Revolution of 1956 and spending much of the day pouring over forensic evidence himself, with no matches appearing on the database and too many potential prints for him to deal with alone, Michael arrives in Victoria a little after 6PM.

The last time he was here was over eight years ago. The last time he was here, Michael thought it would be the last time he'd ever be here, except perhaps for his father's final night teaching, his retirement evening.

He gazes up at the building. The front of it has been redecorated in recent years. It's painted a dark brown, heavy brown, with yellow lines seemingly at random horizontal intervals. Through the window, he sees the man sitting behind the school reception desk, clears his throat, pulls up his tracksuit collar (a plain grey jacket and black and grey trousers) and locks his car. He trots across the road as a London cab approaches and he goes inside.

'Evenin',' the male receptionist greets him.

'Hi.' He walks towards the desk. 'I'm here for the fencing. I know where –'

'Sign in please,' the man, who's in his fifties, bald and

toothless, says.

'Oh, sure,' Michael says, slightly surprised. Times have changed. He lifts the pen, then he hesitates.

Tonight, he's here to work. *To work in secret*. His father, he knows, has already told all the established fencers to pretend they don't know Michael. Michael's job tonight is to watch, to see who turns up, to see if anyone's watching. To try to find a madman who's hell bent on revenge.

So signing in poses a problem. Michael grabs the first name that comes to him and jots it down, in a scrawl most people with lens-perfect glasses would find hard to read. *Rich Clark*.

'Thanks,' he says, and he walks towards the gymnasium.

He's surprised by how busy it is when he walks into the main arena. It's bright blue floor and basketball court lines shine. His father is seated in the same place as over eight years ago, holding a coffee, sipping on it, his legs crossed. Several people, women and men, lean over him, desperate to hear his stories, laughing too much.

He doesn't look at Michael.

But he knew Michael was there. He didn't even look. Like when you're on the piste and you're looking at the blade, you can still see the whole fencer beyond it – peripheral vision, for the best of fencers, is second to none.

Michael introduced himself to a lady who introduced herself as Helen. Helen's job was to take payment for the evening, to tell Michael, slowly, about the course that he could sign up for if he enjoyed this taster evening enough, and to encourage him to join them all for a drink in the pub afterwards.

Like hell, Michael thought.

Michael signed up for a trial of the beginner's group. This, he knew, would give him prime position to observe what was going on in the rest of the gym, for the beginners' group would be positioned against the far wall, with a perfect view of everything that was going on.

'Your coach,' Helen said, 'is Dimitry Petroc. Let me introduce you.'

After a handshake, in very broken English, Dimitry pretended to introduce Michael – or *Rich* – to the world of fencing, at least until Helen left them to it.

'So today you beginner?' he laughed when they were alone.

'*Today*,' Michael said, knowing he could take Dimitry to pieces on the piste if they faced one another.

'Well, I be nice to you, I promise.'

'Thank you.'

'Remember, you know nothing.'

'Yes, I know,' Michael said, not enjoying that Dimitry was enjoying this a bit too much. 'Nothing.'

Not long after Dimitry left Michael alone and Michael was pretending to improve the knot that kept his shoelaces tied, József blew his whistle to indicate the start of the warm-up. One by one, people joined the jog around the gym. Michael was one of the first, jumped up fast as the potential eager new recruit. His act had to be convincing, after all. They're always first up in their blissful ignorance.

Jogging soon turned to running and sprinting, and then a variety of exercises, all of them very familiar to Michael, kicked in. He'd hosted this warm-up twice a week for eight years himself, but rarely had he participated in it. Not since he'd left this fencing club. Not since he'd left Salle Victory.

A quickening heartbeat encouraged drops of sweat to start falling from his face. His T-shirt stuck to his body. His legs started to ache. This, he hadn't predicted.

Fortunately, the speed of the early stages of the warm-up waned, and stretching exercises were the next focus. Michael gasped to regain his breath while he spun one arm forwards then backwards, then the other arm.

He imagined his father looking at him with smug satisfaction. He didn't check. Didn't want to see.

He saw others looking at him. Hated the gaze of their eyes, the knowingness as he knew what they were thinking: *It's hell for a newbie.* They felt sorry for him, his sweaty mass, and he hated them for it.

This spurred him on, so when the pace of the warm-up picked up, his pace picked up, he pushed hard, he wanted to show them all, his father especially, that he wasn't too old, that he was still as fit as he once had been, that he was a Varga, for fuck's sake. He wanted to shout it out. That would shut them all up, their thoughts and their telling looks. Their sympathy.

But he couldn't say anything. Today he was Rich Clark. He was a beginner. He was *nothing, no one.* And he had to be *forgettable.*

The pace slowed down as ground exercise became the focus. József called for everyone to lie on their backs, roll back onto their shoulders and lift their legs into the air. The difficult part was to keep them pointing towards the ceiling as the legs were ordered to step, open and close, and cycle.

Bodies quickly started to sink into the ground. 'Lift,' József said. 'You know where the ceiling is? It's that thing with the lights on.'

Once the warm-up was over, the beginner's session began as the other fencers commenced fencing and their lessons with József. The beginner's group remained lined up, listening to Dimitry's simple instructions, occasionally stepping and moving their arms, with no foils to be seen.

While Michael stood there taking instruction over the next hour, he spied on the men. Men arriving, men fighting, men watching, men speaking to women. There were a lot of men speaking to women and, as with most fencing clubs, there was a lot of laughter and good humour in the relationships. So it seemed.

He watched the other beginners too, closely. The new faces who'd joined the club three weeks ago. Six men and seven women. The men, a range of ages and sizes, everything from the overweight type doing the sport to lose a few kilos (only to put them back on again the moment club night is over and pub night begins) to the adventurous athletes who've swum, rode and shot, wanting another sport to add to their repertoire. They'd be out of the door by the end of the course, or maybe by the time they finished the following intermediate group.

József casually walked over to the beginners. He didn't acknowledge Michael, despite standing only three feet from him. Instead, his attention was purely on one of the men. Stefan, a Frenchman, was in his mid-thirties, with wispy brown hair.

'En garde,' József said to him.

Stefan duly obliged.

József took hold of Stefan's shoulders and tried to shake him lightly. Stefan's body didn't move. 'See,' said József, with all the other beginners looking on eagerly.

'The only place for a fencer to be stiff is in the bedroom.' He waited for the laughter to die down before he added, 'A fencer must be loose, relaxed. Tension kills victory. But looseness is central to victory.'

And without another word, while the beginners stood open mouthed or nodding their appreciation, József casually walked away to resume coaching.

Michael continued looking around, continued pretending to find the simplest things challenging.

No one stood out. Frequently, Michael found himself gazing over to where his father taught: the opposite end of the gymnasium, the line of the basketball court the marker for the feet. His father moved up and down the line, his hand steady, his fingers doing all the work, the arm barely moving, utter concentration on his face, his shoulders slightly stooped, no mask on.

József Varga didn't wear a mask when he coached. It was a mixture of confidence, positivity and arrogance that let him get away with it. And perhaps luck, too – he'd never been injured by a blade. Other coaches could never understand why he took the risk.

He didn't look at Michael, but somehow Michael felt his father's eyes on him. He wanted to get his attention, wanted to grab an electric blade and take the competitive fencers to pieces just to show the old man that he still had the skill to make it in tough competition.

But he was working; anonymity was the key.

Michael glanced at the digital clock that was on the wall above the entrance. Its large green numbers read 21:00. He was running out of time. He started to look around with more urgency now, hoping to locate something odd, something that seemed out of place.

He saw fencers on the piste, he saw others presiding, there was still a lot of talking, now some people were slouched on the ground glugging at bottles of water or sports drinks. Nothing that wouldn't be seen in every fencing club around the country, at his own club.

Then József's eyes met Michael's and Michael sensed disappointment that they'd got nowhere in the aged stare. Michael nodded at him. They were going to Plan B. József removed the whistle from his pocket and blew on it. The gymnasium quietened down.

'There are some things I'd like to say,' said József. 'Tonight and next time. Some announcements. Important club news and some information about plans I hope to introduce. I hope you will give me your ear for a few minutes either today or on Wednesday. Tonight, it's the turn of the ladies. If the gentlemen could retire to the changing rooms, it will be ladies first tonight. Gentlemen, we will meet on Wednesday. Thank you.'

The men, slightly surprised by announcements being made separately but not surprised that József would select ladies first, made their way out of the gymnasium, their movements tired. Michael hovered at the back of the pack. He ensured he was the final person out of the gym while József brought the forty or so ladies together.

When Michael reached the top of the staircase that led to the changing rooms, he checked that he was sufficiently far back to sneak off unnoticed. He quickly returned to the gym whose door his father closed after he entered. József locked the door.

Michael moved to the left so that he stood in front of the wall, out of view of the glass windows at the gym's entrance.

'This,' József said, 'is my son. Detective Sergeant Michael Varga. He must speak to you in secrecy.'

'Ladies, apologies for keeping you. This won't take long, but it's vital I speak to you. I don't wish to alarm anyone, but I'm probably going to tell you what you've already been thinking. So far, two women, Nicole Sarsons and Brenda Harrison, have been found dead. Some of you may have been friends with them and I'm sorry for your loss. They have been murdered and there *is* a connection. That connection is *here*. I can't give you any particular details of the investigation, but there is a greater connection to this place than simply the fact that they both came here to fence.

'There is nothing to suggest that there will be another death. But, at the same time, there isn't something that suggests this is over, so we must not be careless and complacent. So I'm here, first, to warn you. You must be *on your guard*. I'd encourage you all to travel in pairs, avoid dark areas and be vigilant wherever you are. Look around you. Be aware of strangers and where they are. Be aware of anything in your homes or around them that's out of place. And if, for any reason, you're unsure, that you don't feel right, contact the police without hesitation. I'd rather we have false alarms than something else terrible happen.

'Second, I've been here this evening to watch who else is here. I've tried to spot anyone unusual, suspicious. I'm afraid that I've drawn a blank. So now I need to ask you. Think about the past few weeks. Are there any new members who have acted oddly, asked you any unusual questions, anyone who's suddenly shown a particular interest in you or someone else? Did you see anyone show a particular interest in Nicole Sarsons or Brenda

Harrison or both of them? Anyone that spent a lot of time talking to them? Anything at all?'

The women had on their thinking faces. One lifted her hand, a cute young blonde, barely past being a teenager.

'Yes,' Michael said, reminding himself to remain focused.

'A lot of men join, you know. So many of them flirt.' She played with her hair.

Lots of murmurs agreed with her.

'We laugh it off,' she said. 'Some of it can be quite flattering, actually,' she added. Some nodded in agreement, others looked like they were ready to tell her to shut up.

'I'm aware of that,' Michael said, flashing a smile at her, unable to resist. He imagined how her hair would feel, that taut, youthful body. 'What's your name?'

'Chloe Raynor.'

Michael nodded, then looked away. 'Can anyone give me any names, point me in anyone's direction? I will check out any angle.'

The toing and froing began. One name was mentioned, Neil, and then another, Tyler, and another. Names said but little agreement. Until the name *Ethan* was said by someone towards the back of the group. In response, voices rose and people turned around. Then they all spun towards Michael, stepping forwards and calling out various opinions. All negative.

'Lecherous… gets too close to you… almost felt me up… was talking to Brenda definitely.'

Michael handed out his card to all of them, asking them for an urgent call if they came up with anything else. His finger touched the young blonde's hand as she took it from him. He smiled again and received gleaming teeth in return.

'Keep safe,' he said to them all. 'And it goes without say: I'm a new member of the beginners' class and we didn't have this conversation, if any of the men speak to you about what's gone on in here.'

'Tell them,' József interjected, 'I'm arranging mixed-sex competitions and wanted your views before I announced it fully. I suppose we will have to do it. Something to look forward to then.'

The ladies left.

'Show him to me,' Michael said, grabbing his belongings.

They went downstairs into the changing room. Michael took up position in front of the mirror. The changing area comprised three sides of a square. The fourth housed the showers. Most of the men were still in here. József walked into the toilet area, which was accessed through a door. From inside the doorway, he pointed in Ethan's direction. Michael saw in the reflection in the mirror. He nodded, washed his hands and left.

He runs up the stairs and exits the building. He jumps into his car and pulls out into the street. He reverses and puts the car behind another vehicle several metres down the road, with a perfect view of the school's front door.

It's not long before Ethan comes out into the street with half a dozen others. He lights a cigarette and they walk together down the road. Very quickly, they're crossing the street and walking into a side road. Michael guesses that they're going to the pub.

After he's given them enough time to get in, he drives his car into the side street. Again, he finds an optimal vantage point, tucked behind a tree and in front of another car. He turns off the engine and ensures the lights aren't on.

It's not long before another small group, this one containing the cute young blonde, Chloe Raynor, passes by on the other side of the road. The blonde has changed into a white blouse and tight grey skirt that stops above the knees. She has on black high heels, which exaggerate her toned legs, tanned and inviting. She has in her hands a grey suit jacket, which she carries wrapped round an arm. She and the others arrive at the pub's doors and enter.

Michael sits. He waits.

Chapter Thirteen

Michael's there for almost fifty minutes by the time the first of the fencers leave. Three of them, all men, and they head in the same direction, most likely Pimlico underground station. And then it's not long before three women appear. They all spoke to Michael in the gymnasium. And it's only seconds later that their conversation under the street's nearest lamplight is momentarily turned to a haze by the departure of another woman, a redhead, one Michael didn't speak to, didn't even notice, but she handles a small fencing bag, large enough to carry only one blade, so she must have been there. The group says a few words to the redhead while she walks past, a smile across her face. She waves and the group resumes its conversation.

The pub doors open again. Michael springs to attention. The man named Ethan exits, also carrying a fencing bag, but this one larger. He smiles at the ladies, all of whom take a step back. He looks to the right and heads off in the direction of the redhead.

Michael watches him. The three women watch him, whispering to one another. Very quickly, Ethan crosses the main road, then disappears round a slight arc in the road. He's clearly heading for the underground station, possibly just like the redhead. Michael has only a split second to decide: take the car back out of the side road and round onto the main road and try to spot Ethan, or pursue on foot.

He has no option. He jumps out of the car, trots

towards the women who are still outside the pub and passes them. Their voices erupt as he goes by. He darts across the road without the traffic lights giving him way, avoiding cars as he does so. Up ahead, the road edges towards the right and he spies Ethan about twenty metres in the distance. And several metres in front of Ethan is the redhead. Ethan's not rushing; he's keeping his distance, Michael thinks.

Michael follows cautiously, hopeful that Ethan won't remember just another beginner, but wary that he might.

They arrive at Pimlico underground station a few moments later. He follows Ethan, who follows the redhead, into the underground entrance, down some stairs, round a corner and past the red tiles that cover the walls. In the faded light, the tiles remind him of the setting of a dodgy porn movie.

The redhead goes through the turnstile that's directly ahead and Ethan does the same. Michael hasn't got a ticket. He turns to the nearest payment machine, but there's a queue. He quickly locates the ticket booth, but that too has people lining up before it.

He looks back to where the redhead and Ethan were and catches sight of Ethan's bag disappearing down the escalators. He's going to lose them, has to act, has to be quick. He runs to the front of the queue at the ticket booth, around a couple of teenagers and a couple who stand arm in arm. 'Excuse me,' he hears the woman say sharply. They step closer to the booth, cut him off.

'Fuck,' Michael whispers. Again, he turns to the escalators. Now no sign of Ethan. He reaches into his pocket, pulls out the wallet containing his ID card and pushes through those queuing, running to the turnstiles.

He leaps over one of them and is immediately confronted by two security guards, growling and holding their arms in the way. He holds up his identification card. 'Emergency,' he says. 'Back off.'

'Now just hang on,' one of them starts to protest.

Michael's leg starts shaking involuntarily. 'Fuck off!' he shouts. 'Back off, I said! I'm pursuing a suspect.'

He skips over to the escalator and the security guards don't follow. He's thankful he hasn't had to punch his way down here. He runs down the stairs of the escalator, calling 'Police' to clear everyone out of his way. When he reaches the bottom, he has two choices: he takes the left option and runs to the end of the walkway, down some stairs and then has the choice of two platforms. Fortunately, neither is busy. He looks along the first, then the other. Ethan isn't here. No redhead either.

He runs back up the stairs and back to the escalators, pushing through the groups of people coming down. He takes the second walkway, now sprinting. A distant rumbling begins to shake the ground. He fears he's going to lose them altogether. A breeze starts to blow. A train's coming. He still needs time.

The train's arriving at the platform.

Down the stairs.

More people here. The train's coming to a stop. He looks down the length of the platform. Too many people. He jumps back up a couple of steps, uses the vantage point. The train doors open. He needs to get on if they're here. People are stepping off the train. He's stretching to see as far down the platform as he can. People off. People moving. People boarding. The tip of a red bag – the part where the tip of the blade sits – reaches high into the air.

A red bag on the redhead's shoulder. He hopes it's the bag he saw her carrying. He hasn't seen her, but has no choice. He has to get on.

He runs down the platform, knocking into people on the way. The beeping sound indicates the doors are closing. He's almost at the door and can clearly see the bag. She's here.

Michael turns and leaps in through the door, clutches the handrail to bring himself to a stop as the train moves off.

The redhead – she's sitting halfway along the carriage. Michael looks around the rest of the carriage, trying to catch sight of Ethan somewhere. He can't see him, though.

The redhead reads a book for the next three stops as the train travels along the Victoria line. Then she puts it in her handbag, hooks her fencing bag on her shoulder and disembarks at Oxford Circus. She walks along the platform and takes the route towards the Central line.

As Michael slowly approaches the exit staircase, Ethan steps out of the carriage in front of him. Michael halts, pretends to be reading the underground map that's on the wall. When he senses Ethan's out of view, he continues to make his way towards the Central line. There the three of them board another train. This time, Ethan goes in the same carriage as the redhead, so Michael gets into the next one along.

Michael watches them through the end-of-carriage windows. She hasn't noticed Ethan. Michael can't believe she's not paying attention to her surroundings, like he warned them to.

Three stops. Off at Holborn. Up the stairs, then to the

escalator and eventually into fresh air.

The air outside is chill. The redhead crosses the road. Ethan follows on the other side of the road. Michael keeps his distance.

She turns into Great Russell Street. There are people around, but it's quiet. The British Museum, which they're approaching, is closed.

Ethan's much closer to her now. Michael speeds up.

Ethan's closer. Very close.

Too close.

She removes keys from her handbag, looking down as she's walking towards the entrance of an apartment block. Ethan's a metre behind her, no more. Michael's running full throttle now. Charging at them.

Ethan lifts his arm out towards her. She puts the key in the door lock. Michael's gasping for air, his heart pounding, his legs colliding with the ground, a few metres left till he reaches them, till he can save her.

Ethan grabs the redhead by the shoulder. She spins round. Michael throws his arms forwards, shouts, no words.

When the redhead has turned fully, her lips lock onto the man's.

Michael knocks into them, most of the force ploughing into Ethan's body, forcing him into a gate. They fall onto the concrete. The air bursts out of Ethan's lungs, he cries out, the redhead screams.

She screams again.

'Are you all right?'

'What the fuck –' she begins, but she cuts off when she really looks at Michael. When she recognises who it is. She turns to Ethan, clutches hold of him and says

103

urgently, 'Honey, are you all right?'

Pressed against the gate, he's clutching at his back. The grimace on his face can't be concealed.

'Shit,' Michael says.

'Yes, shit,' the man on the ground snaps. 'What the hell is going on?'

'I'm –'

The redhead steps in. 'This is Detective Sergeant Michael Varga. Coach Varga's son.'

'Wait,' Ethan says, 'weren't you –'

'He was at the club undercover. He's trying to find out who killed Nicole and Brenda.'

Ethan rises, slowly. 'You think it was someone at the club.'

'He thought it was *you*,' she says.

Incredulous: 'Me?'

'Look,' Michael says, 'if I could just explain and if I could ask some questions. Can we step inside for a moment?'

They go inside and arrive in a foyer area. There's an office-style counter on the left side, behind which sits a doorman. 'You'll need to sign in if we're to go up.'

There are some chairs deeper into the foyer. 'Here will be fine,' Michael says, signalling the chairs. They sit down. Ethan winces as his back bends into the chair.

'You know why I was following,' Michael says. 'I was warned to keep an eye on you, Ethan. Some of the other women said you'd behaved in a way that stood out – that you're a flirt is what I got most from what they said. What's your surname?'

'Carradine.'

'And your name?'

The redhead answers, 'Lily Gates.'

'The women said they'd seen you paying attention to
_'

'*To me!*' Lily says. 'To me. I couldn't say anything in front of them. He's been paying attention to me because we've been seeing one another and everyone at the club knows I'm married.'

'Hence why you didn't leave together and didn't travel here together.'

'Exactly,' she says, clapping her hands. 'Bravo, Sherlock.'

'So what is this place?'

'It's a company apartment. I have free use of the place.'

Michael looks at Ethan, who freely exhibits how pissed off he is.

'You have my apologies,' Michael says.

'Hey, could happen to anyone,' Ethan mocks. Then he considers, shrugging: 'At least you're trying to find the bastard, I suppose.'

'Look, I may need to speak more to you, but I can see you've had enough of me tonight and I don't blame you.' He stands up and they follow suit. 'Just one more thing. How long has this been going on?'

'Like it's any of your business,' Lily answers.

'What I mean is, do you have an alibi for the nights of the murders? Were you together then?'

'We're together after fencing, yes, regularly,' she says. 'Look, here, if you don't believe me.'

She escorts Michael to the doorman. 'Lionel,' she says, 'can you show the detective the sign-in book so that he can check if we were here on two particular dates?'

Lionel smiles. 'Anything for you, my love.'

He hands the hardback book to Michael. Michael scans the dates. He sees her name, he sees Ethan's name. And the dates match.

'Who fills this in?' he asks Lionel.

'Me.'

Fool-proof alibis then.

Michael nods and turns to Lily and Ethan. They show him out. 'Again, I'm sorry,' he says when he reaches the doorstep, before the door is closed in his face.

He begins the walk back to the underground station. He decides to turn left. Tottenham Court Road station, it'll be.

Chapter Fourteen

Michael Varga is sitting in his car. He's tucked in behind a tree and he's watching the pub. *He's looking for me.* But I'm looking at him, and he hasn't got a clue.

The trouble is, there's an arrogance that comes with the name Varga. He assumes that the person he's seeking won't do research. You see, the name Varga means everything in the fencing world. József Varga first, then his son, Michael. Michael wasn't a slouch when it came to competition and he's not a bad coach. I've read all about him. He's stupid, ignorant and incredibly miscalculating to think he can fool me into believing he's a nobody. *He's a fucking Varga.*

While he's sitting in the car, a group of the fencers pass. He pays particular attention to a young blonde woman. She's very attractive. Actually, she's sexy. Her body demands desire. His eyes linger on her for too long and inadvertently he introduces me to *number three*.

Some time later, a group of three fencers leave. Then three women come out and start talking. A redhead exits next, says farewell to the talkers, then a man follows. Michael comes to life. I thought for a time that maybe he was asleep. From sitting on this wall slightly around the corner, I can't quite tell. I've kept back to remain unseen.

He's thinking about something. He's thinking and then he's out of the car. He moves quickly across the road. The women outside the pub seem to know who he is. He disappears round the corner.

And he gives me my next opportunity. Hands it to me

on a fucking plate.

I don't have to wait for long. The young blonde, the one he was staring at, comes out about fifteen minutes later. The timing's perfect. I'm just starting to get cold out here and the possibility that he might return soon is becoming stronger. I chuckle: she must know how keen I am to get on with it.

She takes the tube to Finsbury Park. She doesn't know me, so I get into the same carriage as her. People come and go. It's busy, and then it's quieter. At one point, I'm so surrounded by people, I can barely see her. When a few of the crowd disperse, I notice the person sitting opposite her leaves the train. I decide to take the seat; today I'm feeling particularly daring, fearless. I sit right opposite her. She's reading a magazine. Her head isn't bent down; her eyes are lowered. The position gives me the first chance to really get to see her face, to look deep into her eyes. Yes, she's pretty, very sexy. Her hair's messy. I'm ready to put my hands in it, to pull. This one, I'm going to enjoy. The others were necessities, had to be done, but this one's special. This one's going to hit him where it hurts.

She must feel my eyes on her because she looks up occasionally, drops them nervously. Three times I let it happen and then I think I'd better stop toying with her. Don't want to make it too obvious; anyway, she's probably used to strange men staring at her all the time and thinking about what it must be like to fuck her. I certainly am right now.

My hands on her body. Then wrapped around her tiny neck.

Soon.

Chapter Fifteen

Finsbury Park.

The call comes in to the police later that night, a little before midnight. The front door of an end-of-terrace house wide open. Darkness inside.

Uniformed officers arrive to search the house. It doesn't take long for them to find her.

The call comes through to Michael before he's had time to reach home. He's in his car, approaching Brent Cross and the M1 motorway. He pulls over, takes the call.

Who? The name is read to him over the phone.

Chloe Raynor.

His gut feels like it's going to implode. He squeezes his eyes together. Can't take much more of this.

'Motherfucker!' His hands collide with the steering wheel.

He slams the car back into gear and waits for space in the traffic to turn around. The journey will be long, his mind filled with the image of Chloe Raynor, the cute smile and the longing he felt for her.

He doesn't want to call his father. Can't bring himself to reveal that there's been another. That can wait.

Michael parks outside the house. The road is dark, but the lights inside the house are on. A uniformed officer stands in front of Chloe Raynor's open front door.

Michael enters after showing his warrant card. He finds himself in a corridor. To his right is a wall and on it is a full-length mirror. It's hanging angularly from a nail and is smashed. Amid the broken pieces of glass are strands of blonde hair and blood.

He got her as soon as she entered the house, Michael thinks. *He incapacitated her. Did he force her head into the mirror?*

Noise comes from a room further along the corridor. Michael reaches the lounge, which is at the end of it. Officers are searching the room. In the corner of the lounge is the kitchen area.

More noise comes from upstairs. Michael wonders if he'll find Stephen Donner there yet. He makes his way back past the shattered mirror and steps wearily up the stairs. Only one door is open. The noise comes from within.

Two officers are inside. The taller of the two tells Michael, 'We're waiting for the crime scene investigators,' when identification is flashed at him.

He doesn't hear the words, *just sees her*. 'Outside,' he whispers.

They leave.

*

'I'll be there in a couple of hours. Keep the door locked.'

Something tells Michael that an end is approaching. That whoever is behind this is getting braver and will soon be coming. For his father. For him. He doesn't know yet. So he'll be with his father for this, ready and waiting for the moment.

Michael still stands in the bedroom. Stephen Donner is quietly at work. He'd been stunned, so horrific was the scene that awaited him, and he isn't easy to shock.

110

While he'd been waiting for Donner to appear, he'd checked for updates. The team back in the office first. Some staff hadn't left but had found nothing of the names András and Dávid yet. Not a surprise. *Needle in a fucking haystack.*

Chloe Raynor, the cute blonde, was no longer cute. She was no longer anything. The mattress from her single bed had been lifted from its base and propped against the wall.

Chloe Raynor was standing, leaning against the mattress. Both her eyes had been blackened. Her nose had been crushed. One cheekbone had collapsed.

She was held in place by snapped fencing blades: one had been pushed through her throat; a second though her breastbone; and a third through her stomach. All blades had gone through her body and into the mattress.

The blade in her breastbone had been pushed through a piece of paper. One word had been written on it, in large capital letters, in smeared blood: *VARGA.*

His father's home seemed like the only place to go. He made the phone call.

Chapter Sixteen

József's head was planted in the back of his armchair. His hands clasped both armrests. His body was stiff, his eyes closed.

Michael picked up both glasses and went to the bottle of whisky.

'Sick bastard,' József said.

Michael filled the glasses then returned to his seat, with the bottle under his arm. 'Tell me something we don't already know.' He put his father's glass on the coffee table in front of him. His own, he kept in his hand. He put the whisky bottle in the middle of the table and then he sat back down.

His father's eyes opened, but Michael knew no one was home. 'She was a lovely girl. So full of life.'

Slowly: 'That I bet.'

Michael watched carefully as his father leaned forwards, his right arm extended, his fencing arm extending, but not in the style that had made him so successful on the piste, now a slight quiver where there was once such certainty.

József lifted his glass and downed its contents in one. He put the glass back on the table and sank deep into the armchair: his hands groped at both armrests, rubbing them. His eyes, once again, closed.

Michael sat perfectly still, watching his father. A man who had inspired awe in opponents on the piste. A man who inspired awe in those who met him in a fencing salle to this very day. A man who had done and achieved so much.

But none of that mattered any more. Now he was this.

Michael stood up again, filled his father's glass. But this time, instead of returning to his seat, he walked over to where his father was sitting and held out the glass. His father heard Michael's breathing nearby and opened his eyes.

They made eye contact. Michael thought, for a second, that he detected fear in his father's eyes, but fear was something he'd never seen in his father, so he wasn't sure whether his eyes were deceiving him or not. And, besides, it was there and gone in the blink of an eye.

'Thank you,' József said, taking the glass from Michael. This time, he sipped from the glass. The whisky warmed his insides.

Relief.

Michael moved back to his seat, silently. As he stepped, he asked, 'What's the worst thing you've ever seen?'

'Dávid –'

'No, not *done*. What's the worst thing you've ever *seen*? I'm not sure I've ever seen, or will ever see, anything like what he'd done to Chloe Raynor.'

This time, it was József's eyes that did the watching, tracking his son as he moved back to the seat, as he sat down.

How to begin?

It was some minutes before József stood up, drained his glass, and refilled it. 'Oh, Michael,' he said, rubbing his forehead. 'Michael.'

'Yes?' he said.

József sniffed. 'These, and everything else, they are all memories I thought I'd been able to forget.' He shrugged mockingly. 'Or I fooled myself into believing I had.' Staring, his eyes not blinking, the glass in his hand, taking occasional sips, József spoke up. 'I killed him, Michael. I killed Dávid, with these very hands. These hands that are responsible for all my fencing skills. All that's good in my life also did the worst. God knows, I didn't mean to. But that wasn't the first horror from that time that I witnessed.'

Michael thought he heard a crack of emotion in his father's voice. The long pause that followed convinced Michael that he had.

The long pause came to an end when József was ready. 'With Dávid, it was an accident, but every one of the people that I saw killed on Budapest's streets, they were all murdered. I dream about them. Their faces. So clear, like it was yesterday.

'What you saw with Chloe, I'm sure it was awful, and I understand how you feel.

'For me, it started just before 6PM on Tuesday 23rd October 1956 when I arrived at Bródy Sándor Street. We all thought that it would be the place of a historic moment: the Sixteen Points, the rebels' list of demands, would be read live on Budapest Radio. You see, they had been fooled into believing this was going to happen.

'A pretend stage, a pretend microphone, had been put up. Everyone thought it would happen. Instead, what happened was members of the ÁVO, the feared secret security force, who were inside the building, opened fire. A young woman who was only feet away from me was hit in the head. Her blood splashed across my face. She fell next to my feet. Then two others fell, hit in the back of the legs as we *ran away*.

'As we fled, an ambulance arrived – and this is how heinous the ÁVO was – so people ran to it, wanting help. The back of the ambulance opened and a dozen more ÁVO officers came out – firing their weapons at random. Fortunately, I was far enough away to escape, but I looked back and I saw. I saw everything they did.

'Somehow I got away from there, but that was the first horror I saw. The first thing I will always remember.'

'What did you do?'

'The only thing I could do. I got home as quickly as I could, cleaned the blood off my face, and I didn't leave for two days.

'But on Thursday 25th October, I decided to join the protesters in Parliament Square. Eight thousand people.

'They fired on the crowd again. Seventy-five killed. Two hundred and eighty-two wounded.

'I helped tend to the wounded, covering gunshot wounds with whatever clothing I could get hold of. I, and many others who had come back, did our best. We did our best.

'I spent the last of my time in Budapest at the Corvin Cinema building and the Corvin Passage. Bizarrely, it was a place where I felt safe, even when I witnessed conflict. Perhaps it was my love of cinema that made me feel this way.

'And then I heard of the first of two things that pushed me out of the country forever. Mosonmagyaróvár, a small town in the northwest of Hungary, where half the town was demonstrating. They marched, shouting 'Russkik haza,' 'Russians out'.

'They reached the local ÁVO base, demanding that the red star flag be taken down. And then machine-gun fire mowed them down. No warning. *Rat–a–tat. Rat–a–tat. Rat–a–tat.*

'Fifty-two were killed. Old men, old women, girls, young mothers, schoolchildren.

'An eighteen-month-old baby was shot to pieces.

'I couldn't take the news. I think I cried like a baby, for the baby.'

Michael got up, filled his father's glass, patted him on the shoulder. 'It sounds like a nightmare.'

'It was worse than a nightmare. Life had changed forever. I had to leave. On Friday 26th October, I knew my time was at an end. I'd heard about fighting in Széna Square, so I went to see if I could help clear up. But I got there too soon, before the fighting had completely ended.

'The square is a vast area with roads going around it, surrounded on every side by buildings. When I got there, gunfire sounded in every direction. I saw the rebels; they were no older than teenagers. They were using a Russian armoured car that had a machine-gun on it and they were using overturned tramcars as barricades. I saw some Russians get mowed down. And I saw some Hungarians fall.

'Something instinctively moved me closer to them. I crawled behind debris, behind bricks and mortar, behind abandoned cars. I had a clear view of the area behind the nearest tramcar. There was just one fighter behind it, a teenager. And a bullet hit him straight in the neck. Nobody was there to help him. Nobody was there to *hold* him. To hold him as he died. I was compelled.

'I charged towards him. As I neared the tramcar, I leapt for the ground behind it. His eyes were wide open, horror, panic in them. He was making gurgling noises, quick, sharp breaths. Struggling. A sound that wasn't human. He sounded like he was drowning.

'I lifted his head in my arms, placed it on my leg as I kneeled. Took hold of his arm. Held it. Moved my hand on it. *Tried* to soothe. 'You're a hero,' I whispered. More gurgling, sinking. 'You're a hero,' I repeated, not knowing anything else to say.

'A fucking hero.'

Michael nodded his head. 'You know better than most what it's like.'

'Oh, I know, Michael. I *understand*.'

'I keep seeing her.'

'I keep seeing *them*. It never stops. But you'll find a way.'

'This helps,' Michael said, indicating the bottle of whisky.

'Always.'

Chapter Seventeen

Michael awoke to the sound of a car speeding past the house, its tires screeching. His head was pounding, his eyes squinting because of the daylight that was forcing its way through the curtained window, and his stiff bones ached while he stretched. When his view of the room and his consciousness of where he was approached clarity, Michael noticed his father, who was asleep in the armchair.

The second bottle of whisky was still on the coffee table. It was empty. Michael grimaced at the sight of it. He got up, stumbled to the bathroom and fell onto the toilet. He couldn't stand. His head in his hands, he felt like crying. His head pounded as if it had been hit by a car.

Once finished, he pulled himself to his feet with a hand on the sink. He turned on the tap, threw water on his face. Letting the droplets run down it, he opened his eyes, looked in the mirror. In a moment, the blur that was there, just like it had been last night, passed and a true likeness of his face came into view. He scoffed at the sight. His hair was standing on end, his eyes were sticky, he stank of booze. He cupped some water into his mouth, swallowed it, knew he needed more to quench his thirst and clear his head.

Determined to go to the kitchen and pour coffee into the largest mug he could find, he opened the bathroom door and stepped into the hallway.

Like there was a brick wall in his path, he halted.

A brown padded envelope lay on the floor. He hadn't seen it when he'd come out of the lounge and entered the bathroom. Had it been there? Likely he hadn't been paying attention. He eyed it suspiciously, as if it was something he'd run over with his car, as if he were curious whether it still had a pulse. Something made him hesitate, something base within him. It wasn't fear, but it was overwhelming.

He walked to the door, peered through the peephole. His eyes remained somewhat out of focus. He saw but didn't see.

Using the door for leverage, he bent down and picked up the envelope. As soon as he had it in his hands, he thought, *Gloves*, and dropped it. Shaking his head, trying to clear his mind, be the detective, he rocked over to his coat. He was still drunk – drunk and hung-over at the same time. He retrieved a pair of gloves from his coat, not the work kind, but the keeping-warm kind. Then he went back to the envelope, lifted it up and took it into the lounge.

As he entered, József stirred. He didn't move, just looked at his son. Looking through him, perhaps.

'Another one,' Michael announced.

Now József saw him. *Really saw him.* He stood up. Quickly for an old man, quickly also for a man with a hangover. He was helped by his Hungarian blood; the whisky would be a distant memory, would have no impact on the present. 'Just now?'

'Think so.'

Michael placed the envelope on the coffee table and got onto his knees. His father stood on the other side of the table, gazing down. The Budapest postmark was visible to both of them. Neither mentioned it. With hands still gloved, Michael unsealed the envelope.

He removed the contents.

Another blade. Rusted. Snapped. Blood on this one. *A lot of blood.* There was blood inside the envelope, too. Michael held the blade in his hands and stood up. He held it out towards his father, whose head moved from side to side involuntarily, whose breathing quickened.

'Another one,' he said. 'Another innocent person dead. Another life lost.'

'We don't know that yet.' He removed the beeper from his pocket. 'There hasn't been a call yet.'

József raised his eyebrows quizzically. 'You believe that?'

'I was being optimistic.' Then: 'No. No, I don't.'

Hopelessly: 'Who this time?'

Michael noticed the blood had ended up on his beeper. From the blood that was on his glove. Looking at it, he added, 'It's fresh.'

Next out of the envelope came a piece of paper. He held it up.

'*Close to home,*' he read aloud.

Placing the note on the table by the side of the blade, Michael dashed to the window, lifted the net and peered out. Searching.

But nothing.

He removed his gloves and put them on the coffee table. 'Wait here,' he said and left the room quickly. He spoke with an authority his father had rarely heard from him.

Michael opened the front door and raced towards the road. But his body came to a stop almost as soon as his feet landed on tarmac. He doubled over as if struck by a poorly executed extension on the piste, a flat blade right into the stomach. Noise came out of his mouth, an exhalation of puff. No words. Vomit welled up in his throat.

'Michael.' He heard his father's voice from inside the house. Couldn't say anything back. 'Michael?' He tried to speak. Was useless. Tears – thought he felt them coming. Wanted them to. *Willed* them to flood from him.

But they didn't – he was simply stunned.

Now with an element of impatience: 'Michael?' The sound closer, approaching. 'Michael?' As he emerged into daylight, József froze in the doorway.

Michael gulped in some air. Swallowed as much as he could, hopeful that it would help him speak, that he wouldn't be sick. As his father reached his side, he struggled and managed to emit words. 'No, don't look. Go in. Inside.' When his father didn't move, Michael pushed him. Released one long, continuous shout as he continued to push, with his father clinging onto him: 'Inside!'

Chapter Eighteen

Michael was in his father's lounge, the empty whisky bottle in front of him, another opened, its contents poured into two glasses. His head was in his shaky hands.

The only sign of life, bar his occasional sloth-like clasping of the whisky glass, was his ribcage extending, deeply, and contracting. Inhale, exhale. *In through the nose, out of the mouth. Try to calm down.* József Varga had taught him that. Right now, Michael was struggling to adhere to that advice.

His father sat in his armchair but faced away from Michael. He was staring at the television, which wasn't on, as if he were watching hypnotic images. Not a moving image, not a film, the news or a programme on television; rather, a still, some kind of staged photograph, so lifelike, so real, but unbelievable at the same time. His mouth was agape as the sight was imprinted in front of him.

Outside his house, on his driveway, in his car.

Blue eyes, shiny skin, long blonde hair. He couldn't see, wouldn't know, but a slim figure, too. Short, fit.

Rachel Bradshaw sat in the front of his car. Her head leaned against the headrest. Her eyes were wide open. Her nose was broken, was bloodied. Her lips were smudged with blood. The blade was resting in her neck. It had been pushed through from front to back. Her hands were taped to the bottom of the steering wheel, with thick grey masking tape.

On the windscreen, spelled out in her thick red blood, the words: *PAPA BEM.*

First the cute blonde who he didn't know, and now Rachel who he did.

Michael saw Rachel speaking to him at the club, in the pub, the smile she always carried, her hand touching his shoulder. He saw her with him at fencing training three nights ago, laughing, the knowing wink before he bade her goodnight and promised her a drink next time.

He thought his heart would melt. Felt something ripping at his throat, thought his ability to speak might be lost forever.

Couldn't breathe any more.

Didn't want to.

Rachel. Those blue eyes. That shiny skin. That long blonde hair, tied back when she fenced.

The smile.

The loss he felt was immense and he had no idea why. He hadn't had a physical relationship with Rachel, but the desire had been there. And friendship. And now, whoever was behind this had picked someone close to him, or someone he had wanted to be close to. They'd made it personal.

And then a sudden realisation hit him: he feared for Sally's safety, needed to call her, warn her.

And then even worse: his son, Ricky. He had to call Julianne as well, tell her to pack and stay with a friend until this case was solved.

Who knew who'd be next. *It could be anyone*, he thought.

'God damn you.' Even Michael wasn't sure whether this was directed at his father or the unknown intruder who had penetrated deeply into their lives.

József didn't turn around, only angled his head in the

direction from which the softly spoken words came.

He held no grudge to be told this, if the words were meant for him. He understood what it meant to feel frustration, to be devastated. Through bad choices, he'd brought this plague on them both. And on Nicole Sarsons, and on Brenda Harrison, and on Chloe Raynor, and now on Rachel Bradshaw, the first of the four he didn't know, but clearly his son did.

József waited for more. When nothing else came, he said, 'I know, I caused this. But I'm not *doing this*. God damn the son of a bitch that is. I've made stupid fucking mistakes. I've pissed off too many people.'

'It's a wonder it's taken this long.'

József nodded. 'Maybe.'

More silence. Michael's head still down. Head shaking. His shoulders tense, his feet pressing into the ground, rising onto the balls and then back down.

'Everybody makes mistakes.'

Michael, eventually: 'Everybody does.'

'And, believe me, mine have kept me up every night for years. And now this guilt, I can assure you, this fresh guilt will see to all the years I have left. So I ask you, please stop this bastard.'

'Stop him?' Michael said incredulously. 'We don't know who he is. The Revolution leads are dead ends. He's a ghost, nothing more. He'll keep on and on –'

'No, Michael.' József got up and stepped towards his son. 'No.' He paused. 'This is a game to him. He's played with my mind, now he's playing with yours. There will be no more killing. Not here, anyway. He's made that clear in his message. Now I understand what we need to do next. What *you* need to do.'

'What?'

'Papa Bem.'

'Who is Papa Bem? I presume it's a person.'

József shook his head. 'Not who, Michael. What. Papa Bem *was* a person – Józef Bem, a Polish general in the eighteenth century who inspired Hungarians through two revolutions – but all it can mean is the *Bem Statue*. The statue that's in Budapest as a memorial to him.'

'I see,' Michael said.

'Yes?'

'I need to go to Budapest.'

'Yes, you do.'

Chapter Nineteen

Outside, the light is bright, the air fresh and the breeze chilly. There's no more rain, but dew layers the grass. The pavement and road shine, puddle-ridden. Michael lifts the collar of his coat as he stands, dizzy, the air hitting him with its post-heavy-drinking effect. He puts his hand onto the side of the house, leans on it.

He surveys the crime scene operatives who are working on the car in the driveway. Rachel's body has already been checked, photographed, swabbed and taken away for further examination.

Michael moves slowly towards the car. Blood remains on the seat. At the sight of it, he turns away and vomits into the flowerbed. It makes him realise how hung-over or drunk he is, or perhaps how much Rachel's friendship meant to him; the sight of a body has never made him reel like this, even Chloe Raynor's. Vomiting, however, refreshes him somewhat.

He's left his father behind physically, but not in his mind. He could despise the man who's in the house, just metres away – because of how he is, because of how he's spent his life behaving, because of the father he's been, the fencer he's been, the arrogance he's exuded – but he feels sympathy for him.

Michael leaves. While he walks home, he phones Julianne and then Sally. He warns them. Then he's satisfied they'll be safe, if they do as he's asked.

He hopes the walk will help him shake off the hangover and the pain. He hopes.

Chapter Twenty

It was pitch dark when József's eyes prised apart. He was in his bed, but he couldn't remember getting here. It took several moments before his ears adjusted, before he got his bearings, heard the scratching sound again.

His body moved slowly as he got off the bed. The alcohol. He remembered finishing the bottle and then starting, and finishing, another. He didn't feel steady on his feet, had pushed himself too far, rare for him, so he put his arm out and took hold of the wall in an attempt to keep steady.

Slowly, that sound – the scratching – became clearer, more deliberate, more intense. Like metal scraping along wood. And, as suddenly as he'd realised it was there, the sound became piercingly loud, with a screeching accompaniment. Like violins ravaged against your ear.

And then it stopped, no warning.

He pushed himself from the wall and walked towards the closed bedroom door. His hand reached towards it, then came to a stop as his body came to a stop. He took one more deep breath, readying himself, still not fully in control at a moment he knew he had to be.

He opened the door, cautiously, revealing himself to the corridor and whatever was in it. After the door opened fully, he stepped into the hallway, the staircase in front of him. He stood still, his eyes adjusting to the slight light that came through the bathroom window, the result of a distant streetlamp.

As his vision became clearer, he peered down the

stairs. His eyes focused and widened. The first thing he saw was the woollen shape of the balaclava. Then the eyes and then the whole form.

The eyes – they looked up towards him. The form – it didn't move. And *he* didn't move. He remained rooted in the carpet upon which he stood, staring into the eyes that, with tilted head, looked into his, with distant familiarity. A welcome to the past. A hello. A stare-down. Eyes, and eyes locked on one another. He tried to recognise them.

And then the figure's right hand moved, lifted to the side of the neck and then, slowly, across it. The thumb grazed the skin as the arm pulled it across the neck. Even filled with alcohol and its effects, József recognised the signal. He knew: a sign of death. And this was when he suddenly felt exposed, glanced into his own hands and realised he'd not picked up his blade. His legs unsticking from the carpet, he moved as quickly as his body would take him back into the bedroom, grabbed the blade from next to the bed, and hurriedly returned to the corridor.

But as soon as he reached the second step down, ready to fight to end this, he found he was alone. The figure, with the unrecognisable eyes from the past, had gone.

Chapter Twenty-One

József awoke a little before seven in the morning. His neck was stiff. He had no memory of returning to bed, but he remembered the figure. He remembered the hand moving across, cutting, the throat. Warning him, showing him how it would end.

Or did he?

He asked himself, *Was there really someone here, a masked figure, eyes I know but couldn't recognise? How did I get back to bed?* He couldn't remember. *Did I search the house, check that I was safe and alone, that he'd really gone?* He couldn't remember.

He got up and went downstairs, cautiously again, the blade in his hand. He reached the front door and tried the handle. It was locked. He checked in each of the rooms. Nothing. He searched for any sign of disturbance. Nothing. Searched for any sign that he'd been visited. He could find none.

He went outside and stretched in the early-morning sunshine. The rays radiated through his body and somehow he felt anew. His eyes squinted as he lifted his head towards the sky, wondering *why*. It was a surprisingly pleasant morning.

'Who are you?' he whispered to himself. His eyes moved towards the house across the road. He gazed at each window. Then he looked at the property to its right, again considering each window. 'Who?'

He arched his eyebrows as a car drove past. It was moving slowly. Dark blue, a Ford. A man in the front seat. The man's head, with eyes that may or may not have been familiar, turned towards József, and then the car disappeared down the road. József's gaze followed it until it was out of view.

He heard birds singing. The air was crisp despite the sun. József might have shivered, but instead he opened his arms wide, letting the sun seep further in. The blade fell from his hand, landed on the grass. The thud grabbed his attention and his eyes came to rest on the fallen steel form.

The blade. A sabre, one he'd had for thirty years, give or take, given to him by his father shortly before he'd passed away. The blade, and all it represented. The source of so much pleasure for him. The source of so much pain. He contemplated it, thinking whether it had been worth it. Had it been worth pursuing the sport so much, to the detriment of most of what had been around him, when he considered what had become of his life, this final phase, alone in the home he'd called his and his wife's, and now as the target of someone prepared to kill and kill and kill? Had it been the right choice, all those years ago? A different lifetime, it felt like, a different place from here, a different mind. Somewhere along the way, he'd contracted a disease, something rotten, something that right now had infected his soul and was tearing away at him. This person, whoever it was, had infected him.

But the sun, it made him feel different, more alive than he'd felt during the past few years. Ever since his wife had left him to continue the course of life alone.

No, he thought. *The blade is here for a reason.* He knew what the blade meant, to him and to those who had revered his skills over the past seven decades. He knew how to use it like no other person. So he planned to use it – he'd use it to defend himself and those around him. This unknown person wouldn't be able to prevent him from doing the one thing he could do better than anyone else. Fight. He'd find a way to stand tall and respond. And Michael would, too. If he'd taught his son one thing in life, it was how to fight with a blade. And once they started, there'd be no stopping them.

Drifting back into the house, he stood in the hallway, stopped and looked up towards the upstairs landing. Was he standing on the very ground that his mysterious adversary had been perched on only hours ago? He thought but still wasn't sure. Perhaps he'd never know.

But one thought was clearer than all others: if he appeared again, real or imaginary, he wouldn't be allowed to leave this time, not alive.

Chapter Twenty-Two

'No signs of forced entry anywhere. It doesn't look like there was anyone here.'

József had called Michael and told him about the might-have-been intruder. Now the two stood in the hallway downstairs. While he welcomed Michael's comments, he felt only confusion. He still wasn't sure what had happened, what he had – or hadn't – seen.

'The officer in the police car down the road didn't see anyone. I'll make sure the car moves right outside the driveway for the next couple of days while I'm away. And there'll be two officers. At least that'll put off anyone who's planning to do anything stupid. That is, if you saw what you think you saw.'

'I think so.' A pause as he turned and took in the framed pictures on the wall. Family snaps from trips when Michael was younger: Turkey, Spain, Malta, Austria and, of course, Hungary. Lake Balaton and Budapest. Having been young meant that Michael didn't remember most of the trips, but they'd been a well-travelled family. 'I don't know.'

'Well, a police presence on the doorstep should help either way.'

József nodded but didn't make eye contact. Still finding it hard to say, he repeated, 'Thank you.'

They walked outside, Michael leading the way. When he was a few steps into the driveway, József asked, 'Do you have anything at all? Anything else to go on?'

Michael stopped and turned to face his father. 'Aside

from the envelopes and the blades, no. They're covered in prints, but there are no matches on file. We're giving them a closer check for fibres, but I don't think that'll lead anywhere. The envelopes were manufactured, stocked and sold somewhere. Maybe they were posted and then handled countless times, but I have my doubts about them actually arriving from Budapest. That's more about the message. It just doesn't make logistical sense. Whoever it is, he's careful. And he's close by.'

József put his hands on his hips. 'What's the likelihood?'

'Of what?'

'That you're going to find this son of a bitch.'

Michael exhaled. 'There's always hope.'

József stepped forwards, this time maintaining eye contact. 'You can do it.'

Michael nodded his head. 'You have my word –' He broke eye contact, turned towards the lawn. 'I won't stop trying. I'll fly out tomorrow. Can you connect me with someone who knows the Budapest of your past?'

'István, of course.'

Twice during his early teenage years, Michael and his father had stayed at István's home, but Michael couldn't remember István.

István Novák was the grandson of József's father's brother's daughter. He was the closest to family that József had in Hungary. József's brother was rarely mentioned; Michael didn't know the reason why the two were barely in touch.

'And as it looks like we're starting at the Bem Statue, someone who knows the history of the Revolution.'

'István studied history at university. You won't find

anyone better informed about the Revolution than him.'

'Perfect.'

'Do you want to stay at his apartment?'

'No, I'll be at a hotel. I just need someone to help me with any clues that might be waiting. I assume there'll be something for us at Papa Bem. The force has been in touch with the local detectives' bureau and they're putting me in touch with a detective over there. They'll meet me at the airport and take me to the hotel. Keep it formal. The detective will take me around, help me make my inquiries.

'Have you spoken to István about what's going on?'

A pause. Then, finally: 'Yes. He knows everything.'

Spotting the blade that József had dropped earlier on the grass, Michael walked to it and crouched down. He picked it up, ran his fingers along its sheen. He aimed the point at the ground, eyed the line of the blade, the slight bend. Then he stood up and went back to his father. 'I won't stop,' he repeated and he handed the blade to his father, adding, 'Yours, I think.'

József took the blade, cracked a smile. Weak but genuine.

'I'll call you when I arrive.'

'Look after yourself.'

Michael nodded. 'You too.'

Michael left József standing on the lawn. József's gaze didn't follow Michael's car as it departed but remained on the blade.

Part Two: Allez

Hungary

Chapter Twenty-Three

A late-morning Malev flight departing London Heathrow at 11AM means Michael arrives in Budapest's Ferihegy International Airport at just after 3PM local time.

Although Ferihegy is the name of the neighbourhood where the airport is located, it was named in honour of Ferenc Xavér Mayerffy, a former estate owner in the area who in the early-to-mid-nineteenth century established vineyards and was a key player in the development of viticulture in the city. *Feri* is a diminutive form of Ferenc and *hegy* translates as hill. Today, the area is almost completely flat, but in the past there was a sandy hillock standing 147 metres tall, which was destroyed in the 1940s during the airport's construction.

Exiting Ferihegy International Airport's customs declaration zone in Terminal 2, with baggage in hand, Michael walks round the corner and through the doorway that leads to the arrivals area. A crowd of at least fifty people is waiting for loved ones, business acquaintances, visitors of all kinds.

It takes Michael a few moments before he spots the card that has his name written on it in thick black felt pen. And then his eyes lift and come to rest on the face of the person holding it, the detective who'll be his guide around Budapest: a woman of about thirty, with long, wavy brown hair, the ends cupping her breasts, part of the hair in front of her shoulders and the other part behind, hazel eyes, tanned and gleaming skin, and a beaming smile when she sees that her guest has arrived. She has on a beige shirt, a tight grey skirt, black tights, black shoes with high heels.

'Mr Varga?' she says, walking towards Michael, arm outstretched, her hips swaying.

Michael knows it's customary in Hungary for the man to wait for the woman to offer her hand. 'Yes.' Taking her hand, he feels the smoothness of her skin.

'Gizi Orbán. Very good to meet you.'

'A pleasure.'

She leads Michael out of the terminal building and into the sunshine. It's warm. It makes a surprising and pleasant difference from the dreariness of the majority of the past week in London. And, as she leads the way, the view he's afforded of her backside piques his interest.

He hasn't been in Budapest since he was fourteen. Doesn't remember it at all, doesn't remember the airport and its surroundings, doesn't remember anything he sees during the drive.

They make their way from the airport to the centre of Pest, which is the airport side of the city. Gizi drives a red Volkswagen Polo. She swerves in and out of the traffic, rarely releasing the accelerator, rarely pressing the brake. And when she does, she does so with force, as if she's trying to punish the pedal.

'How much do you know about why I'm here?' he asks.

'It's been explained. I know what I need to know to be useful to you. I'm sorry, especially for your father. We want to help.' She has a slight American twang to her accent; no trace of the brutal Hungarian lilt that's often noticeable.

'Thank you,' Michael says, nodding, blinking several

times. After a lengthy pause, he glances at her, notices her elbows locked as she clutches the steering wheel, and adds, 'So how long have you been a detective?'

'Not long.' Michael glimpses her jaw tighten as she swerves to the left, then to the right. 'Six years almost.'

'And how do you find it? What's being a cop in Hungary like?'

She shrugs. 'It's a job. It's not quite what I thought it would be when I was signing up. We're not especially popular with the public. And there's a fair amount of corruption in this country. It's to be expected where salaries in law enforcement are low. You can't really blame the public for being wary, or even angry.' She turns towards him, only for a fraction of a second, and smiles.

'Well, don't let that carefree attitude get me killed, okay?' A smile from Michael, too.

'I care. I care.'

'Good.'

'But it *is* a job.' And she laughs.

As they go along Andrassy Avenue, she points. 'That's the Terror Háza. The House of Terror. It's a museum dedicated to the Hungarian Revolution. It commemorates the lives lost. Many pictures of victims are on display, and there's a preserved Russian tank. It's haunting. If you want a fuller understanding of your father's escape from Hungary, this is the place to go. It was once the headquarters of the ÁVO, the dreaded, evil secret police. They made hundreds of people, thousands maybe, disappear.'

Gizi turns onto Üllői Avenue, one of Budapest's longest and main roads. Michael glances to the right. He's surprised to recognise a sign he notices: *Corvin*.

'Can you turn around?' he asks.

'Why's that?' Gizi says, signalling and turning without waiting for the road to be clear.

'The sign. My father was telling me about it, I think.' As two signs come into view, a horizontal sign sticking out high over the pavement and another, vertical, clinging onto a building, Michael says, 'Those.'

Gizi parks the car further down the road, they get out of it and they walk towards the signs.

As they approach, Michael says, 'Is it the Corvin Passage?'

'Yes, and the Corvin Cinema. It was a cinema in 1956 and it still is today.'

As they reach the Corvin Passage, a fairly narrow pedestrian-only walkway with buildings lining each side, they encounter the cinema, which is a yellow oval building that sits in the centre of the area. They walk towards it, slowly, Michael looking up at the buildings on both sides.

In front of the cinema is a memorial dedicated to the 1956 Revolution, a young man holding a rifle pointed downwards, standing atop a rock, with two round boulders on platforms on either side of him. He looks like he's on guard.

Behind him is a triangular block and beyond that are several plaques dedicated to leaders of the Revolution whose lives were lost. These are fixed on the Corvin Cinema building. As he walks along scanning them, Michael recognises several of the names.

Michael and Gizi stand next to the soldier. He points at the triangular block. There's writing on one side of it. 'What does it say?' he enquires, thinking about his father potentially standing right here all those years ago, thinking about the fighting that took place in this very place, the deaths.

'It says: 'On the fortieth anniversary of 1956, in memory and in honour of the Budapest Boys and the revolutionaries and their fight for freedom'. They were called the Budapest Boys because so many of those who fought and died were so terribly young, yet patriotic to the end.'

There are a lot of people around and there's vibrancy in the air. To Michael, it feels like a different world from the one his father spoke about. 'It's hard to think there was such devastating fighting here.'

'Yes, it is *now*.'

They circle the building, moving round it anti-clockwise. To the right is a passage that creates a walkway under the building that lines the right side of the cinema. It seems like a small courtyard. The building towering above is five storeys high.

'I could see how tanks would struggle to get in here,' Michael says, pointing to the passage. 'It's narrow and low. The rebels could fight off the soldiers from here. They *were* brave.' Where once there would have been shelling and destruction, now there are small trees, plant pots and benches.

'Yes, they could, and they did. The cinema was also connected to a collection of underground alleyways and secret corridors that linked to roads and other nearby buildings, so getting in and out was very straightforward for anyone who was a local. It gave the rebels the element of surprise. Arrive suddenly, remain unseen, throw a Molotov cocktail or fire a weapon, and then disappear into the darkness. The Russians struggled to deal with it and for days they were losing the battle here.'

'Brave, brave men,' Michael repeats, leaning to inspect another plaque on the cinema.

'*Boys.*'

Michael stands still. His head moves from left to right and back again. 'A waste.'

After they've taken it all in, they return to the car. Michael feels strangely emotional, the poignancy between what he's just seen and what he's recently heard from his father difficult to absorb. They don't speak when they get back into the vehicle, when Gizi fires up the engine, when they re-join the traffic.

They continue on, arriving at the Hotel Ketto after another ten minutes. 'You check in,' she says, 'and I'll pick you up again in an hour. Meet me in the lobby.'

'First stop, the Bem Statue?'

'Absolutely.'

He thanks her, gets out and enters the hotel. The lobby is quiet, the wait to be welcomed very short.

In only a matter of minutes, Michael is opening the door to his room. It's a simple set-up: a double bed, a wardrobe, a small television, a desk on which sits a telephone, and an attached bathroom. He quickly unpacks his suitcase, hangs up his shirts and jumps in the shower.

As the hour mark approaches, Michael, dressed in fresh clothing, a white shirt and dark grey suit, no tie, makes his way from the room, down the stairs and into the lobby. Gizi isn't here yet, so he decides to go outside, save her parking and coming in herself.

She pulls up a few minutes after he arrives on the

curb. He notices her smile when she sees he's waiting for her. As soon as he gets into the car, she thanks him for his courtesy, tells him it isn't necessary, that she really doesn't mind parking and coming inside.

'Perhaps for a coffee later,' he jokes. But he knows how his mind works: he's serious and wouldn't say no.

After several minutes, Michael speaks. He's still thinking about the Corvin Passage. And he's fighting thoughts of Chloe Raynor and Rachel Bradshaw. 'It's so odd to think that not so long ago this city was ravaged by war.'

'Destroyed. Utter devastation.' She thinks. 'Look, we'll go into Buda, which is where the Bem Statue is, via a bridge that takes us to where it all began.'

'Where what began?'

'The Revolution. 1956. Let's stop and walk the walk they all took that day.'

'Okay. Where do we start?'

'The Petőfi Statue.'

Over the Elizabeth Bridge, they enter Buda, a very different area from the city-like style of Pest, hilly and green in contrast.

Originally three cities, Buda and Óbuda on the western bank of the Danube, and Pest on the eastern bank, Budapest was born upon unification of the trio in 1873. There are a number of theories suggesting how Budapest came to possess its chosen name. One, from the Middle Ages, suggests Buda was named after Attila the Hun's brother Bleda, who was also known as Buda. With regard to Pest, it's said it originated in Roman times when a fortress called Contra-Aquincum was in the region and referred to as Pession by the Greco-

Roman writer, mathematician, astrologer and astronomer Claudius Ptolemy, who died in AD 168.

Gizi parks the car when she and Michael arrive at Petőfi Square. Roads on all sides surround a raised square section of grass.

'He was a poet and a revolutionary,' Gizi explains. '*Arise Hungarians* is his most famous poem. It had something to do with starting the earlier revolution that happened in 1848. Petőfi himself was a leader then and died in the Battle of Segesvár.'

Erected in 1882, the bronze statue of Petőfi stands two-and-a-half metres tall. Michael positions himself in front of it, gazing up towards the scroll that's in Petőfi's right hand, his left arm proclaiming in the air.

'Twelve thousand people were standing here on the first day,' she says.

'Twelve thousand? Bloody hell.'

'Was your father here?'

Michael shakes his head. 'Not that I know.'

'Let's walk it.'

They walk along the Buda embankment. To their right is the Danube and parallel to it is a road that lines the river's side. The embankment is at least ten metres above the road. On their left are cliff edges raised high above. Szt Gellért Szobor, or Gellért Hill, Budapest's highest point at around one hundred and forty metres, towers above them. At its peak is the St Gellért monument and slightly further back is the Citadel fortress.

Named after Saint Gellért, who came to Hungary as a missionary bishop at the request of King Stephen I in approximately AD 1000, the hill is host to a monument that was erected in his memory. Gellért was killed in

1046 by pagans who were angry that he was trying to convert Magyars to Christianity: placed in a barrel, he was rolled down the hill straight into the Danube.

Gellért Hill is also home to Szabadsag Szobor, or the Liberation Monument, which was erected after World War Two, in 1947, by the Soviets to commemorate the defeat of the Nazis. Standing fourteen metres high, it depicts a woman who holds an olive branch, a symbol of peace, in her hands.

Legend states that witches used to visit the hill every night, riding on the back of a human being.

When Gizi sees Michael staring at the fortress, she says, 'During the Revolution, the Soviets occupied the citadel. From there, they fired tank shells over the river into Pest. But now it's a hotel with the most stunning views.'

The construction in 1851 of Citadella, as it's known by Hungarians, was led by Julius Jacob von Haynau, a commander of the then-ruling Habsburg Monarchy, after it had successfully quelled the Revolution of 1848. At the time, a demonstration of sheer size and power, Citadella had a complement of sixty canons.

After several minutes of continuous walking, Gizi instructs, 'Over here.'

They cross the road, Gizi telling Michael what she knows about the history, and the statue comes into view. In the centre of Bem Square is the Bem Statue, which was erected in memory of József Zachariasz Bem, a Polish general who fought with Hungary in the 1848 Revolution against the Habsburg Monarchy and Austrian rule. Grass fills the square and in the centre of it are oval flowerbeds. There's a section of gravel and some benches. Cars drive on all sides of the square – the roads are busy – and tall buildings surround it.

The statue, which feels like it stands taller than Petőfi's, even though Michael isn't sure, points towards Pest with an arm. 'It's like he's encouraging anyone who stands in front of him,' he says.

'To the youngsters fighting in 1956, he was like a father figure. They called him Bem Apó.'

'Papa Bem.'

'That's right,' she says, impressed. 'You see the writing on the statue there? That's what it says.'

Michael nods. 'There's got to be some kind of clue here. This is where the message said to come.'

Gizi frowns. 'It looks the same as it always does to me.'

They circle the statue and, when they find nothing of note, they search the grounds of the small square.

Nothing.

Michael returns to the statue and faces it. He looks up, into the eyes of Papa Bem, and he thinks about his own father. Papa Varga, the reason he's here now. And, frustrated, he has no answer.

'I'm sorry I can't help you more with this,' Gizi says after some time.

He turns to face her. 'Me too. Hopefully István will have some ideas.'

'Let me take you to him.'

They return to the car, a fifteen-minute walk. She pulls out a piece of paper containing István Novák's address, turns the car around, and they return to Pest. Shortly thereafter, they arrive outside a large apartment block. Gizi says she'll come in with Michael in case István's

English isn't up to much. He can't remember. Shamefully, Michael has never learned Hungarian. He's never been taught it.

They leave the car in a car park outside a row of shops. It's a large area, not tarmacked, and off the main road. The main road, which they have to cross, comprises two three-lane carriageways that open up to five lanes yards ahead where there are traffic lights and turnings into other roads.

The apartment complex is old and dark but clean. They enter through the exterior double doors, walk up six steps, and come to a lift. Taking it to the third floor, they go to apartment twenty-two. Michael knocks on the green door.

A white-haired man, a bushy moustache above his lip, a cardigan wrapped around his shoulders and a newspaper under his arm, opens the door. His head peers round before the rest of his body is visible.

'István?' Michael asks, not remembering what the man looks like.

But István immediately knows it's Michael: 'Michael Varga,' he says, stepping forwards, his arms open wide, and embracing Michael in a deep hug, one he holds for several seconds. He kisses Michael, first on the left cheek and then on the right.

When István releases Michael, his eyes land on Gizi. Michael introduces her but is quickly cut off by Gizi who, in her Hungarian tongue, begins a conversation with István that soon has them both sniggering, sounding, Michael thinks, almost mischievous. They shake hands and István bows his head slightly. Michael watches Gizi, impressed. And he quickly finds himself keen to know what they're saying. Hungarian, which belongs to the Ugor branch of the Finno-Ugric language family, goes straight over Michael's head. When, amid so many words foreign to him, he hears his name, once then twice, his curiosity increases and he glances from one of them to the other, an expectant grin on his face, waiting to be told what's being said, waiting for a long time actually, waiting and never receiving the answer he craves. Now he remembers what it's like to be a non-speaker in a foreign country.

István invites them in and offers them coffee. They settle in the kitchen on two benches that line a corner, a table before them. István lights a gas ring, places a stovetop espresso maker on top of the flame and waits patiently.

When he's poured three espressos, offered milk and sugar, he asks, 'Okay if I smoke?'

Michael nods. Gizi withdraws a packet of cigarettes herself, saying, 'I'll join you.'

'Coffee and cigarette,' István explains. 'Man's great pleasure.'

'Not only man's,' Gizi adds, leaning forwards with a cigarette between her lips. István holds out his lighter. He brings her cigarette to life, repeats the process with his own, and both lean back, inhaling deeply, quickly following the inhalation with a sip of extremely strong and black espresso.

Michael sips his milky and sugar-filled own.

István's English isn't fluent, his sentences not entirely accurate, but he can make himself understood and he can understand much of what Michael says. Gizi's language skills, it seems, will only be needed in an emergency, and

Michael's pleased by that.

István sits on a stool on the opposite side of the bench from Michael. The walls, wooden, have patterned plates mounted on them. Beautifully decorated, no doubt collectable porcelain.

István sees Michael looking at the plates. 'My mother's,' he says. 'She give to me. Her mother give to her. Is many more in box and in dining room. Hungarian porcelain most wonderful.'

Michael agrees.

He's eager to get on, so he soon asks, 'István, do you have any idea why we might be told to go to Papa Bem, to the Bem Statue.'

'I think. I think very hard and I no have reason.' He shakes his head vigorously. 'No, no.'

'Please, keep thinking.'

'So while we think more, is there anywhere we can take you today?' Gizi asks after a silence has fallen on the room, filled with more sipping and puffing.

'You know, I'd like to see my father's fencing salle. That is, if it's still here. Does it still exist?'

Gizi repeats the request in Hungarian, the word *salle* creating the need. István's face immediately lights up, he smiles and he guffaws, a chesty sound, frothy. He's been smoking for a long time.

'Of course,' he says. 'Of course. I take. We go. Spartacus.'

And as soon as the words have escaped his lips, he's up, energy abounding, taking his cup to the sink and washing it. When Gizi and Michael's coffee cups are empty, they're snatched from the table and also cleaned.

'We go,' István says. 'We go.' Repeating himself is, it seems, a habit.

Michael doesn't remember anything about István from when he visited as a child. Growing up, his life in England has remained almost entirely separate from his father's in Hungary. One or two of his father's friends visited their UK home when Michael was a child and teenager, but his and his father's time in Hungary has been limited. Michael wonders whether this has anything to do with his father's and uncle's relationship, but only blank spaces plug the gaps where there are answers to his questions.

They leave the apartment, wait patiently for the lift, István coughing occasionally, a loud hacking cough though, something that sounds like it emanates from the base of his gut.

István speaks to Gizi, more streaming Hungarian lilt filling the air, as the lift descends, but he keeps his gaze on Michael. He wears a big grin, as if he's recounting an amusing anecdote about the man in front of him. Then Gizi laughs.

'What?' Michael asks.

'He says you've grown up so much, that you were such a scrawny teenager. Now you're a *ma-an*.' She plays with the word, keeping her tongue between her teeth as she emits the final sound.

'All for the ladies,' Michael says coolly. 'It's all for the ladies.'

The lift door opens and they exit, lady first, István indicates, then Michael, the younger of the gentlemen. There's something about sequence in Hungary – be the gentleman to the lady and then be the older gentleman to the younger one. Age really does bring with it some responsibility, a leadership that's visibly and honourably maintained.

They walk through the dark foyer towards a powerful sunlight. As they emerge, it takes a few moments for Michael's eyes to adjust. István and Gizi don't seem to register the change in light.

Michael keeps still for a moment as he shields his eyes from the sun. Needs just a moment longer. Traffic roars by. Each vehicle yields a wave of air that presses into anyone on the pavement. Michael's jacket lifts in the breeze, his body feeling a chill in the afternoon warmth.

István and Gizi wait for him a few feet on, still talking among themselves.

As the traffic passes by – cars, buses, motorcycles; it's much busier than when they arrived – Michael's eyes start to adjust to the light. He suddenly realises the vastness of the main road that's in front of him. There's no central reservation, no lane markings, just six lanes in total. Drivers swerve in and out, making it difficult to tell where one lane begins and ends. Pedestrians walk along the pavement on both sides of the road in both directions.

Then Michael's eyes, fully focused, come to rest on a man who's in front of the shops on the other side of the road. A man dressed in a beige jacket, jeans and a white baseball cap. Michael can't see his face, because of the distance, the bright sunlight and the cars darting across his eye line. But he can see that the man, swaying from side to side, is watching him. No – *staring at him.*

Michael squints some more, tries to make out the other man's features. He must be thirty metres away, the road's so wide.

'This way,' István calls, and he starts to walk along the

pavement. 'We take metro.'

Michael relinquishes his view of the man on the other side of the road, looks towards István and Gizi, sees their backs as they walk away, and calls after them, 'No, just a –'

Before he finishes the sentence, his head twists back towards the other side of the road, and the swaying man isn't there any more. Michael looks to the left and then to the right. He squints deeper as he tries to see into the shop windows. He scans the car park. Nowhere. Nothing.

'That's not possible,' he says to himself and, automatically, he walks forwards, forgetting the cars that are racing from left to right.

As Michael steps into the road, Gizi turns around. Seeing Michael, trance-like, stepping onto a devastating Hungarian main road, she shrieks, 'Michael, stop!'

Michael flinches back to life, spots a car hurtling towards him, and jumps backwards, landing safely on the pavement, just in time. He shakes himself clear, can't believe what he's just done. He turns towards Gizi who's running towards him.

'What are you doing?' she says. 'Do you know how dangerous this road is?'

István, too, is shuffling back towards Michael.

Bewildered – by the man he's just seen and by his own actions – Michael asks, 'Did you see him?'

'Did I see who?'

'*The man*,' Michael says. He points across the road. 'The man over there. Watching me.'

'Michael, I –'

But Michael isn't listening. His head turns to the left, he steps forwards while he judges the speed of the traffic, and navigates his way across the road. He has to weave in and out of cars that sound their horns in frustration, cars that don't slow down regardless of the man in their midst.

'Michael!' Gizi shouts.

Michael is several metres ahead of her, approaching the middle of the road before she, too, decides to brave it. Cautiously, she lunges onto the road, holds her hand in the air with her police badge visible to the approaching cars. Some come to a violent stop, some swerve and speed on, some drivers ram their horns deep into their steering wheels. Car windows open, men shout. They stop shouting at Gizi when they see the badge, continue shouting at Michael when they see nothing from him.

Dizzy, Michael reaches the other side of the road. He presses his face against the nearest shop's window, opens the door and scans the three aisles, the face of the shopkeeper showing nothing but bewilderment. Then he repeats the same with each of the five shops.

Gizi reaches Michael while he's searching the third shop. He doesn't answer her pleas to explain what's going on. He just pushes past her, goes to the next shop and when no fruit is borne he makes his way, jogging, to the car park. He scans each car, bends low to seek the feet of anyone hiding behind one.

And nothing. Nothing at all.

'Michael,' Gizi says once more. 'Talk to me, Michael.'

Michael stops and turns back towards the main road. His eyes, glazed over, are on the traffic, but he doesn't see anything. Gizi stands beside him. 'There was a man,' he explains. 'Someone strange, the way he rocked from side to side. He was wearing a white cap. A beige jacket, jeans. Somebody's watching me. What the fuck is going on?'

But then Michael thinks: the light. *I was squinting. I couldn't see properly. There were plenty of people walking. Reflections in the shop windows. All those cars. Buses. The noise.*

So maybe not.

'Let's go to the metro,' Gizi encourages. 'Let's get to the fencing club.'

'Yeah,' Michael concedes. 'But you keep your eyes open, okay? And be careful.'

Chapter Twenty-Four

They take the metro to Ferenciek Square, the underground station nearest to Spartacus Fencing Club, which is located on Kossuth Lajos Street in Pest. On the train, Gizi and Michael sit down while István stands without the need to keep hold of something to maintain his balance. The energy the man possesses, despite his sixty-year-old frame and the repeated coughing caused by the cigarette habit, is surprising.

There are only a handful of stops until it's time to exit. All the metro stations seem to have low ceilings, circular support pillars scattered, and dull yellow lighting, and this one is no different. The platform is between both the inbound and outbound lines. The station is surprisingly clean, and vast in size, which also seems to be routine, but there's graffiti in the carriages.

István leads the way off the train and again they emerge into a bright, although not as affecting, sun.

'Will be no training now but maybe lessons,' István explains. 'Training is every night. Usually six to nine-thirty. Lessons in day as well.'

The dedication of the fencers, Michael notices before laying his eyes on even one of them, is far greater than that shown by their British counterparts. No doubt that's the reason for the difference between the countries with regard to their levels of success and their standards in the sport, both nationally and, most important, internationally.

'Your father,' István continues, ' he train six nights, and

lessons in day as well. And competition every Sunday. All the time, he fence.'

Gizi is amazed. Michael doesn't respond.

'How does somebody keep that up?' she asks.

István says, 'Takes remarkable man.' And then he adds more in Hungarian.

'Takes a stubborn man,' says Michael. 'Takes *dedication*. The greatest… that's what they're always like. They're amazing people, but they're amazing because they think the world only revolves around them.'

Gizi is taken aback. István doesn't appear to have understood everything Michael has said, looks inquisitive.

Then Michael adds, 'And the irony: when they manage to become the greatest, everything *does* revolve around them.' He shrugs and smirks, hopeful to soften the force of what he has said.

They continue walking in silence, the streets busy. Michael keeps his eyes near and far, on this side of the road and the other, occasionally behind them. If he spots the man in the cap again, he'll be ready to get after him.

Chapter Twenty-Five

Spartacus Fencing Club has been in the same building for over sixty years. Its heritage, like its reputation, precedes it. Known among everyday Hungarians, since before the 1950s and until today, it has produced some of the country's greatest fencers, champions, Olympians. It has produced József Varga, the teenage sensation who toppled adults. It's renowned for building fencers of eminent skill, those who can do with the blade what few have ever dreamed of, those whose footwork never falters, those whose hand movements are so slight they're barely visible to the human eye.

It has produced József Varga.

Michael is on the pavement, peering up at the building, a faded white concrete, neglected, its tattered roof peeling. *This is the place of champions?* he thinks but doesn't vocalise.

As István and Gizi wait patiently, making small talk in the doorway, Michael feels small compared to the building, the memories of his father's early glories radiating from every inch of the decrepit shell. *So many years ago.*

He tries to visualise his father arriving, striding up these very steps, his fencing bag on his shoulder, or a blade in his hand, eager to practise, to fight, to win. And then leaving, the bag again on his shoulder, or the blade in his hand, the sweat dripping from his forehead, his hair wet, a smile on his face, satisfied, pleased with the practice he'd completed, pleased with the fights, pleased with the wins.

His eyes scan the building. He doesn't notice the occasional vehicles that, traditional to Hungarians' style of driving, rocket by behind him. He doesn't notice the other pedestrians who walk past him, the few on their bicycles. He sees only this shell, what was once his father's habitat, perhaps even more important to him than his home, the place that made József Varga the fencer he became and the man he became. The place that engrained not only the skill in him, but filled him with the arrogance, the confidence and the determination that every champion has. That every champion needs.

Michael's eyes: left, right, up, down. And then he squints. Looks more closely. His head presses forwards, his whole body following, then a couple of steps.

'Is that…?' he starts, but he doesn't need to finish.

Gizi steps down from the doorway and stands beside him. 'Oh, yes,' she says, taking a look herself. 'You're going to see those in several places around Budapest.'

'Bullet holes?'

She nods. 'Bullet holes. Caused by the Revolution of '56. They haven't been filled in as a sign of respect. So many people lost their lives, so the bullet holes will never be removed. We will never forget our fallen heroes, no matter how much time goes by.'

The moment they enter the building, all heads turn towards them, all eyes curious. There are about two-dozen people in here, surprisingly busy for the daytime. They've been notified about Michael's visit, no doubt about it.

An old man approaches, a beaming smile on his face, his right hand extended.

'Ah,' says István. 'Michael, this Tibor Benkó.'

Tibor shakes Michael's hand with vigour. He speaks very good English. 'It is a pleasure. Thank you for coming.'

'Thank you for welcoming me,' Michael says.

'Your father, may I enquire about his health?'

'It's good, thanks. Quite good.' Michael will reveal no more about the state of things back home. The need for secrecy is paramount to his investigation. 'He still coaches, still loves the sport. It's still like a drug to him.'

'Good, good,' says the old man, nodding his head as keenly as moments ago he shook Michael's hand.

Michael decides to veer the conversation into a different direction. 'How do you know my father?'

'Oh goodness, your father. I fenced with him, many, many moons ago. Oh, we were young men then, merely boys. He was the most technically assured fencer, the greatest fencer, I'd ever seen, that I've ever been on the piste with. I was two years his senior, had been fencing some years longer, and he was still able to beat me within a year of picking up a blade for the first time.' He chuckles. 'And I was no slouch, I can assure you. I tried hard, very hard. Every time. I wanted to win so much.' More chuckling, to himself. 'So much. I would have done anything.' A long pause as he contemplates the past. 'Oh, listen to me: I'm an envious old man. Anyway, I wasn't the only one to be on the losing end of the piste when József Varga stepped on it, I can tell you. I can still remember how it felt.'

Michael doesn't have a response, so he turns his attention to the building in which they're standing. 'So this is the place, then?' and he steps a few feet further in, circling, and leading his eyes from corner to corner. The building's interior is in as poor shape as its outer layer.

While fencing may have a strong uptake in Budapest, it certainly doesn't have the investment. 'This is the place where it all began for him.'

'Yes, indeed,' replies Tibor, stepping to Michael's side. 'Right here. It hasn't changed much. We are a poor country in comparison to England. The sport is a poor sport, even though we manage to have so much success. Your father, he was one of many great fencers to come out of this club.' A pause. 'But he was the greatest, that much I must tell you. No matter how much we all tried. And many of us did. I tried so very hard and I failed. So many years have now passed since, but no one has come even close. You must be very proud. And your mother.'

'Yes, she was,' Michael replies casually. 'She died a couple of years ago. It's just him and me now.'

'Oh, you have my condolences. It seems that over the years we lost touch. We did, for a few years, have contact, about five years after your father left. He wrote to the club to see what was going on. A few of us wrote back. But we were not close beforehand – we only knew each other on the piste – and that, along with distance, meant we lost touch.'

'Don't worry about it. It happens.'

'I still remember. I still reminisce a lot.' Tibor crosses his arms, smiles to himself, chuckles again. 'Oh, those were the days.'

'I'm sure.'

'Here.' Tibor leads with his hands outstretched. Michael follows him. They arrive at the ground markings of the nearest piste. 'This was the piste your father fought on the very last evening he was here. The night before he left Hungary because of the Revolution.' Tibor engages

160

Michael's eyes with his. 'It was a great loss. But England's gain, eh?'

'Quite,' Michael says, feeling even more unsure about how to deal with the gushing, gushing, gushing, trying not to tire of it, trying to prevent the heat within him from increasing. He knows he's acting like a spoilt brat, but he can't stop himself. Another change of topic, perhaps, the answer: 'Do you coach here?'

'Yes, I am in charge. I've coached here for thirty years now. As soon as I stopped competing, I started coaching.'

'And are any of my father's other former colleagues still involved in the club in any way?'

'No, I'm afraid not. Several left when József left and moved abroad. Some others over the days that followed. A few died during the Revolution and many have died since. There are their relatives, some close, some distant, who compete here or work here as my junior coaches. Many know of your father simply by reputation – their fathers or their uncles or their grandparents spoke about your father frequently. A talent like that keeps people speaking, even after it can't be seen any longer. One, Benedek, is the son of Konstantin Sebestyén, who was one of József's main club competitors. They fenced also on the same team in competitions. They were a formidable team.'

'Really? My father's never mentioned him.'

Tibor shrugs. 'That's surprising. They got on very well and they fenced beautifully together. Unfortunately, Konstantin died almost ten years ago. He was still a young man. A heart attack took him from us much too early. But I know he told Benedek all about his fencing career and Benedek fences in his father's memory and honour here every week. He would, I'm sure, be honoured to meet you.'

'Please. And I'd like to meet anyone who knows about my father, if you're able to arrange that?'

'Of course. Come back tonight after six. We train for the evening session. Some will be here then. I will send word round and try to get more people here. Anyone else, I can try to arrange for tomorrow onwards. How long are you planning on staying in Budapest?'

'As long as is necessary.'

'Here,' Tibor says, handing Michael a small metal broach that he takes from his pocket. 'It's our fencing logo.' Gold in colour, the lapel broach is the shape of a fencer extending a thin, long blade, knees bent. 'Please accept this as a gift to thank you for being here.'

Michael thanks him, looks at it for what he thinks is long enough and then places it in his trousers pocket. Then he's in the process of making his excuses when Tibor asks, 'Tell me, do you fence, Michael?'

Michael hesitates. The expectation, it'll be there again, he knows it. 'Yes,' he says, finally.

'Perhaps you'd like to bring some training clothes tonight. Did you bring your equipment?'

'No.'

'Not a problem. I'm sure we could arrange a blade, a mask, glove and plastron and lamé. Maybe some breeches, but shorts or tracksuit trousers would be fine if not.'

Michael stands, now flanked by Gizi and István, both keen to hear agreement from him. After a moment, considering but ultimately understanding that he has no option, Michael says, 'Why not?'

Chapter Twenty-Six

After returning to István's apartment for more coffee and a light meal, Gizi and Michael say goodbye to him, content after a bowl of Hungary's national dish, a meat stew known as pörkölt or tokány, along with dumplings filled with cabbage. Michael, like most foreigners, initially mistook it for goulash until Gizi corrected him; goulash, or gulyás, is actually a soup made with meat and paprika.

István's wife reminded him about a dinner invitation they'd accepted for tonight some time ago, so he's not able to join Michael and Gizi at Spartacus.

Gizi drives Michael to the police station, where she shows him round and introduces him to some colleagues. This will be their base for the next few days, until either Michael discovers what the Hungarian connection to the murders in England is or until being here becomes futile.

When the clock strikes five, he asks Gizi to take him back to the hotel so that he can get ready for the evening's visit to Spartacus and the fencing that it appears is going to be necessary.

As she drives, she asks, 'Do you fence well?'

'How capable do you think I am, looking at me?'

She turns to him and then back to the road. 'Oh, I don't know. You look like you can take care of yourself, I think.'

'I guess you'll find out soon enough.'

'You get frustrated a lot, don't you? When you hear them speak about your father?'

The question surprises him, not least because it

comes across as a statement. But he answers honestly. 'Sometimes I try not to.' A moment's silence. 'Wouldn't you? It's been all my life.' He peers out of the window and adds in a whisper to himself, 'All my life.' Then louder: 'This is my chance, you know, to step out of his shadow. Being a detective is something I can do well, and where the name Varga doesn't mean a thing.'

'I used to date an athlete. He was a water polo player. He competed for Hungary on a national level. He still does, I think. He used to train five times a week and he was amazing at the sport. Everywhere we went, people told him how great he was. Most of the time, they didn't notice me by his side. So I know, to a much lesser degree, how you feel. I felt small. I felt like I didn't matter. I felt *ignored*. But I imagine you have skills yourself that you can show off. Skills that make you special.'

'I have skills,' he nods. 'Oh, I have those.'

'So focus on them. I focused on being the best girlfriend I could be when I realised things wouldn't change.'

'Right now, I'm focusing on being the best cop I can be. I need to sort out this mess.'

They look at each other.

'And I will help you.'

The wind has picked up. Michael can feel it batter the sides of the car. It doesn't affect Gizi's driving; she clings onto the wheel and veers from one side of the carriageway to the other.

'We're almost there.' A couple more turns and the hotel comes into view. 'I'll stay here,' she says, as she pulls up outside the hotel.

Michael wants to tell her that it isn't necessary, that

she can go and he'll make his own way to the club, but he has no idea where to start. He thanks her, assures her he'll be no more than fifteen minutes, but then hesitates. 'What happened then? With you and the water polo guy.'

'He got bored of me. It turns out that being a good girlfriend isn't always enough.'

'His loss.'

'That's what I told myself. It was hard to believe at the time.'

'And now?'

'Now I might just agree with myself.'

Michael gets out of the car and jogs up the steps leading to the hotel entrance.

In the hotel room, he quickly changes, sprays himself with deodorant and then stands in front of the mirror. *Expectation*, he thinks. *They're going to expect a lot. Tonight you're going to have to be on form. Get focused.*

For a moment, he leans against the glass, its surface becoming smudged by the grease that's built up on his forehead. 'Come on,' he says to himself. Then he turns to the right and, seeing the fridge, pauses. He contemplates, but hardly at all, then stoops down towards the fridge, opening the door. He pulls out a small bottle of vodka, downs it in one. Sharp, burning, he winces.

'Thanks for waiting,' he says as he gets back into Gizi's car.

There's something in his eyes. 'You okay?' she asks, noticing.

'Of course.'

He isn't convincing. She says, 'What's happening in England, I'm sorry about that. And I'm sorry for what you might have to put up with tonight.'

'Nothing for you to be sorry about. Nothing you or I can do about it having happened and there's certainly nothing we can do about the *greatness* of the past.' Inverted commas with his fingers. 'The fact is, some time in his life, my father, the one everyone here remembers with such fondness, pissed someone off to such an extent that they're willing to kill in the name of revenge. Not just kill, but *kill and kill and kill.* There've been four so far and I'm awaiting the call that tells me there's been another. And you know, I'm expecting it at any moment, that's how bad things have got.'

'Well, I'm still sorry,' she adds with a smile, which somehow makes him feel slightly better. 'No one should have to endure such a thing. Not him and certainly not you.'

'The smile makes it all worthwhile.' And he smiles. His eyes run down her chest and along her legs as they work the pedals.

Traffic holds them up, so they arrive about twenty minutes late to find Tibor standing in the middle of the gymnasium, with all the fencers lining three walls of the space, warming up as their coach calls out various instructions.

Once the warm-up is over, around fifty fencers retreat to their bags, fall to the ground and drink profusely. Several others come in, thankful to have missed the torture. Many of the fencers have with them supporters: perhaps other coaches, or family members, friends or girlfriends. Some attractive women are in here; typical Hungarian women, well dressed, well looked after, make-up to define features, hair done, tight clothes, shapes on show. Good bodies, so many of them.

Tibor greets Michael and Gizi, says he put up a notice earlier in the day to announce Michael's presence this evening and made some phone calls, and explains that a few non-regulars are here, people who have heard of József Varga's legacy. People want, Tibor says proudly, to pay their respects. 'This is a big thing for me and Spartacus.'

He makes a brief announcement to introduce Michael and Gizi to the masses and then the evening begins. It's a busy place; more fencers come in, more spectators too, as strangers approach Michael and Gizi, chat with them, mostly through Gizi as translator, a few in broken English.

After his first lesson of the evening, Tibor returns and says, 'Don't forget, when you're ready, get on a piste. Perhaps the nearest one, in honour of your father?'

Michael attempts a kindly grin.

'Really, you don't have to wait,' he says to Gizi, after another banal conversation, another that leads nowhere.

'It's not a problem.'

'A woman as beautiful as you surely must have busy evenings.' Michael means it, but he also wants her to leave him to endure this evening on his own.

She laughs. 'You flatter me.' Then she adds, 'Not busy, no. Besides, the chance to see you in breeches. That I can't pass up.'

Something verging on a laugh comes out of Michael's mouth. It contains a hint of despair.

'Plus, I think you need me. The last time I listened carefully, your Hungarian wasn't too hot.'

They stand at the side of the first piste, next to the benches. A handful more people come up to them, introduce themselves. Gizi was right: it's important for him to have her with him. And he also believes what he said to her before: she's incredibly attractive. He enjoys her company.

Two of the people who introduce themselves have heard of József Varga, have heard ravings. Michael thanks them, asks some questions, through Gizi's translations, but garners no additional information. Dead ends.

And then Tibor comes towards them enthusiastically, his hand hooked on the arm of the man accompanying him. 'Michael,' he calls. 'Michael.'

Michael and Gizi turn to the approaching voice.

'Michael, this is Benedek Sebestyén.'

'Ah, yes.' He extends his hand. 'Pleased to meet you.'

'Very good to meet you, too.'

They shake hands warmly.

'This is Detective Gizi Orbán, my colleague.' She also shakes hands with Benedek and they greet one another in Hungarian.

They speak briefly about the pasts they've each heard about from their fathers. 'My father,' says Benedek, 'told me about your father many times. He had a display of all his trophies and medals in our home. The majority of them were for team championships. He, another man who I also never met and who died several years ago, and your father, they were a great team. I still have my father's awards – I display them in my dining room. Your father's name is on many of the trophies. Perhaps I could offer you lunch tomorrow and I could show them to you.'

'Now that *would* be interesting,' Gizi interjects.

'Okay,' Michael concedes. 'Thank you.'

'I have some other bits and pieces that might be of

168

interest to you.'

They speak a little more and end the conversation with a question. 'Did your father ever speak about anyone who hated my father, anyone who might wish him ill?'

'Are you a fencer, Michael?'

'Yes, I coach now, but I competed for several years.'

'A champion?'

'I won some titles in Britain, yes.'

'Well, then, you will understand. Names, I don't remember, but yes, of course. There were many who hated them *both*. They were champions, and champions upset people when they win. Champions have enemies. There are a lot of jealous people in this world.'

'Indeed there are,' Michael muses.

Gizi and Michael agree to visit Benedek for lunch tomorrow and then Benedek excuses himself; he has to get home.

A few others come and greet them and, for some time, Michael and Gizi stand watching the fencing.

'He's good,' she says, pointing at the fencer on piste number one on the opposite side of the gymnasium. For the first time, Michael pays attention to the actual fencing. He sees the slim figure advance, retreat, leap backwards, balestra, fleche, with the speed of a car at full acceleration. There's aggression in each of his movements, perhaps too much; perhaps his weak point. Michael recognises technical skill, too, not perfect, but a degree of accuracy that's rare in fencers in England. There's much to admire.

The bout comes to an end when the fencer at the far side executes a beat attack, feint to the low line, then balestra followed by a flick hit, which is struck with such force that when it connects with the shoulder blade the sound of metal on bone reverberates around the gymnasium, hard enough, Gizi thinks, flinching, to crack bone. An immense cry of 'Allez!' radiates around the gymnasium and he pulls off his mask, drops it to the ground and jogs past his opponent.

His eyes land on Michael. *Those* eyes. The eyes from earlier: the man who was watching Michael outside István's apartment block. Michael hadn't seen him earlier when Gizi and he arrived at Spartacus; this individual must have arrived after they'd turned up. Michael wonders if it's possible that they've been tailed.

He fights the urge within himself, manages to refrain from revealing surprise on his face. He maintains a neutral stare, merely nods his agreement with the win he's just witnessed. The man, breaking the connection between their eyes, turns round and heads back to his opponent. Face to face, a salute of the blades and a handshake between them, it's all over.

The man wipes sweat from his forehead, clutches swathes of overgrown curly black hair in his hands and tugs at it, then shakes the sweat from his hands. He presses his fingers against one side of his nose and forces the air out. Whatever has accrued in it and caused a blockage flies out. Michael doesn't wince at the sight of snot falling onto the floor; he's seen enough to turn any man's stomach. Instead, he keeps his eyes on the man. Now, his task for the night has turned out to be simple: *find out who he is.*

After stepping away from the piste, putting his mask on the ground and drinking some bottled water, the man approaches Michael and Gizi. He greets them in

170

Hungarian. Gizi replies.

'Impressive,' Michael says, not waiting for them to conclude the words they're speaking.

The man makes a face that indicates he doesn't understand and turns to Gizi for support. She says a few words, which come out as sounds to Michael. Then Michael hears his name spoken, as she introduces him to the stranger so that they are as such no longer. The stranger reaches out a hand. Michael takes it. The man says, 'Ferenc.' It's pronounced Ferents.

'Michael,' Michael retorts.

The grip is firm, held for slightly too long, by both of them, eyes locked the whole time.

Releasing Michael's hand, Ferenc says some more words to Gizi. She laughs, shuffles on her feet, tucks her hair behind her ear. Michael senses jealousy building inside himself, as this man indicates with his hands that the moves he's just exhibited were nothing special. Gizi makes some hand signals, imitating fencing with a blade. Again, Ferenc waves off whatever it is she's saying. *It was nothing*, Michael finds himself thinking for Ferenc. *Nothing at all.*

Gizi turns to Michael. 'I've just explained why we're here. Unfortunately, he's never heard of your father, but he's noticed you're wearing a tracksuit.'

Michael says, 'I don't have any equipment,' and he holds his arms in the air, as if proclaiming absolute ignorance in something.

Gizi translates and before she has finished Ferenc is making his way over to the other side of the gymnasium. Michael catches Gizi's gaze, which follows the stranger. 'Oh, please,' he says.

'What?' she asks, innocently.

'He's not that bloody good, you know. Stop swooning.'

'I don't know what you mean.' But she has turned a shade of pink.

Ferenc, from across the hall and on his knees next to a bag, calls over to them and pulls from the bag a blade and mask. He holds them in the air, shakes them, almost victoriously. A call to arms, perhaps. He stuffs a glove into the mask, zips up the bag and trots back to Gizi and Michael. They near one another in the centre of the gymnasium, when he throws the foil in Michael's direction. Michael catches it, notices the force with which it has been lobbed. He takes the mask from Ferenc, ready.

'We fight to five,' Ferenc explains to Gizi, who duly translates.

Michael catches Ferenc's eye. Says nothing.

Chapter Twenty-Seven

They stand opposite one another, one on each end of the piste. Michael is suspicious. Those eyes. *It's him.*

Ferenc isn't wary of Michael. He's ready for this.

Michael lunges slowly, stretches his hamstrings. Winds up his arms, forwards then backwards. Feels a stretch is needed. Pulls his arms behind his back, his neck forwards, stretches the area between his shoulder blades. Tries to release the tension. There's so much of it, it won't budge.

He takes hold of the blade, which is leaning against his thigh, presses its point into the ground and applies pressure. The blade bends. He repeats the motion, bending the blade further, pushing into the ground. He likes a nice curve to the blade, something to facilitate a flick hit.

'En garde,' the president speaks, his voice loud and crisp.

For a moment, it sounds and looks like time has stood still for the remainder of the gymnasium. The air is heavy, it's enveloped, clasped hold of, everything in the space.

The two men salute with their blades, first to each other, then to the president, neither pair of eyes flinching, neither releasing its grip of the other pair. Then the masks go on and, suddenly, the eyes aren't clear any more, although both men believe they still have a firm grip on the other's.

Michael jogs then runs on the spot before coming to a halt and jumping, landing with his knees bent, into the en garde position. His opponent, well warmed up from his previous bout, lowers himself to en garde like a submarine going under on an exploratory expedition, so effortlessly and meaningfully.

Michael's heart is beating. An alien sensation: nerves. He's taken back to the first day he ever participated in a competition, when he was a novice, and then subsequent competitions, until he got a handle on winning, until he figured out how to deal with the gnawing that ate at his insides, gnawing that clutches with its teeth and won't let go. He hasn't had to deal with it for many years, so it's odd, an unusual sensation, he wants to laugh, he wants to tell it to fuck off, he wants to walk out of here and forget all about this bloody sport, this fucking investigation.

But he needs to find out who Ferenc is, he wants to know why this man was following him earlier today and, above all, he craves victory. Not only that, but he wants to show Gizi that flirting with this bastard was a mistake, he wants to show all the onlookers – for the gymnasium is still filled with them, now repressed of voice and movement – that he is more than the shadow of his old man, that he can hold his own, that he can impress, damn it, that *he* is something special.

'Allez.' The familiar call to action, the sign: this is it, breathe carefully, *in through the nose, out of the mouth*.

His father taught him that.

The aggressiveness that Michael recognised in Ferenc from observing his earlier fight has not waned. The Hungarian moves forwards with dexterousness. Michael backs up, but not quickly enough. A feint to the low line, which Michael doesn't fall for, but a double balestra lunge gets through because Michael fails to retreat quickly enough.

His legs feel stiff, like lead. *What is this?* His body's heavy, like a bag of stones. *What the fuck?* The air, non-existent. Suffocating. The people, everywhere. Glaring. He sees them as he walks back to his starting point, embarrassed. *What a piss-easy hit.* He hasn't heard it, but Ferenc has already made a sound of victory, grunted, thrilled with the opening point. One-zero.

The president raises his voice. The competitors are ready. Michael silently urges his legs into action, urges the lead to decompose. *Move.*

Speed comes at Michael again, but this time he applies the effort needed to retreat successfully, and he parries, deflecting the blade, when there's another double balestra lunge from Ferenc. Michael's riposte is short of the target; Ferenc's retreat is as swift as his attack. But Michael keeps the momentum going, following his opponent with an attack comprised of a series of complex feints and attempted attacks. They fail, his express-train of an opponent back on the attack the moment the third attempted strike doesn't land, but Michael extends his arm, leaps into the air and twists his body. A counter-attack, the blade landing square centre on Ferenc's chest while he's mid-attack, secures the second point for Michael. One point each.

By the time of the third point, both men are breathing heavily. Michael has forgotten the pit of his stomach, he's forgotten the lead, he's forgotten the oppressive silence, the stifling heat. This is his moment.

'Allez!'

Michael attacks, as hastily as his opponent had attacked previously, so fast that Ferenc is momentarily startled, doesn't expect it. Michael binds the blade, then disengages, a sixte beat and a lunge, successfully hitting the low line. A second point.

Gizi smiles. Michael can see her on the opposite side of the gymnasium, behind his opponent. He smiles in return, knowing she can't see him gleam at her, pleased with the effect he's having on her, pleased with himself and with the ease of that last point, such a simple idea yet so effective.

'Allez!'

A tangle of blades, some beats for feelers, steps back and forth, feint attacks, then finally Ferenc goes for it, applying the force of a strong wind, but Michael manages to avoid it. Then from Michael: croisé, a semi-bind forcing the other blade into the high line. Their bodies are close together, too close, and Ferenc steps further in, cutting off all the space between their bodies. They're only inches apart, could whisper to one another, could share the deepest of secrets, their blades pressing together in the air, each man applying force with all his might, trying to wrestle his blade free. Michael feels the pressure from Ferenc on the sixte side, he pushes back, Ferenc disengages and attempts to come round it, but Michael applies the pressure in the opposite direction, cutting off the blade. When he feels Ferenc push the accelerator towards the reverse side, he disengages and leaps backwards, lifting his blade high in the air and dropping the point. A tight, uncomfortable angle to hit from, but it comes down on Ferenc's shoulder. A third hit against the Hungarian's one.

As Ferenc stalks back to his starting position, he reveals his frustration, swiping the blade angrily at the floor. The whipping sound careers around the still-silent gymnasium, makes Gizi flinch, and the inhabitants seem as if they've all just been on the receiving end of it.

There are murmurs, excited whispers, in the gymnasium now, from the onlookers.

'En garde.'

Michael lifts his blade, ready. When 'Allez' is called, he casually moves forwards, his arms relaxed now, the leading arm with blade in hand dropped and pointing towards the ground. Then he stops moving and keeps the point aimed at the ground. Utter stillness from him, the only movement his chest rising and falling. This is confidence. *Psych him out.* See who'll give in and move first.

Suddenly, to Michael, Ferenc's feet sound like a large animal's, and he hears the first, the second, the third step. When Ferenc is close, his blade attempting a direct attack, for Michael's blade is so low and near to the ground that a beat attack is impossible, Michael lifts his blade in one sweeping motion, picking up Ferenc's blade and sweeping it aside to sixte, bringing his blade in direct. Centre of the chest. Four hits in a row. A smile that won't leave him, a cry of 'Allez!' for good measure, and a lot of cursing in Hungarian from an embarrassed, frustrated opponent.

The final required point. Michael prepares himself. He sees Gizi watching. She's standing, her hands clasped under her chin. Then he turns his attention to his opponent. The mask stands in front of him. And imprinted on it, he sees István, then Tibor, then Gizi, then Chloe Raynor. Then Rachel Bradshaw. And, finally, his father. The face is neutral, the eyes dead. But then they're mocking, they're telling him he hasn't got what it takes, that his club, Salle Worth, will always play second fiddle to Salle Victory, that even if he'd had all the time in the world, even if he'd started fencing while in his mother's womb, he'd never have matched up to the incomparable József Varga, that *you'll never match up to me, or the memory of me*.

Michael hasn't heard the call of 'Allez.' He's seen the face of his father approach, but the movement and his own reality haven't registered. A direct attack. He's hit before he switches on.

Michael looks down at his chest, observes the blade pull away. Watches the tip, carefully, as it returns to Ferenc's side, as he turns around and walks back to his starting point, now satisfied.

Two points to Michael's four.

'En garde' is called again.

Michael sees nothing but his father again, doesn't bend his knees, doesn't ready himself. He sees the face that's inspired yet plagued him, the face that's represented the name that's inspired yet plagued him, the face that's inspired so many fencers yet plagued one far more than others, a killer, someone to whom revenge is all that matters, for whom life means so little that he will snuff it out in an instant, to cause pain, yes to the victim, but more importantly to József Varga, to the man who, for whatever reason, deserves it.

'Allez!'

Michael lifts his head. This time, he recognises the brisk approach of Ferenc's form. Still, the face is there. József Varga. *Father.*

Sweat drips down Michael's forehead, creeps into his

right eye. He brings it closed, tries to suck in the sting caused by the facial excrement. Through one eye, the face is still there, almost waving as the body advances, the attack coming. And now he feels his cheeks flush, there's rage, it builds up inside, the pit of his stomach besieged in a totally different way. István, Tibor, Gizi, Chloe Raynor, Rachel Bradshaw, József Varga again. The faces change, like a rotating film. And then the final face remains.

Knees bend. Fury inside. Bent low, springboard off the floor.

Ferenc is only three feet away now, desperate to land the hit that'll level the match, to take it to sudden death.

With a fleche, Michael erupts from the ground, charging into Ferenc's attack, a delicious counter-attack that catches the local man by surprise. His attempt to parry is too late, futile; Michael's blade has connected and he's run past his opponent, leaping into the air, pulling off the mask, throwing it into the air and catching it, like a student celebrating graduation, as Gizi claps, she celebrates, the audience claps, some even cheer. Michael inhales, absorbs it all.

'Halt!' the president calls. Then, with arm extended, he awards the fight to Michael.

Michael, wiping the sweat from his eye and forehead, returns to his side of the piste. The two men stand face to face, neither blinks. The gloves come off, the hands extend, they shake. Ferenc says something in Hungarian. It sounds like a long sentence but must be congratulations or the like, even though it's growled in venomous tones.

And they part, Michael returning to Gizi. She places her hands on his arms, kisses him, embraces him when she congratulates him. He feels a different kind of excitement, not the thrill of a fencing victory, but the threat of a victory of other sorts that he now believes will soon come. He will have her.

Chapter Twenty-Eight

They hang around for the rest of the evening, talking, asking questions, allowing a couple of members of the club to reminisce on behalf of their fathers and uncles, and Michael has two more fights, both with equally impressive opponents, in a club full of impressive athletes, competitors, fencers. He manages to win both bouts.

'Keep your eye on him and if he leaves,' Michael said not longer after beating Ferenc on the piste, 'fetch me straight away. Don't wait for anything. I'll explain later.'

Despite all the conversations and questions asked and answered, they learn nothing of use, except the identity of the mystery man from earlier, but Michael gets a lot out of being in the building his father trained in so many years ago. It, somehow, helps him to channel his skills, step out of himself and who he is by reputation, and deal with the opponent in front of him as himself, not as a Varga.

With club night finished and Tibor thanked for his hospitality, Gizi and Michael retire to her car. They leave the building while Ferenc is still in it, get into the car and move it out of the car park and to a space on the side of the road some distance away. Close enough to keep the building in sight in the rear-view mirror, yet far enough away to remain unseen.

When Ferenc emerges a few minutes later, he doesn't get into a car but turns left and walks down the road.

'Shit,' Michael says. 'He's on foot.' He tries to work out their best next step. 'That doesn't make any sense. How could he have known we were here if he didn't follow us? No car means he didn't follow us, right?'

'Do you want to tell me what you mean, why we're watching him?'

'The man,' Michael says. 'The man I saw earlier. The one who was watching me outside István's apartment block. It's him.'

'Ferenc?'

'Yes, him,' Michael says incredulously. 'Ferenc.' Watching the figure disappear into the distance, he adds, opening the car door, 'We've got to follow on foot.'

Gizi gets out of the car as if she were sitting on hot coals. She locks the car and trots to catch up with Michael, who is already several metres ahead. They increase their pace to a jog, passing Spartacus as Tibor steps out and starts to lock up the main door. 'Good night,' he calls, and they repeat their thanks without slowing, waving. Tibor watches them as their figures, like Ferenc's before them, disappear into the distance.

They come to the end of the road, stop and look both ways. Some way off to the right, as the road curves, Gizi spots Ferenc, his fencing bag draped over his right shoulder. 'There,' she says, pointing.

Now they're running, until they gain to an appropriate distance. 'Enough,' Michael whispers, and they slow to a steady walk. They remain thirty or forty metres back, far enough to remain nondescript.

They're on a long main road. Traffic whizzes past them, all headlights blazing. Every so often, they take cover in shop doorways, or in road turnings, careful not to get too close, careful to remain unseen.

'Oh no,' Gizi says to herself.

'Oh no what?' Michael asks.

'The metro.'

'What?'

'I know where he's going. He's going to get on the metro.'

'Shit.'

Budapest's metro connects all parts of the city, a vast network of stations that are used by many residents for their daily commutes, and is the world's second oldest electrified underground railway system, after the City and South London Railway of 1890 in the UK.

'Then how the fuck?' Michael is bewildered. 'How could he have possibly known we'd be there?'

Ferenc descends the steps that lead into the coincidentally named Ferenciek Square underground station.

'This is going to be fun,' Gizi says, and Michael looks at her, senses the excitement she feels. Feels it, too. They're getting close.

As they reach the top of the stairs, Michael says, 'Forget the translating shit, now I'm glad you came.'

She laughs as they go down the steps. She flashes her identification, the security officers who guard each station step aside, and they run down a corridor.

'How many train lines?'

'Just one.' Both directions are reachable from one large open platform. 'This way.'

She leads him down an escalator and into a short dimly lit corridor that precedes the platform. They come to a halt at the end of it, Gizi holding her arm out. 'Stop,' she whispers. A lot of people are on the platform, and about halfway along Ferenc is standing, the fencing bag on the ground by his feet. 'Now we wait.'

They hear the train approaching only a few minutes later. 'Let's take the last carriage,' Michael suggests.

'Got it.'

When the train reaches the platform and comes to a stop, they wait for Ferenc to board. Before he steps in, he looks to the left, to where Michael and Gizi are standing. Their heads bolt back, out of view.

'Did he see us?' Michael asks.

Gizi doesn't answer.

More agitated now, hissing: '*Did he see?*'

When she threads her head back round the corner, Gizi can only see a crowd of people who have got off the train. She can't spot Ferenc. 'I don't know. He's not on the platform any more.'

'Shit!'

They jog to the train and board the last carriage. The carriage doors close and the train starts moving. For a moment, Michael and Gizi stand next to one another, holding on to different handrails. 'Is it possible to move from carriage to carriage on these things?' he asks.

Gizi tells him they'll have to. They move to the carriage's interior door and step through to the next carriage. They have to tread air to get through. 'Don't look down,' she tells him.

He makes a mistake and glances down. Train track appears to move beneath his feet. He feels weightless, sick, dizzy. He leaps through to the next carriage, offering his hand to Gizi. She doesn't take it. 'You've done this before,' he says.

'It's been necessary, yes.'

They arrive at the next station and Michael steps out.

Gizi goes through to the next carriage. Ferenc isn't in sight. Just as the doors are about to close, Michael leaps into the carriage where Gizi is. They repeat this process at the next station. They advance three carriages, but Ferenc is nowhere to be seen.

When they arrive at the next stop, West Station, Gizi starts to walk towards the interior door. Michael moves towards the main door, but as he does so he sees Ferenc on the platform, the fencing bag on the ground. He lifts up the long bag and as he does so he makes eye contact with Michael. Instinctively, Michael spins around and closes his eyes. 'Fuck,' he says, hopeful, but knowing he's been seen and that his reaction would make the fact that he was tailing Ferenc all the more obvious.

'Gizi,' Michael calls. He turns back towards the platform. Ferenc isn't there, but the fencing bag is on the ground again. 'Gizi! Bag!' He runs onto the platform and Gizi follows. 'Shit!' he shouts. 'Where?' They look in both directions, scanning all parts of the platform.

'There!' she calls, pointing at the stairs that lead to the station's exit.

'Secure the bag,' he says, and before she can protest he's away. Michael takes the stairs two at a time, reaches the top and enters the wide foyer area, running as fast as he can, knocking into people who are blocking the way. 'Move! Police!' he shouts, forgetting that for many it will be a foreign tongue.

When he reaches the centre of the area, he spins round to look in all directions. Small shops line the circular structure. There are several exits he can choose, but at the one directly opposite he notices the fast-moving shadow of someone running up the stairs. He charges to it and as his foot hits the first step he sees Ferenc's feet leaping up the final few steps.

He's up the staircase in no time and runs along the passageway that leads onto St Stephen's Boulevard. It's raining now.

Ferenc has reached the other side of the road and is running in the direction of the Danube. Michael crosses, having to slow down because of oncoming cars. But then he's on the other side of the road, probably thirty metres behind Ferenc, his heart racing, his breathing heavy, for this is a different kind of competition from the one they shared earlier. Michael is in his stride, however, his right and left arms moving forwards and backwards at a pace that keeps his body moving quickly, in a manner that keeps his weight centred, his body steady.

They pass shop after shop, bus stops and lots of people, some milling about, some walking. Cars continue to whizz by.

Then Michael notices a bridge up ahead. Margaret Bridge. Michael knows they're close to the Danube.

They've been running for about eight hundred metres when Ferenc suddenly makes a sideways tear and crosses the road, leaping over the central reservation. He tries to squeeze between two cars, but the second catches his leg, perhaps his hip. He careers further into the road, lands on the ground in a heap.

Michael spies his opportunity, urges his legs to move faster. A bus is coming. Does he run or does he wait? He's not sure. He hesitates, his body freezing as his head moves forwards, then he goes for it and the rest of his body follows. The bus driver reacts, slams on the brakes. An almighty screech fills the air, piercing, and smoke from the wheels billows into the air. The bus skids towards Michael. He dives to escape its path, landing heavily just feet from where the behemoth comes to a standstill. His hands scrape on the ground, his tracksuit trousers tear. He curses and lifts his head.

Ferenc is stumbling to his feet.

'Hey!' Michael calls after him, to no effect. 'Fuck!' He struggles to get himself on his feet, his hands sore, his knee throbbing. Ferenc, too, is limping, but more severely. His body is bent double, like an aged hag, like a beggar too embarrassed to make eye contact, or physically unable, the torment of too many winters having taken its toll.

He reaches the pavement on the other side of the road. Michael isn't far behind him. Ferenc makes urgent, chaotic glances over his shoulder, his body writhing. He notices that Michael is gaining. There are only, maybe, ten metres between them now, and Michael is closing the distance every second.

They're running onto the bridge, the hills of Buda in the distance. Parliament is behind them and to the left. A tram passes their charging forms, its passengers staring intently at the tumult outside.

Realising he has no choice, his eyes giving the game away as he continues to glance over his shoulder almost as often as he steps, Ferenc stops moving along the bridge, grabs hold of the yellow side fence and lifts himself on top of it. As Michael reaches out to grab him, he jumps. His body falls, his person upright, and he lands in the water, feet-first, as Michael leans over the side of the bridge, watching, helplessly and despairingly, as the Hungarian disappears into the darkness below. His one lead, gone.

He waits for Ferenc to surface, squints into the darkness of the river, desperate to see, leans further over the bridge's side, but cannot spot him emerge, cannot make out the lame form of Ferenc, if indeed that is his name.

Chapter Twenty-Nine

The flashing lights of three police cars and an ambulance illuminate the bridge. Michael sits on the pavement, his leg being attended to by a paramedic. Gizi sits beside him.

It's been twenty minutes since Ferenc leapt into the Danube. Officers are, Michael has been assured, down there searching for him and have cordoned off the road that lines the river below the embankment.

Ferenc's fencing bag is on the ground next to Gizi. Michael has already explained what happened after he left her in the metro station. 'Only a desperate man would take on that jump,' she says.

'What's in the bag?'

'Fencing gear. Everything you'd expect. And an address book. It's *really* old. The pages are coming apart and the writing in it is really faded. In pencil. I can't read all of it, parts of it are so worn. I don't know how old it is, but it must have been written many, many years ago. We'll look at it back at the station. We'll get István to look at it, too. We'll see if anything stands out.'

'Can you get it dusted for prints?'

'As soon as we get back to the station.'

'We need to find out who this guy is. Can we go back to Tibor before the station and ask him some questions?'

'I've called him and he's returning to the club. Two officers are already on their way to him. They'll start until we get there.' She runs her eyes up and down his leg. 'And what about you? How are you feeling?'

'Been better. It's going to play hell with my lunge for a few weeks. Still, nothing like what happened to him.'

'Better him than you.'

'Well, thank you,' he says with a smile.

After his leg is cleaned and bandaged, they get into Gizi's car, which has been picked up and brought to them. They don't say much as they drive to Spartacus. Both are preoccupied and equally confused. They need to find out who Ferenc is. They need to understand what's happened this evening.

When they arrive at Spartacus, they park directly in front of the building and enter. Only one officer is speaking to Tibor. They're sitting in the office, which is at the front of the building, adjacent to the main entrance. A glass partition separates the office from the foyer. Tibor has made tea, which they're both drinking, legs crossed, casual, calm. They're laughing and sipping when Gizi and Michael enter.

Gizi asks the officer a question. He replies. Then they speak for a few minutes more. She does all the questioning. During this time, Tibor comes out to re-greet Michael. He leads Michael into the office, leaving Gizi and the officer in the foyer, and starts making Michael a cup of tea. 'I'll make one for Gizi, too,' he says.

'What is Ferenc's last name?' Michael asks as Tibor stirs sugar into the tea. No need to reheat the kettle; still warm.

'I don't know,' Tibor says with a shrug of the shoulders. 'Tonight was the first time I've seen him here. The first time I've seen a few of the people who came. All, I believe, because I said you were coming. It's been a special evening for the club. People came. People whose relatives knew your father, or had heard about your father. That's what I thought when I saw so many arrive tonight.'

'Is there anyone who might know who he is?'

Another big, elaborate shrug. 'It's possible. But I have no idea.'

'He's a good fencer. He's obviously had a lot of training. Where could he have trained to become like that if not here?'

'Budapest is full of excellent fencing clubs. Hungary, too. He could have trained anywhere in country. Or even elsewhere in Eastern Europe.'

'Bloody hell.'

Her conversation concluded, Gizi comes into the room. The officer goes outside. After taking the cup of tea from Tibor, thanking him and tasting it, she says, 'The second officer is outside in the car park. It looks like Ferenc came here by car. I guess he suspected somehow that we were going to follow, so he abandoned it and went on foot. The car is in the car park, near where we were originally parked. We've called for it to be towed away. We'll have it checked out carefully.'

Again, the question about how fills Michael's mind. Gizi's too. 'So that means,' Michael says, 'he could have followed us here. He probably did. I think he arrived after us. I don't remember seeing him when we first came in. Maybe walking away from here was just precautionary. But he genuinely didn't look like he knew we were following him until the moment he ran in the metro.'

'And he's never been here before.' She sits down on a stool.

'I know, Tibor was just saying he doesn't know who he is.'

191

She says a few words to Tibor in Hungarian. Tibor nods in response.

'Is there any way everyone here tonight could be questioned?'

'Most of them, but some haven't been here before. And even to speak to most will take quite some time.'

'I know,' Michael acknowledges. 'Can we have any help?'

'I'll request it. I don't know. I doubt it.'

Michael turns to Tibor. 'Can you organise a meeting here tomorrow? Invite along everyone who was here tonight.'

'I'll try. I'll try.'

Michael and Gizi leave, after announcing they'll return tomorrow evening at the same time as they'd arrived tonight. As they emerge from the building, they discover the rain has intensified. They go to Gizi's car. Michael stands on the pavement, waits for her to go round to the driver's side on the main road to unlock the door. As she arrives at the door, she looks up at him and then looks beyond him. 'Merde.' Her eyes are wide. Her hair's covered in rain. It's dripping down her face.

'What?' Michael asks.

She doesn't answer. 'Merde,' she repeats, louder. She steps around the car, then she picks up the pace. Michael turns as she runs towards the car park. Before he even moves towards it, he sees. He sees what she sees, what she's running towards, what she arrives at, what he's now running towards.

The police officer who was in the club building ten minutes ago and talking to Gizi is lying on the ground. The rain that surrounds his body in puddles mixes with his blood. As Michael nears Gizi's kneeling form, he sees the officer's throat has been slit. The man's eyes stare at the sky, surprise and horror speaking through them. Tilting his head up at the police car, Michael sees the other police officer sitting in the driver's seat. His head is leaning back against the headrest. The car door is open. A faded interior light casts shadows.

After checking the pulse of the corpse on the ground, Gizi walks towards the car and round to the open door. Michael follows her. He looks in, over her shoulder. The officer's head is bloodied, the left side of his skull crushed. His eyes are closed. Gizi leans in, checks his pulse. 'He's still breathing.' As she leans further in, her foot knocks into something. She bends down, searches the ground. A police baton. 'It must be his,' she says, pointing at the officer lying on the ground. 'Wait here.' She pulls out her mobile phone, dials and steps away, moving into a trot towards the club building.

Michael looks around the car park. Aside from the police car, he's the sole occupant. Ferenc's car is nowhere to be seen.

Chapter Thirty

The address book has been dusted for prints. Only partials have been discovered, will likely lead nowhere. Now it's over an hour after midnight, and Gizi and Michael sit at István's dining room table, the book perched on it. There's a lingering smell in the air, teasing: batter, a frying pan, pancakes cooking away.

'We need you to look through the book. Tell us any names that mean anything to you. People you know, people you've heard of. Perhaps most important, people you know who have a connection of some kind with my father.'

'Of course,' István says. A few words in Hungarian, then, 'I understand.'

He carefully turns each page, searching the entries. Gizi sits next to him, her notepad open and ready on the table, a pen in her hand. Michael sits on the opposite side. Without thought, his hand is rubbing his knee.

István makes some noises, shakes his head, coughs, as he turns the pages. Nothing so far. His wife, Ilona, comes into the room, carrying a large plate, waiter-style, and three small plates, on top of which sit knives and forks. She sets the table and places the large plate, which is full of rolled pancakes that are filled with chocolate sauce, in the middle. The smell is overpowering, exhilarating. 'Good appetite,' she says, as is customary. Michael and Gizi thank her and she leaves the room.

The dining room is large. The dining table is oval-shaped, big enough for twelve people, and is surrounded on three sides by cabinets. On the fourth side is a set of large double doors that lead to the hallway. On the walls are pictures of István, Ilona and their children, who must be about Michael's age.

The far corner of the room, where there's a small corner table, is a Sacred Corner, something that's a common feature in Hungarian homes. It's an area that's decorated with pictures of saints, and items that have been brought back from Catholic pilgrimages, a sign of the family's faith. A picture of Maria hangs on the wall. A blessed crucifix, from Częstochowa in Poland, is balanced on the table and there's an unlit candle next to it.

They begin eating the pancakes and, not long after, István's wife brings in freshly filtered coffee. She places the cups and saucers on the table and then, coffee pot in hand, fills the cups. She repeats, 'Good appetite', and, again, is thanked by Gizi and Michael. She leaves as soon as they're served.

Eating and drinking in silence, Michael and Gizi watch István working his way through the book. His head is bent low, his eyes close to the page. Disappointment, frustration, pain – these are what Michael thinks he can read on the old man's face. It's clear how hopeful he is to prove helpful to the duo of detectives, one of whose father he would lay down his life for.

After a while, he holds a page open and, through a strained voice, he says, 'I think. Maybe, I think. Moment.' He straightens his back and breathes out heavily. 'Moment. Something I get. I want to show. Wait, please. One moment.'

Gizi and Michael nod as István goes out of the room, leaving the address book on the table. Michael picks it up and shows Gizi the page that's open. 'Puskás, J.,' she reads. '*Puskás* means *gunsmith* in English.'

'Maybe that'll end up being appropriate.'

Michael starts flicking through the remainder of its loose pages. 'Here,' he says finally, when he gets to the inside of the back cover. 'Look at this.' He hands the book to Gizi, pointing at something. 'Two letters. And then two numbers and a letter. And in ink, the only part of the book that is. Some kind of biro, it looks like. And clearly written. It looks far more recent than anything else in the book.'

Gizi folds the book into the table. She focuses on the letters and numbers. *I* and *T*. And then *65C*. She's puzzled by them, Michael can see.

He knows it's a redundant question, but he asks nonetheless. 'Any idea what it means?'

'Not a clue.' She blows air between her lips. 'It could be anything.'

'Needle in a fucking haystack.'

István arrives back in the room. 'I look, but I no find. I want find old newspapers. Name, I think I recognise, but no remember. But I find this.' He shakes his arms, which carry a black shoebox. It's aged, worn. Michael and Gizi sit expectantly.

First, István pulls out a pile of pictures. Old photos, on card stock, black and white and sepia, the lot of them.

Michael doesn't think now is the right time to be reminiscing through old photos, but he doesn't say anything, hopeful that there's a point to this.

Politely, Michael nods his way through about thirty photos. István explains who's in most of them, but the majority of the names that Michael hears are unfamiliar to him. They're all family, though. His grandparents appear in two, the most faded and battered of all the photos, probably ninety years old. There are a few of József with his brother, Ákos. They're smiling in all the photos, but there's a noticeable distance between the two in how they stand, even though they're the only two in the picture.

'Can you take me to see him?' Michael asks. 'Tomorrow?'

'Ákos?'

'Yes, Ákos.'

'Is difficult.' He doesn't expand. 'But I try.'

'Why's it difficult?'

'He likes to drink. A lot. Maybe he not able to see us. I try.'

'Why don't my father and he speak? Don't they get along?'

István answers in Hungarian. He seems to be trying to convince Gizi that what he's saying is right, that it's true.

'What?' Michael says.

'I don't know. I don't.'

'What?'

Gizi speaks up. 'He said you won't believe him, but he doesn't know.'

'Well, maybe I bloody don't believe him. But if that's what he says, who am I to question it?' He faces István. 'So you don't know why my father and his brother almost never speak and, judging by this photo, more or less never did, and you don't know who this Ferenc guy is and why he followed me.' He takes and pushes the book towards István. 'Do you know what this means? These numbers and these letters?'

'Please. Michael.' And more Hungarian.

'He says he knows you're upset. He understands. But believe him, he loves your father, truly he does, but he knows your father was a difficult man. He believes it would have been possible for him to have enemies. He doesn't know why your father and his brother have rarely spoken, why they've always been distant, but he knows it's been that way since he was young. Your father never said and he never asked. He respected your father too much to pry. Michael, he wants to help us. Give him time and be patient.'

'I know. And thank you. I appreciate it. Look, can you think about this more? Who or what is this, *Puskás, J.*?'

'Is name I remember. József. Jakob, maybe. I no know. Yes, Jakob sound right. But is too long time ago. I recognise.'

Michael turns to Gizi. 'Can you find out if anyone named József Puskás or Jakob Puskás lives here and is the right sort of age?'

'What's the right age?'

'Sixty or seventy.'

Michael turns back to István and nods, glum. He indicates the box. 'Do go on.'

After the photos, there's a notepad. István doesn't open it. Instead, he pulls from under it a small stack of newspaper clippings. 'Ah,' he mumbles. And he starts scanning them. As he finishes each one, he places them on the table. He doesn't hand them to Michael or Gizi, but the way he places them softly and near them is inviting.

Gizi is the first to pick up an article. A report on a

fencing tournament. József Varga is mentioned as the winner. She hands it to Michael. 'They commend his skill, and another great win in this one.'

There's also an article from during World War Two. 'There was a bomb that landed right outside this apartment?' Gizi says, surprised.

'Yes,' István answers, his eyes scanning pages. 'Only miracle it no explode, no kill anyone. And during Revolution, tank fire, it comes through here.' He points at the wall behind them to the left side of the room, without lifting his eyes from the articles. 'And it go through there and through next wall.' With his hands, he indicates that shellfire entered the building through the exterior wall, into the dining room, and then through the wall into the lounge and then through another wall before it came to a rest in a bedroom. 'We in bomb shelter in basement at time. Lucky for us.' He looks at the final article in the pile, disappointed. 'No Puskás.'

Gizi hands the bomb article to Michael. His eyes scan it, but he absorbs no meaning. All he wants is sleep.

Confused, for he's angry with his father and with all the reminders of greatness, but he also feels sorry for his father, for being a memory, a revered one, yes, but one that also, for some as-yet-unknown reason, inspires so much hate.

Chapter Thirty-One

They arrive back at the hotel at almost 3AM. 'Drink?' Michael says, exhausted.

'The bar will be shut. Hungarians like their drink, but not that much.'

Michael turns to face her. They're side by side. His hand leans on the handbrake. 'I have a *fantastic* mini-bar.'

She laughs and turns away, peers through the windscreen, shrugs her shoulders. 'For one. Why not.'

They reach Michael's room. She takes off her coat and places it on a chair. Michael hangs his in the wardrobe. He offers her a seat. She perches on the corner of the bed.

'Your drink of choice?'

'I'm Hungarian.'

'So whisky it is then,' he laughs. She laughs, too. He helps himself to a whisky as well. 'Mixer?'

'Neat is fine.'

'Well, you *are* Hungarian.' He takes the drink to her. In unison, they turn the lids and the familiar cracking sound creeps into the room. 'Well, here's to us. To solving this. Egészségedre.'

'Egészségedre.'

Down in one, both of them. 'You know,' Michael says, leaning against the wall, 'you are an *attractive* woman.'

'And you're an attractive man, Michael.'

'And you can knock back a whisky impressively.'

'So can you.'

'I have Hungarian blood, too, remember,' he says. He looks up at the ceiling. 'Music to my ears.' It's only been one drink, but he feels as if he's had a caseload. Too tired. Too consumed by the fumes of physical and mental exhaustion. Pain in his leg. Memories of his father. Of Rachel's lifeless body. Of Chloe Raynor's. This whole mess. He wants to forget. *Make it all disappear.* He touches her leg. 'Another?'

'Another what?'

He pulls open the fridge. He removes every drink that's in it, drops the small bottles on the bed, eyes them expectantly as if they're his lovers lining up. 'Another whisky, of course.'

'Maybe one more,' she says.

He hands one to her, then picks up three bottles, a whisky, a Bacardi and a vodka, for himself.

'Cheers,' she says.

'Egészsége fucking dre.' He knocks back all three in a row. Then he takes a fourth, knocks that back, too.

'Michael, shouldn't you –'

'Do you know, all my life –' slurring, he takes on the physicality of a pantomime dame, his hands and arms doing much of the talking, his words only just comprehensible – 'I've followed that man's name around like a *fucking tail.* He's made me feel inadequate because, in comparison, *I am. Everyone* is, don't you see? I was a good fencer. Now I'm a bloody good detective.' He lifts two bottles from the bed, doesn't pay attention to what they are, throws one to Gizi and opens the other for himself. He feels like shit, sounds like shit, looks like shit. 'I need to solve this, Gizi. I need to show him I'm worth something. I can't be a disappointment. Not any more.' His bottle is empty, hers is untouched. He picks up another two, knocks them back. 'I have to figure out what he's done that's come back to haunt him. The way the memory of his achievements always haunted *me*.'

With two empty vodka bottles in hand, Michael stumbles to the bed.

'I understand why you're upset,' she consoles. 'I'd find it difficult, too.'

He's about to fall, she can see, so she stands up and catches him, a supportive arm around his shoulder.

He grinds deep into her eyes. He's not all there. 'You are… so attractive.'

'And so are you.'

His eyes close and she guides him onto the bed, his head onto a pillow.

'So are you,' she repeats, leaving his sleeping form on the bed, softly closing the door behind her.

Chapter Thirty-Two

It was a coaching night for József. He arrived at the club before 6PM and followed his usual routine. Coffee in hand, he sat on a chair in the corner of the gym. People gravitated towards him, talked to him, but he couldn't absorb anything they said. He couldn't get his mind off what was going on in his life. What had *become* his life. He couldn't stop thinking about how much hope he'd placed in Michael being able to discover what was going on. He wasn't sure his son was up to it.

As soon as an individual or a group finished speaking to him, another person or group of people were ready to fill the space. As usual, he made some witty remarks, cracked some jokes, received resounding laughter, but his heart wasn't in it, nor his mind.

Distracted, he blew his whistle to indicate the start of the warm-up. Members of the club lifted themselves, some wearily, some keenly, from their rest points, pulled themselves from their conversations, and started to jog around the hall.

As he gave each instruction, he pictured Michael in Budapest, wondered how the investigation was panning out. He knew István would be an almighty help, would make sure Michael would get to where he wanted to go, would find answers to any questions he'd have. And he also knew István wouldn't say what he shouldn't say.

After half an hour of gut-wrenching exercises, time came for the footwork part of the warm-up, the final fifteen minutes. It wouldn't be longer than fifteen minutes, not tonight. With the fencers lined up on one side of the gym, József stood in the centre, calling out instructions. As he did so, his eyes scanned the fencers, not in their usual guise as unyielding coach, but suspiciously, with uncertainty. Could one of the people in front of him be involved somehow? What about the people who only joined a couple of weeks ago? That would have been the perfect time to join, to discover his routines and the routines of a few club members, to then threaten and kill. He made eye contact with several, questioned whether there was something other than physical strain in their eyes, whether there was a seething hatred, some kind of clue that said, *I can and will kill to get at you.*

He thought he saw it several times, in that man and in this woman. And then, in an instant, whatever he had seen was gone. And then he thought he saw it again. It started to make his head spin. He reeled on his feet as the fencers were completing ten balestra lunges across the hall.

Started to fall, to topple to the right. Going down.

Caught by one of the fencers. Didn't know who.

He was helped to his seat by several eager members. Given a drink. Sipped on it. Looked up to see lots of concerned faces staring intently at him.

Coming fully to his senses, he searched the faces again, so many now, it seemed like the whole club was standing above him. Could he see anything, any clue in them? Still wanting to know. Getting desperate, and starting to feel enraged.

'What I need,' he said, getting up as quickly as he could, 'is a cigarette. Alone.' And he walked out of the hall, unaided, snapping at someone who tried to take him by the arm.

Alone outside. Isolated. *Look at yourself. Stop this. Sort yourself out.* He lit a cigarette, took slow, deep drags. Wallowed in the smoke as it consumed his lungs. All he needed now was a strong coffee to go with it, get the blood flowing, the heart racing. Or better still, a tumbler of whisky. He looked forward to reaching home for one of those, if not several. Make this day more bearable, somehow.

He went back in. Back to normal, he was determined.

When training finished, he didn't go to the pub. It was rare that he missed the social conclusion to the evening – the first time had been two years ago, when he'd received the call from Michael that his wife's illness had taken too firm a grip. That night, after József raced home, when he sat by her bedside, held her hand, kissed her forehead, he listened to her final breaths.

Now, in the rented car that replaced his own while the police carried out further tests on it, rain falling, the windscreen wipers doing their dance, his mind started to travel again. A mixture of thoughts: nothing about himself being in danger, but the faces of the women at Salle Victory, alive and then dead, their faces caked in blood. He started seeing all those still alive. Potential victims. Clarissa, Michelle, Devon, Beatrice, Angel, Bronagh, Fiona. So many possibilities. *Who's going to be next?*

And then strong headlights in the rear-view mirror. Really strong, blindingly so. He lifted his hand, tried to adjust the mirror so that the light wasn't such a problem. Couldn't seem to find a way out of the bloody light stream. He shook his hand in the air, hopeful that the other driver would realise how intense the lights were. But the message didn't get through.

József put on his hazard lights, and gently and intermittently applied pressure to the brake. A warning sign. But the light remained, piercing.

They were nearing Finchley Road. There'd be plenty of space to pull over, József thought, or stop if necessary, and let the car pass. He sat at a red light, the light remaining the whole time. He tried to make out through squinted eyes how many people were in the car behind, whether he could discern any features. The mirror failed him, so he twisted round and, clasping the headrest of the passenger seat, pulled himself fully round so that he could look directly behind. He was blinded instantly by what were clearly not just main beam lights but the bigger lights being applied either deliberately or accidentally. He could see nothing of the car, so he turned back.

A car horn. Two, three times.

Unable to see clearly, then dots and colours. He could see blurred green. The traffic lights had changed. Slowly, he released the handbrake and pushed on the accelerator. The car lurched forwards. He needed to pull over, not just to rid himself of the bastard, but to give his vision time to return to normal.

Lots of cars were parked in the bus lane, which wasn't a bus lane this time of night, but as soon as he made out a fairly large space, one that could occupy at least five car lengths, not yet trusting his vision, he indicated to the left and pulled over. He applied the handbrake and immediately rubbed his eyes. Then he removed his hands and widened his eyes, staring hard into his lap, his head bowed. He stared until he saw two legs distinctly.

Two tracksuit bottoms, two trainers. All there, all now clear.

He lifted his head, put his hand onto the handbrake. But the light: still piercing. He froze. *What the fuck!* The car that had been following him had also pulled over, was parked about three car lengths behind, the lights still digging into him. Like a weapon, *like a blade*.

He shivered and considered what to do. The car was just sitting there. The light was unrelenting. He tried again to turn around and to look. And again, he failed to see anything.

'Fuck this,' he said.

He turned back to the windscreen, grabbed the door lever and opened it. He kicked the door open and stepped out. The second his feet reached the tarmac, the engine of the other car revved. A foot was on the gas, to the floor, the whirring of the engine revolting, painful to the ears. It sounded like it was pleading to be released.

Undeterred, József took confident steps forwards, closing the distance. He didn't think of consequences, didn't worry about weapons. Just marched towards the car, marched tall. At which point, the handbrake was released and the car rocketed at him. He had nowhere to go. Jumped sideways and pressed himself tight up against the tail of his car.

He recognised the car behind him, now that he could see clearly, was a Peugeot saloon. It missed him by inches, centimetres perhaps, hit his car's open driver's door and tore it from its hinges.

József Varga was left pressed into the car, watching the Peugeot speed into the distance, disappearing from view.

József's rental car was towed home. The officers outside helped him inside. Others arrived and took a statement. Showed concern, but had no answers and no ideas.

When they left him alone, he knew what he had to do next. That had been decided for him, for when he arrived home, not a package but an envelope waited for him on the carpet behind the front door. He opened it and pulled out a sheet of plain A4 paper.

Three words, handwritten, the first in capitals.

József phoned Michael. It was clear that Michael had missed something. The message was for him, that much was obvious.

But the phone rang and rang. No answer. He left a message, explaining what had happened on Finchley Road, asking for an update on the Hungarian end of things, and urging Michael to return the call. 'I have news, Michael. Ring me back.'

Chapter Thirty-Three

Michael's eyes open slowly. His head pounds. The daylight that's streaming through the gap between the curtains is painful, troubling, an agonising reminder of what he'd hoped was a nightmare. He remembers how he behaved with Gizi, what he'd said and done, before he even tries to think about it. Shame – he's full of it. He places his hand to his head, presses hard. His flesh is taut, just. He sighs, or groans. He rolls onto his back and, through squinting eyes, stares at the ceiling, focusing on the cracked off-white paint.

His vision blends into a different picture. He sees Ferenc at the club last night, on the opposite side of the piste, a foil extended, punching, punching. He sees Ferenc hurtle towards him at speed. He sees Ferenc's blade collide with his chest, and he sees the hits he lands on the Hungarian's frame. He sees their handshake, something about it striking him as deathly false. He sees the Hungarian leave the building. He sees the incognito pursuit. He sees Ferenc spot him and he sees him run. He sees the car collide with Ferenc, his legs giving out, the Hungarian falling. He sees the bus plummeting towards him, diving for cover his only choice. He watches, helplessly, as the body leaps over the edge, falls into the darkness below.

He sees *nothing*.

Then he sees his father. József Varga. The one and only.

And he remembers the difference he can make by solving this mystery.

He places his hands over his eyes, flexes his shoulder blades. Time to get up. Time to apologise to Gizi for being a sleazy drunk last night.

As he gets up, he sees his mobile phone indicating a message has been left. He doesn't remember it ringing last night and he doesn't remember seeing the message signal when he arrived back in the room.

He dials his voicemail. He hears his father's voice, hears the message. 'I have news, Michael. Ring me back.' His head's pounding, but he realises how serious the information he hears is: there was an attempt on his father's life. He thinks about calling, but then he thinks about Gizi, who will arrive soon.

He decides that giving an update to his father can wait an hour, until he's fixed things with Gizi, until he feels more like himself. Instead, he calls Sally Davison and tells her to make sure the uniformed officers are doubly attentive outside his father's house, that if his father moves they should too. He knows he should say more to Sally, but it's too awkward and he can't get his mind off the embarrassing conversation he'll have to have with Gizi any moment now.

He showers and is downstairs before Gizi arrives. He asks in reception where to find a florist, then he runs there to beat Gizi's arrival. Some tulips, an odd number of them traditional, but not thirteen, which Hungarians count as an unlucky number. They'll probably be dead before she gets home to tend to them, but still, it's the thought that counts. Or so he thinks.

He returns to the hotel moments before Gizi pulls up in front of it. She leans across to unlock the passenger door. He gets in.

'For you,' he says, 'for the fool I was last night. You have every apology under the sun.'

She thanks him, takes the flowers, places them on the backseat. 'Don't worry about it. I've seen worse. Far worse, believe me.'

'That's refreshing.'

As Gizi drives, and amid a silence, Michael repeats, 'I *am* sorry.'

'Don't mention it. Anyway, the fingerprints on the fencing bag and the address book have come back. They don't lead anywhere. They're partials as I said last night and they don't match anything on our database. So let's get to István, see if he remembers anything more about *Puskás, J.* after a night's sleep.'

'And then to Ákos.'

'Absolutely.'

Amid further silence, Michael says perkily, 'So tell me about yourself to shut me up.'

'What would you like to know?'

'If there's such little respect here for police, and if there's so much shit to put up with, what with the corruption, why be one? Why fight the public when you already have to fight the crooks?'

She keeps her eyes on the road. They gleam in the daylight – Michael isn't sure whether it's because they're welling up or they have a natural shimmer. 'My father. He was a good man. I was twelve when he died – when he was killed. He was in a local newsagent buying some cigarettes when the shop was robbed. The thieves didn't want any witnesses. They shot my father and a woman who was also there, as well as the cashier. They just executed them. And they were never found. As I waited with my mother for news of arrests, I got more and more frustrated, angry that the police didn't seem to act quickly enough. They were so casual.'

She doesn't speak for a while. Michael gives her time.

'Within two months, I thought I could do that job and do it better. Within six months, and with no arrests made, I knew I *had* to be a cop. So I am. They never found my father's killers and every day I turn up for work in his memory. And I always will, no matter what it's like, no matter what challenges and difficulties are thrown at me.'

Michael doesn't know what to say. He feels he should comfort her.

She sniffs, but she's composed.

'I'm sorry,' he says simply.

'That's life,' she says simply.

'Well, it shouldn't be.'

'That's *my* life.'

They're interrupted by the sound of Michael's mobile phone ringing. He pulls it from his pocket, sees his father's name as the incoming caller. 'Shit,' he says. 'Shit.'

'What is it?'

He shakes the question off and answers the phone.

'Michael, where the hell are you?' József asked. 'Didn't you get my message?'

'Yes, sorry. Look, it's crazy here. We're just on our way to István. What's up?'

'What's up?' Irritation was clear in his voice. 'What's up is that this bastard tried to kill me last night.'

'Yes, you said. I'm sorry.' And every word sounded hollow.

'I didn't call for your concern, Michael. And I know I don't have it. Are you any closer?'

'Bem Statue was a dead end. Someone going by the name of Ferenc is involved.' He briefly explained the previous evening at Spartacus and the pursuit that followed it. 'Any ideas?'

'No. None. But here's something you need to know. You have to go back to the Bem Statue.'

'Back? Why?'

'Because when I got back last night, there was an envelope waiting for me. Only it was for *you*.'

Michael felt his heart speed up. He swallowed. 'What did it say?'

'It said, "Follow Papa Bem". And the word *follow* was in capital letters.'

Michael repeated the words, getting Gizi's attention. 'Statue?' she says.

'Get us back there right now.' To his father again, realising: 'So if there was a message for you *there* and if Ferenc is *here*, how's that possible? There's got to be two of them.'

'Oh, merde. Michael, this is just –'

'No, listen. Sit tight. *Do not* leave the house. The police will be right outside and they won't be complacent. You have my word. I'll get to the bottom of this. Papa Bem has to show us something.'

Driving at speed, a blue light flashing atop the dashboard, Gizi gets them to Bem Square in little over ten minutes. She parks in the road adjacent to the square. They get out and rush over to the statue.

'There's no difference,' he says. 'It looks just like yesterday. Nothing visibly different. What is all this?' he says, pressing a hand through his hair, clinging on to strands of it.

'I have no ideas,' she says, shaking her head. She steps towards the statue, climbs up to the base on which it's erected. 'I can't see anything unusual,' she says, searching around the higher parts of the statue.

Michael scans the square. 'Fucker's watching,' he says. 'I bet.' Slowly: 'Motherfucker.'

'I wouldn't be surprised,' she says, jumping down, wiping the dirt off her trousers after she lands.

'What else do you know about this statue, this place?'

'Just what I told you.'

'István,' Michael says. He pulls out his mobile phone and searches for a number. Handing the phone to Gizi, he instructs, 'Ask István to tell you everything he knows about this thing.' He jabs a thumb in Bem's direction.

Gizi's soon speaking in Hungarian. Listening, she nods. Michael keeps looking round. Gizi repeats some of the history she's already told Michael. He doesn't take in the words properly. *Inspiration to the young freedom fighters.* He's desperate to see Ferenc, a man in beige swaying from side to side as he stands across the road. But he sees nothing out of the ordinary, even though he feels dozens of eyes on him. *He's pointing, directing the revolutionaries to Parliament.* He needs to see something, anything that will –

'What did you say?' he says, springing back to life. 'Parliament?'

'Yes, he's pointing at it.' She, in turn, points. 'Look.' With her hand, she draws an invisible line from Bem's outstretched hand across the Danube and then beyond buildings in the distance. 'Parliament Square's just over there.'

Michael's running back towards Gizi's car before she's

214

finished speaking with István. '*Follow Papa Bem*,' he calls out.

When they get inside the car, she switches on the blue light and accelerates. It's not long before she makes a right turn onto the heavily worn Margit híd, or Margaret Bridge. Twenty-five metres wide, it carries four lanes of traffic, two tramlines in its centre and pavements on both sides. Designed by French engineer Ernest Goüin, with construction that began in 1872 and was completed four years later, it's the city's second oldest bridge, an example of French neo-baroque bridge building. Six steel spans, with a lattice structure, rest on pillars. The bridge's pillars are decorated with statues of galley prows, which are adorned with large, winged female figures. Unusually, the bridge lies in a V-shape; it's placed at an angle of 165 degrees at the point where it branches off Margit sziget, or Margaret Island.

Gizi's car makes the more than six-hundred-metre-long journey in no time, passing the spot where last night Ferenc leapt to his escape. There's a right turn and she slams the car to a halt.

'Here,' she says, pointing and moving forwards at pace.

They enter Parliament Square, a vast area with the main parliament building on the riverbank side, the Ministry of Agriculture and a museum opposite it, and other buildings on the far side.

Michael drifts away from Gizi, towards the middle of the square. His ears are filled with echoes of his father's words. *This is the place.* 'Why here?'

Gizi walks to his side. 'On October 25th 1956, day three of the Revolution, five thousand people were fired upon, seventy-five were killed, and almost three hundred

215

injured.'

'So what's the significance? My father wasn't here when the incident happened. He told me he got here *afterwards*.'

'Just like us. After Papa Bem.'

'Yes, but why are we here now? What's the next clue?'

She shrugs her shoulders.

'There has to be a reason. Something we're not seeing.' He stands and turns, looking all around them. 'There's a reason we've been sent here. There's got to be another message.'

'I don't know. I can't tell you anything else.'

'It's too big a place to search for something small. It's got to be a signal of some kind, like the statue. We've got to be able to work it out. This has become a game to him.'

'Yes, but what?'

'I don't know.' Michael's eyes don't stop scanning the area. 'I know,' he says. 'Can you call István again? This time, let me speak.'

Gizi dials her mobile, speaks and then hands the phone to Michael.

'István, what happened here at Parliament Square on October 25th? I'm looking for any reason why we might be here right now. What's the next message? What should we do next?'

The deep voice sounds, rarely pausing for breath. 'Three thousand protesters, they march along main boulevard and wish to meet with other protesters group outside the Parliament. When they approach the Astoria Hotel, which on Kossuth Lajos Street, they find passage blocked by three Russian tank. No one budge. Protesters stand opposite huge tank and no back down.

'Men at front talk with soldiers in tanks. Many men just students. They give leaflets to soldiers, leaflets written in Russian. These explain. I tell you words.' There's a moment of silence, and then some rustling, and then István returns on the line, slowly and deliberately reading, '"You are not fighting against counter-revolutionaries. We Hungarians want an independent, democratic Hungary. You are not shooting at fascists but at workers, peasants and university students." The Russian soldiers, they let men pass and they go together to the Parliament. Some of the men at the front, they jump onto tank. They arrive at the Parliament Square together, where already five thousand other people wait. And then someone shoot on protestors. They shoot from Ministry of Agriculture and they kill without moment to think.'

Michael crouches down, hanging up the phone, his hand reaching for the ground. He thinks back to what his father told him. *This is the place, where it happened.*

'Are you okay?' Gizi asks.

He nods, possibly instinctively. 'Students. Tanks. Huge crowds. Gunfire. One of them, something about them…' He sees his father arriving amid news of the massacre. He sees his father tending to the wounded. He sees his father, at nineteen, carrying corpses.

'Are you okay, Michael?' A hand on his shoulder.

'This is the place.' He shakes his head slowly. 'Tourists today, everyone's happy, taking photographs. Without a care.'

'Yes. It's a history no one could speak about publicly for so long. Not until the nineties. Just quiet discussions at home, nothing in public. And no one has ever been able to believe it, not even today.'

217

Michael stands up and turns to face Gizi. 'I don't believe it. And now we're here with another inhumane fucker calling the shots.' His line of vision goes over her shoulder and he points. 'That one? That's the Ministry of Agriculture?'

'That's right.'

'Maybe there then.' He moves towards it.

It's a dull-cream block building. A walkway, with oval arches at either end, lines the front of the building, the upper floors perched on pillars. 'Somewhere up there. That's where they fired from?'

'Somewhere there, yes. No one knows where exactly.'

'It's too big a building to search. Why did no one do anything? Britain? The States?'

'The Americans, the British, the French – people were pleading with them for support, they were even pounding on the doors of the embassies, but it fell on deaf ears. America's President Eisenhower was far more concerned about his own re-election campaign, and the British and French were embroiled in the Suez Canal crisis in Egypt. No one wanted to get involved.'

Michael starts walking along the walkway, searching. Gizi follows. Only concrete. Some posters in frames on the building's exterior walls. But nothing else.

'It was a massacre,' he says. 'Just like what this guy, whoever he is, is doing to those women in England.'

Gizi takes a few steps away, starts circling. Then, together, they walk the whole of Parliament Square, stopping intermittently, looking.

Finding nothing.

Chapter Thirty-Four

With no answer to the puzzle placed before them, Michael asked Gizi if the day could resume as planned. But not long after their search of Parliament Square, a call had come to Gizi's mobile phone, alerting her that an address had come up in the search for *Puskás, J*, so that interrupted their plans and became their next destination.

Jakob Puskás, aged sixty-two.

Like so many of Budapest's residents, Jakob Puskás lives in an apartment block. It's in the centre of the commercial district of Pest.

Gizi parks on the roadside and they enter the building. They find themselves in another dimly lit foyer. Michael squints, brings his arm close to his eyes, to make out the time on his watch. It's a little after 9AM.

'Third floor,' says Gizi.

Michael holds the lift door open for her. She makes the floor selection and the lift takes them up. When they step into the hall, they face a wall. There are four apartments on this floor: two to each side.

'It's number fifteen.'

They make their way to the right. It's as dark up here as it is downstairs. As they approach the apartment's front door, they can hear a dog's bark emanating from within. Barking incessantly.

Gizi knocks. When there's no answer, she knocks again. And then a third time. The barking gets louder, as if it's just behind the door. Its howl is unrelenting.

'No letterbox,' Michael says. 'No way to peer through.'

He moves to one of the windows, puts his hand against the glass and leans his forehead on it. 'No, can't see anything.'

'Letterboxes are always on the ground floor in one collection, near the entrance, in apartment blocks.'

'What about a neighbour?' They have to raise their voices, so loud is the din. Now there's scratching, too, gnawing against the other side of the door. 'Surely someone can tell us if this is normal. How the hell can anyone put up with this bloody racket?'

They knock on a neighbouring apartment's door. An old lady answers. Her head creeps round the side of the door. She winces at the sound that's filling the corridor, points her ear towards them.

Gizi speaks to her in Hungarian, says something with a smile after the old lady answers, then politely nods her head and walks back towards apartment fifteen.

'And?' Michael says, following, but still with his mind on Parliament Square and its potential message.

'The dog is always barking, she said. It's always loud and it's perfectly normal and she's as disturbed by it as we are. Although she said the scratching is odd. But it's a dog, after all. What can you expect?'

She knocks again. Still no answer.

'Okay,' Gizi says, 'we'll keep our appointment with István, then return here later.'

'Can you get a uniformed officer to keep an eye here and call if Puskás returns before we get back?'

'Absolutely.'

As they walk away, the dog gets even louder, scratching, barking, demanding. *It's normal*, the old lady says.

They arrive at István's apartment a short while later.

From the main road, they can see him, up on the balcony of his apartment, smoking. He waves.

Looking tired, István appears at the front door. Once they're inside, he offers them espresso.

'Thank you, but no. I'd rather we get on with this.'

István bows his head to acknowledge Michael's wishes. 'We try Ákos. Maybe is too early. Maybe he no answer door.'

'Or maybe it's too early to be pissed,' Michael says hopefully.

They enter the lift, discussing Parliament Square, Michael probing István about possible clues there. Every dead end is quickly discovered. The lift begins its descent.

'He live alone. He have one son, but he live alone. Wife leave him many, many years ago. Last time I see him, he a dirty man, beard, dressing gown all day, drinking all day. He no leave apartment much. Sometimes he fight in veteran tournament for fencing, but not many time. Last time your father here, they meet at tournament and he tell your father they drink whisky together. This before eight o'clock in morning.' He laughs. 'Still, we try see him, if he have conscious.'

Gizi drives, István sits up front, Michael behind.

Much to everyone's surprise, Ákos opens the front door. He steps back when he sees István but doesn't acknowledge Michael and Gizi. It's a small apartment they step into, like a studio flat, and dark: the curtains are drawn, but a slight gap remains. The walkway outside can be seen from inside.

The lounge is the immediate area, and a small kitchen, completely visible from the area near the front door, comes off it. There's a sofa and an armchair in front of a tiny black-and-white television. A cabinet shows off some porcelain figurines, several chipped and all covered in dust, and plates and cups and saucers, likewise chipped and dusty. A bookshelf stands filled with old, dilapidated hardback books.

Ákos's mass falls into the armchair. In front of it is a coffee table no larger than a folded newspaper. Some folded paper sits underneath one of its legs to provide equal balance. On it is a bottle of whisky, three-quarters empty, and a scotch glass. Next to that is a cup and saucer, coffee filled to the brim, and an ashtray, likewise at bursting point. On the floor is an empty vodka bottle.

To a stranger, Ákos would appear to be eighty, but his actual age is sixty-eight. He speaks to István, his eyes closing involuntarily and frequently. His skin is loose, his eyes are dead. There's no tone in his voice, no feeling in the words. Every so often, his hand robotically rubs the side of his face.

István is pointing at Michael and Gizi while speaking to Ákos, obviously explaining. It sounds like he's stressing key points.

József Varga's brother doesn't look at them; they might as well not be here. When István has finished speaking, Ákos grumbles a few words. Then he turns his head and fixes his glare on Michael, not relinquishing it. Dead eyes remain. When he's finished speaking, he doesn't look away from his nephew. Michael thinks he can identify an odd grin beneath the death-like mask.

'What?' Michael says to István. 'What did he say?'

'He ask, 'Why don't you speak Hungarian?''

Michael smirks. 'I was never taught.'

But Ákos has stopped looking at him; he's closed his

eyes.

'Nice to meet you, too,' Michael says, and he leaves the apartment. He stands in the corridor outside, understanding a little why maybe his father has no relationship with the man on the other side of the wall.

He's been outside for fewer than five seconds when the calm, comatose environment inside erupts into a fiery outburst. He hears shouting, a constant roar, the name *József* said again and again, and a crash and thud as glass smashes and an object of weight is displaced. He hears István and then Gizi speaking in soothing tones, but the roar, a voice he doesn't recognise, refuses to subside.

He dashes back into the apartment to encounter Ákos on his feet, his arms flailing, his cheeks a deep red, his forehead purple, his eyes exploding, his temper ricocheting off the walls.

'What the fuck?'

István and Gizi spin round. 'Michael, please,' István says. 'Go, please.'

'What the fuck?'

Gizi speaks up. 'Michael, he's crazy. Just wait.'

And then Ákos surprises them all, his actions suggestive of a man much younger than his appearance, by lunging at Michael, his fist lifted. István grabs the old man's arm. Gizi steps in between them.

Michael, initially startled, steps backwards then forwards. 'What?' he calls. Then louder: 'What?'

More Hungarian is shouted through gasps for breath, as Ákos struggles to get free from István's grip. The barrage of Hungarian words is relentless.

'You come to my home to ask about that fucking bastard! The son of a bitch and you come here! Who the fuck do you

think you are? You come here for József. József can rot in hell! He can rot in fucking hell!'

'What is he saying?' Michael directs his question to Gizi, who doesn't respond. Then to Ákos: 'What? Come on then.' And he presses forwards.

'Back off, Michael!'

But Michael gets round her and grabs the old man. 'What?'

Ákos doesn't back down, but Gizi charges past Michael, her gun withdrawn, and she pushes Ákos's chest. He allows himself to fall back into the armchair.

And then he's silent. They're all frozen. And now, as he returns to the state Michael originally left him in – the still, stony figure – there are light, delicate tears in his eyes.

'What the fuck,' Michael whispers.

And then, slowly, Ákos closes his eyes. They won't open again.

Chapter Thirty-Five

'He won't speak.'

'Well, why don't we fucking force him?'

'Michael, be reasonable. What he said made no sense. It certainly didn't give us reason to arrest him and interrogate him.'

'What did he say?'

'He cursed your father, again and again and again. Like I said, it didn't make any sense. But you being here in the name of your father made his blood boil.'

'You know, sometimes I know how he feels, but that's not good enough.'

They're outside the apartment block. Michael's pacing up and down a small section of pavement. Gizi's smoking a cigarette. They've left István with Ákos, whose eyes, once closed, wouldn't open again, no matter what was said to him.

'He's not going to talk. We have to be patient and see if István can get somewhere with him.'

'He's a prick.'

'He's certainly difficult. He's a strange man.'

Michael says the words slowly: 'He's a prick.' Then he stands still. 'We need to find out what caused that. Just the alcohol or a genuine rage and, if a rage, why? You know, maybe he's got more to do with this than we thought possible. He's clearly not the frail old man he appears to be.'

István joins Michael and Gizi not long after. 'I sorry,' István says.

'Don't worry about it. Hell of a greeting, though.' He mimics, '"Why don't you speak Hungarian?" Bloody idiot. And then that temper. I thought he was going to try to clobber me.'

'He was,' Gizi says.

'*Try* is the word of importance here. Wouldn't have had a fucking chance. Any luck with him, István?'

He shakes his head. 'Nothing. Eyes still closed. We come back.' He takes a deep breath. 'We come back.'

Michael nods. 'Yes, we will, just as soon as we work out what could have caused that. I need to call my father.'

Chapter Thirty-Six

'Do you have any more news?'

'Tell me about Ákos.'

'I asked for an update.'

'I want to know why Ákos hates you so much.'

'How is István? Has he been a good host?'

'Host? This isn't a fucking holiday.'

'Language.'

'This is a murder investigation.'

'How is it going?'

'What's up with you and Ákos?'

'What do you mean?'

'I want to know why, when I just met Ákos, he flew into a rage, why he cursed you, why he damned you to hell.'

'Because he is a son of a bitch.'

'Tell me.'

'Ignore him, he's crazy. He's an alcoholic.'

'That much I saw for myself. Now stop stalling and tell me.'

'There's nothing to tell.'

'Why does he hate you? Why do you hate him? I presume you do, don't you?'

'It doesn't matter what I think.'

'It matters very much what you think. And it matters what *I* think. I'm investigating here and I need to know.'

'Lay off.'

'Tell me now. He could be behind all this shit.'

'He isn't.'

'Listen, you're not to –'

'He isn't! He might be a son of a bitch, but in Hungary family actually means something. It's the centre of a person's world, it's sacred. He just wouldn't.'

'You can't –'

'He wouldn't! Now enough!'

'He hates you, you know. He's sick of living in your shadow. No, in the memory of your shadow, because you're only a memory here. But the memory's lasted. He cursed you and wished you dead. Why would someone do that, huh? A brother, someone supposedly close. Why would he spit on your memory, claim you were a blight on the family, say your parents were ashamed of what your life became?'

'He's just a jealous son of a bitch who's never got over the fact that I could wipe him off the piste after only a year of training. Stole his thunder? That's right, it was there to be taken and I took it.'

'Oh, it's not just jealousy. Jealousy's there, absolutely, but the hatred is so *deep*. Yes, you made him feel like shit, you humiliated him and continued to humiliate him every time you beat him on the piste or won a tournament, or every time people lauded your talent while forgetting his – he was good, remember. He felt like shit, but this goes way beyond that. Tell me how.'

'You're not listening.'

'That's all I seem to be doing at the moment. This prick, whoever he is, has sent me on a wild goose chase. If there's even a possibility that it could be Ákos, I need to know.'

So long a pause that it seemed like József had disappeared.

'He's angry because I left…'

Pause.

'Because you left Budapest?'

Pause.

'Because you –'

'Because I left *him*.'

'Impossible. He couldn't care less that you're not here.'

'Not left him home *alone*. Don't be stupid. Because I left him behind, in the street.'

'Tell me what you mean.'

'What I told you is right, he has got nothing to do with this. He is an alcoholic and a bitter old man. And, in a way, I can understand why. Yes, I stole his thunder, and I enjoyed doing it. I was better than him and I still am, and that gave me great pleasure when we were younger. Maybe it still does today.

'But that is only scratching the surface. The truth is, when I told you about the Revolution, I didn't tell you about one part of it. Something that is *not* important. Again, what I said before is right: family is sacred in Hungary. Full of hate he may be, but that's the total extent of it.'

'I need to understand *everything*.'

One final pause.

'On the day I made my way out of Budapest, Ákos worked out what I was up to. He read my thoughts, because they were his thoughts, too. He followed me from our home that day. My journey was a slow one as I dodged tanks and soldiers, so he couldn't stay hidden for very long. I spotted him. I froze in the middle of the street.

'He told me he knew what I was doing, that I was

abandoning our parents, that I was being selfish. And, without hesitation, contradicting what he'd just stated, he said, "Let me come with you". I laughed. It was a laugh of surprise; I wasn't mocking him or being spiteful, I just couldn't believe what he'd said.

'We'd never been close, we weren't friends, barely brothers, and he was asking to come with me. He must have felt desperate.

'I didn't want to be with him. It's that simple. So I made him believe we would find a way out together. And then, in a large crowd, I managed to sneak away.

'I later found out that he was picked up by some soldiers. He was taken away and locked up. My father's contacts were perhaps the only reason he was released. He spent two days in a cell. And I destroyed his chances of escape.

'That's why my brother hates me. That's all, and that's enough. End of discussion.'

Chapter Thirty-Seven

'I want to see him again.'

'Michael, I don't know.' Gizi sighs. 'István, what do you think?'

'No. No good idea. Today he no speak. In morning. Maybe after he sleep. Wait for no alcohol.'

'Fine then, tomorrow,' Michael says.

Gizi breaks the silence that builds. 'Why did you tell him he'd shamed his family?'

Feigned ignorance: 'Who?'

'Your father. Why did you tell him that?'

'I had to try to get him angry. Calm, I knew I wouldn't get anywhere with him.'

'Well, you got what you wanted. Just not in the nicest _'

'Yes, I did.' He doesn't pause and directs his next words to István. 'What about his wife and son? Where are they?'

'His wife, I no know. His son, he work in bank.'

'I want to see him.'

'Edvárd?'

'Yes, Edvárd. I want to see him.'

'Now?'

'Right now.'

Edvárd Varga lives in an apartment building that's one block parallel to the Buda embankment near Margaret Bridge. Michael and he have never met; until today, they've never heard of one another. But Edvárd greets Michael with a smile, shakes his hand and welcomes him, Gizi and István into the small home. It's on the third floor of three storeys, and there are two main rooms, a kitchen and a bathroom. The lounge doubles for a bedroom: the parents'.

Edvárd and his wife, Magdolna, who isn't home when the visitors arrive, have a three-month-old daughter, Szilvia, whose room contains a small cot bed, which she doesn't sleep in yet.

After Michael briefly explains why he's in Budapest, deliberately omitting almost all the key details, and asks Edvárd about his father's relationship with József, Edvárd responds in fairly good English. 'May I be open?' he asks. 'Open and honest.'

'Please.'

'My father doesn't speak very often about your father. Perhaps I remember four or five times in my whole life. Now I'm forty. He has only spoken about him when he has been very, very drunk. But one thing he always makes clear in such cases is just how much he hates József Varga. I would go as far as to say *loathe*. Every time I have asked why he has ill feelings towards his brother, he does not want to talk about it, even though he has always been very drunk at these times, but he says a few things. He doesn't use sentences, just words or phrases. He says things like *betrayal* and *thief* and *arrogant* and *disloyal*. He spits the words out. And he has also said things like *he showed me up* and *he humiliated me* and *he double-crossed me*. Again, I have never been able to fully understand the circumstances surrounding these words, but the feeling is clear enough. It's pal… What is it, when you can feel it?'

'Palpable.'

'Yes, *palpable*.'

'Yes, it is,' Michael says, understanding more about feelings like these than he's prepared to admit.

They drink coffee as they speak and soon the conversation turns to general matters. Edvárd, Gizi and István, sitting on a settee, smoke a cigarette each. They converse in Hungarian and English, flit between the two casually. Michael sits on an armchair. At times, there's even laughter. It's clear that Edvárd wants to help, but it's not clear whether he can be any help.

They speak about his new family – he's been married for almost two years and a father for such a short time. His father has only seen the child once. Edvárd doesn't foresee a second visit any time soon. But Magdolna's parents are both helpful and caring; that's where his wife and daughter are right now. Edvárd, an accountant for the bank, works from home twice a week, so he's been given space today, on one of those two days.

'I'm sorry we've never met,' Michael says. He likes Edvárd. He senses he has a kind soul, is friendly and good-natured. He makes Michael feel comfortable. Both, it seems, have difficult parents.

'Well, it's good to meet you now.'

Cheers is signalled with their coffee cups. Michael finishes his; it's richly aromatic.

'Four women have died in England, Edvárd. Four women because of something my father did in his past. Your father didn't want to know when I visited him earlier.'

'I'm sorry about his behaviour.'

'He's more similar to my father than I imagine both of them know or are willing to admit. My father assures me Ákos would have nothing to do with what's happening in England. Do you know anything that might suggest my father is wrong? After meeting Ákos, I'm not sure.'

'I like to think he is a harmless old man. He *was not* always harmless, however. He used to hit me, when I was a child.' Edvárd's eyes fix on the coffee table's patterned narrow tablecloth whose ends hang off two edges. '*Beat* is probably the better word to describe what he did to me. He would *always* drink a glass of vodka here and there, in the morning, in the afternoon, in the evening, from as soon as I can remember. But eventually there came a time when he drank almost all the time and he just seemed to be permanently relaxed. Much slower, much calmer, much looser, much more different from how he had been before. So, now, he usually sits at home drinking, in some kind of trance. You can talk to him, but he usually doesn't talk back. I can't see how he could be involved. He could not hurt a soul. He does not have the energy any more.'

'The rage is still there. He exploded.'

Edvárd looks at István, who nods his head and says some Hungarian words of confirmation. Then looking at Michael, he adds: 'So he's like a volcano, then. What's that word?' He clicks his fingers. 'Dormant.'

'He was very active today.'

'Well, then.' There's a lengthy pause. No one says anything while Edvárd chews his bottom lip. 'Years ago, this is, I'm talking about *years ago*.'

When he realises there's going to be another pause, Michael says, 'Yes?'

'I was only a teenager. Very young. It was maybe only the second time my father had spoken about his brother. About József. He was incredibly drunk. I had returned home from school and there he was, sitting in front of the television, and three quarters of a bottle of vodka finished. He was mumbling. *József this, József that.* I did not know what he was saying. It did not make sense. I just knew who József Varga was. Mostly because of what my mother had said, to be honest, I knew a bit about him. I think I already knew my father was jealous of him. I think I sensed that from a very young age. Whenever the name was mentioned, he changed the subject.

'So that day, when I came home and he was so very drunk, being young I tried to question him about it, to find out what was bothering him so much. This was before he had become much calmer, and immediately he slapped me on the face. I fell on the ground and he shouted at me, but he was confused. A few times while he was shouting, he called me Edvárd and a few times he said József. But he stalked over me like a hunter, and when he was mixing our names I got very scared. I wanted to run, but I could not – there was not space to get past him. He shouted for about ten minutes and hit me again. When he dropped back onto his chair, I ran. But before he did, he said something that did not mean anything to me then. Maybe it does now, though.'

Silence. He doesn't finish what he wants to say. The anticipation is too much for Michael who, calmly, despite his inner feelings, says, 'What did he say?'

'It wouldn't cost much to shut you up forever, József.'

Chapter Thirty-Eight

They arrive back at Ákos's home within the half hour. Michael takes the lead, doesn't wait for the lift and leaps up the staircase two steps at a time. He arrives outside Ákos's front door and bangs on it. There's no answer. After he has pounded on the door three more times, Gizi and István, who took the lift, catch up with him.

'Maybe he's not home,' Gizi says.

'Bullshit. A drunk who suddenly goes out for a lunchtime stroll?' His fist collides with the green door again. 'Ákos!' he calls. 'Open the door.' Then, remembering the gap in the curtains, he walks to the right, to the window, and peers through. 'Asleep,' he says.

Gizi looks. 'Or dead,' she jokes.

Ákos is still in his armchair, but his head is tilted back, his mouth is open wide and his eyes are closed. Michael listens carefully: there's snoring.

He quietly curses. 'Okay. A bomb probably couldn't wake him, the amount he's no doubt drunk.' He looks at his watch. 'It's almost twelve. Let's go to Benedek's for lunch and come back later in the afternoon. Time also to think more about Parliament Square and what the hell could be going on there. And maybe he'll be awake and just hung-over by then.'

*

Benedek Sebestyén lives in Kenyérm Street in Pest, not far from Elizabeth Bridge. En route, they stop at a small shop. 'What kind of gift is customary here when you're visiting someone for lunch?' Michael asks.

'For a man, a bottle of some western alcohol. And for a female, a box of good-quality chocolates or flowers. An odd number, remember.'

Michael dashes into the shop and buys a bottle of Irish whisky for Benedek and a box of Lindt chocolates for his wife. He picks up a small cuddly toy for their daughter.

There's no parking available in the street outside Benedek's apartment, so Gizi drives to the end of the road and parks facing some grass that verges on a square.

'Another interesting place for your Revolution tour book, this is Republic Square,' Gizi says. Pointing: 'Behind us here is the Erkel Theatre. It's named after, coincidentally, Ferenc Erkel, and has on operas. It was, for many years, the largest public building in the city. It dates back to the early twentieth century. Next year, it will close and be renovated. As you can see, it hasn't aged well.' The light grey building, marked with signs of age and smog, is in need of urgent attention. 'Now this,' she says, pointing towards the opposite side of the square at a grey rectangular building, 'is the headquarters of the Hungarian Socialist Party, back then the Greater Budapest Communist Party.' A dull mass, its ground floor is lined with large vertical-rectangular barred windows, and four storeys above are lined with squat, almost-square windows.

'The basement was full of cells where prisoners were held,' Gizi says, crouching down and placing the palms of her hands on the ground. 'It's actually believed by some that the cell system stretched out underground into the square, right here, and that, from underneath the grass, when there was fighting in the city in 1956, people could hear cries for help. Later, the area was dug up, but no bodies were ever found.'

'There's an air of sadness here,' Michael observes, looking around at the space that's empty of people. 'Something in the air.' He looks round to see where István is, but the old man isn't near them and, instead, is waiting, smoking a cigarette, on the corner where the square connects with Luther Street.

Gizi notices Michael's gaze. 'He won't want to be here. For his generation, it's a time to forget about. For people who lived through the Revolution, or those who were born soon after it, this is a place where one doesn't feel quite human, where no matter how hard the government tries to make it pretty, it remains ugly.' Greenery and benches have been laid in the square, inviting visitors but failing to attract them. 'Even all these years later, death hangs in the air and unhappiness sits by its side.'

'What happened to make this place worse than all the others, or is it because of the cells?'

'There's more to it than the cells. The ÁVO had been officially disbanded, but inside the building were some ÁVO officers who hadn't wanted to leave. Maybe they'd feared for their safety, I don't know. Anyway, the soldiers who had been protecting the building left as per the ceasefire agreement and people were going about their business in the square. Some were queuing for food. A fresh delivery of meat arrived at the headquarters and the people queuing became angry that it looked like a special favour was being given to the communists – their food was being delivered, lots of it, but the regular people were made to queue and wait.

'Some rebels were told about this, so they came here and went into the building to question why this delivery of food was still happening. Inside, they noticed two ÁVO officers and all hell broke loose.

'With extra support, the rebels overpowered those in the building. All those inside were shown no mercy – there was no hesitation. A high-ranking officer was hanged from a tree and set alight. In total, twenty-three of them were killed. The rebels called it 'instant justice'. So you see, it wasn't just the Russians who did unspeakable things.

'And then there was the image that ended up shocking the world the most: the picture of a young member of the ÁVO, barely a teenager – his name was László Elek – hanging upside down from a tree, with a group of rebels kicking him. That was the Revolution: children killing children on both sides.

'This place is the ultimate symbol of the horrors caused by both sides. It is the place where *everyone* was inhuman. That is why no one comes here, and why István is over there and not here.'

She stands up and, without waiting for Michael, walks across the road and into Luther Street, past István and to the entrance of the block in which Benedek lives. The two men join her and she presses the buzzer.

'After lunch, back to Parliament Square, okay?' Michael asks. 'We must have missed something. The answer's there.'

Gizi nods.

Benedek's voice sounds through the intercom, Gizi speaks and they're given access. As they make their way up in the lift, she checks in with the officer at Jakob Puskás's property.

'No sign of him yet,' she tells Michael after she hangs up.

Benedek is standing on the other side of the lift door as it arrives at the floor on which he lives, the fifth. 'Welcome, welcome,' he says, his arms extended either side of him, his smile beaming.

'Good to see you again,' Michael returns, offering his hand.

Michael offers his gifts, to be told that Benedek's wife and daughter are away for a couple of days, but he's thankful for the gesture nonetheless.

Benedek escorts them into a dining room in which the table is already laid with an afternoon snack. Traditional Hungarian choices have been made: there's sliced bread, paprika butter, large yellow peppers, cabbage stuffed with pork, some boiled vegetables and, as something sweet, mákos, which is a light and fluffy poppy seed cake. There's also a carton of orange juice, a freshly brewed pot of coffee and a sealed bottle of vodka.

'Please, make yourselves comfortable,' Benedek says, and they all sit down, Michael and Gizi next to one another, and Benedek and István on the other side of the table.

'This looks wonderful,' says Gizi.

Michael shifts forwards on his seat. 'Yes, absolutely. Thanks so much. You shouldn't have gone to so much trouble.'

'Please, help yourselves. Good appetite.'

As they fill their plates with food, they make small talk. The food is tasty.

Michael surveys the rest of the room. To the left is a large unit, which goes from wall to wall and contains a metre opening in the centre in which trophies and medals are placed on a shelf. Others are attached to the wall.

Benedek notices that Michael has spotted it. 'Ah, yes, you've seen my little tribute to my father's glory days.'

'Yes, it is… impressive,' Michael says, finding what he reckons is an appropriate word.

With his mouth full of food, Benedek leaps to his feet and trots over to the display. He points at each one in turn and explains what they were awarded for. Michael switches off and only comes back to the situation in front of him when he feels Gizi elbow his arm.

'Michael?'

'Yes, quite,' he says, stirring.

Benedek, a smile exploding from every pore on his skin, has in his hand a trophy and he's holding it out towards Michael, who nods his head.

Michael feels Benedek beckoning him, so he rises awkwardly. *What, does he want me to hold the fucking thing?* With slow steps and trying not to appear uncomfortable, he crosses to the side of the room and stands face to face with Benedek. The smile hasn't subsided; in fact, it may have erupted further.

'Take it,' he's encouraged.

Michael nods and takes hold of the trophy, a glass fencer with knees bent and foil extended atop a porcelain base. He looks down at what he's holding and turns it in his hands. It's weighty. On the base at the front, there's a plaque. Three names appear on it and a year. *Barabás, Ambrus; Sebestyén, Konstantin; Varga, József. 1955.*

'This is one of three trophies they won together, the

most impressive, and there are several medals. They were a wonderful team.'

Without averting his eyes from the trophy, Michael says, 'Yes, they must have been. What happened to Ambrus Barabás?'

'He moved to the north of the country when I was a child. I attended his funeral a few years ago.'

Another one to scratch off the list of possible suspects.

Michael pictures his father and the two other men – then teenagers – holding up their trophies in triumph, pleased with themselves, basking in the glory of victory. He wonders whether József Varga held this trophy in his hands, whether Michael's actions at the moment are merely a repetition of his father's. Just like much of his fencing life has been.

But this investigation is going to be different.

Handing the prize back to Benedek, Michael says, as he walks back to his seat, 'I need to find out if there was anyone who ever made it clear they might one day come after my father. If our fathers fenced together a lot, that means they trained together a lot and that most likely means they partied together a lot, from what I understand. Is there anyone in your family who was around then who might know more? Or did your father keep a diary? Is there anyone he could have revealed anything important to?'

'Aside from me?'

'Aside from you.'

'My mother, she died before my father, but she didn't know him in those days. There's no one else. There's just everything he told me.'

'But you don't know anything regarding what I'm

242

speaking about?'

Benedek shakes his head and sits back down. 'Nothing specific, no. Unfortunately. Because I would love to help you, I really would. But there is something that might be important, a piece of, how do we call it, character witness, that might be useful to hear.'

Without saying another word, he stands up and walks back to the unit, crouches down and opens a drawer that's little above floor level. From it, he extracts an A4 brown hardback envelope and, leaving the drawer open, goes back to the table. He remains standing, opens the envelope and pulls out a ten-by-eight black-and-white photograph. He holds it in his hands, stares at it and then turns it around so that it faces Gizi and Michael. István, chewing on a piece of mákos, twists uncomfortably to get a clear view. In the picture stand three men, masks in arms, blades in gloved hands, serious stares on their faces.

'They meant business,' Benedek says. 'You know better than most what your father managed to achieve in only a short and young time. He didn't waste time and he didn't mess around and, because he was the natural leader, as the best fencer on the team, they didn't waste time and mess around. Or, at least, that's what they and everyone else thought. You know, my father admired your father greatly and he still did on the day he died. But they stopped competing as teammates, and they stopped training at the same club, about six months before your father left Budapest.'

Michael sits patiently. He chooses not to look at Gizi, but he can't avoid István's flickering glances that shift between him and Benedek again and again.

'Character witness, that's right. You see, my father had

a girlfriend. Her name was Ema. They had been together from school, since the age of fifteen.'

Shit. Michael already sees where this is going.

Benedek points at the glass trophy, the fencer with the extended blade. 'That one, it has pride of place in the display. It did when the display was in my father's home. Right up till the day he died. You see, that trophy was the last one they ever won together. They won the tournament and celebrated. But your father celebrated in an additional, separate way. His own special way. My father's girlfriend, Ema, went home with him that night, not with my father.'

Michael stands up abruptly. 'Why are you telling me this? Your father's dead. What good can come from this?'

They oppose one another, one on each side of the table.

'It's simple: If your father would do this to his teammate, his *friend*, what would he do to strangers? The point I'm trying to make is, the person you're looking for, it could be anyone. *Anyone.*'

Michael nods his head. 'Thank you for the lunch. We ought to get moving.'

Michael leads the way from the dining room and into the corridor. As he reaches the front door, Gizi, István and Benedek appear in the corridor.

'Before you go,' Benedek says urgently.

Michael turns around, his shoulders tensing. He raises an eyebrow, the only signal that he's willing to listen to one more thing.

'You asked me why I told you. Character witness, I said. That is the man your father was. He was a *playboy*.' He considers, then laughs. '*Playboy Varga.* That was right.'

'What?' Michael says, confused.

'But no matter what he did and even though our fathers never spoke again, my father respected József Varga until the day he died. He did not hold a grudge, even though most reasonable people would say he should have. He had great respect for your father and his talents. And I have great respect for my father, so I have told you in his memory. It is one small thing I can do for him. Somebody must know, and now you do. But it should, I hope, also serve a purpose for you. Now you see what József Varga was like and now you know the person you are looking for could be *anybody*.'

'But –'

'And now I think lunch is over.'

Chapter Thirty-Nine

Michael tries to breathe in the thick, humid air outside the apartment block. Gizi and István stand next to him, smoking cigarettes.

'I'm not enjoying this,' Michael says. 'I'm finding out just a bit too much about my father and what an arsehole he was.'

István makes a noise that sounds like he's growling, drops his cigarette on the ground, stamps it out and moves in front of Michael. 'One thing to realise,' he says. 'With József, can be no surprise. I love your father like no other, but he very difficult man. And when he…' He speaks to Gizi in Hungarian, frustrated with himself and inquisitive.

'When he was at the height of his success in fencing,' Gizi finishes for him.

'He was most difficult then. But I love him. He my best friend, always before and always now. Sometimes I wonder in past how your mother manage with him.'

'So how many more surprises? You know, the way things sound, it could be anyone in the whole of fucking Budapest who's doing this.'

After taking a deep drag, Gizi says through the exhale, 'So what do you make of him as a possibility?'

'Benedek?'

'Yes.'

'I don't see it. Regardless of what my father did, the respect was always there from Konstantin – I believe that. I think this was his one opportunity to get it off his chest. To do something in a very odd way for his father. I don't know.'

'But it's possible he could want revenge. Maybe he wants to do more in his father's memory than just tell you a damning secret.'

'What about his father? Is he definitely dead, not lurking in the shadows somewhere?'

Gizi and Michael look at István. He answers, 'Maybe I meet him when child but not when adult. I no know.'

To Gizi: 'Can you find out?'

'Let me make a call.' She steps away and removes the mobile phone from her pocket.

When she finishes the call, Michael says, 'Okay, hold Parliament Square for another hour. Let's try Ákos again. Maybe the answer's closer to home.'

The drive takes only about fifteen minutes. En route, Gizi's phone rings. She answers it and speaks while she drives. After hanging up, she says, 'Konstantin Sebestyén died nine years ago. His death's registered.'

Michael nods.

After thinking, amid the silence, about what's imminent, he says, 'We get answers from him no matter what.'

'No matter what.'

'Even if that means putting your gun to his head, we make this fucker talk.'

'Michael –'

'I'm prepared to do anything, Gizi. *Anything.* Just don't react surprised by how I act at any time.'

'Michael, you're not going to –'

He turns to her. 'I'm going to get answers. I'm going to get to the bottom of this.'

Gizi parks outside the apartment block, puts the car on the wide pavement. She speaks to István. He nods.

Only she and Michael get out of the car. 'Isn't he coming?' Michael asks.

'Maybe it's better if he stays here.'

'Maybe you're right.'

'Do anything?'

'Anything.'

Chapter Forty

With his hands up against the glass and his head pressed against it, Michael peers through the window of Ákos's apartment. The old man is still asleep on the armchair, snoring, mouth wide open, head leaning back.

'We'll try it the nice way first,' Michael says, knocking forcefully on the window. With no answer forthcoming, he asks Gizi, 'Can I have your gun?'

'Michael! What are you thinking –'

'I'm not going to do anything stupid. You'll see. Can I just have it?'

Reluctantly, she hands him the weapon.

'Is the safety off?'

'Michael!'

'Just kidding.' He turns the gun in his hand so that he's holding the barrel and, using the grip like a hammer, he hits the small windowpane that lines the side of the door. A few more hits and it shatters enough to put his arm through. The glass landing on the floor also fails to wake up Ákos.

Michael unlocks the door from the inside. He leads the way in and stalks over to Ákos, the gun now in his hand the right way round. When he arrives at Ákos's side, Michael taps the gun on the old man's head again and again and again. After a while, Ákos starts to stir, his eyes opening slowly, and he soon realises there's a weapon pointing at his forehead. His eyes break open. Startled for a moment, it doesn't take him long to figure out the full extent of what's going on. His body presses backwards into the chair and his mouth opens wide. He shouts, something incomprehensible to Michael, no doubt swearing in Hungarian.

'Translate for me as I speak,' Michael tells Gizi.

'I'm investigating four murders in England. Perhaps you already know that? My father – your brother – is being targeted by a madman. Maybe that's *you*. I've spoken to your son, Edvárd. He confirmed what I already thought about you: that you're jealous of your brother, that you hated the glory he stole from you. And, you know what, perhaps I understand you. You were the older brother, the one the younger's supposed to look up to, the one who's supposed to lead the way. But he overtook you. So I can see how that could drive a person insane. I wouldn't be able to take it. Just being his son, with that reputation preceding me everywhere I go in the world of fencing, is bad enough. But to be the brother, the one who's the entire reason he took up the sport in the first place, now that would be horrendous. Waking up every day, knowing it was because of me he started, and it was because of me he's better than me. It was my own stupid fault that my little brother could beat the shit out of me on the piste. So, yes, I understand the jealousy. He took the attention away from you on the piste. Maybe he took attention away from you in the home; he most definitely took away the attention of girls from you. A right Lothario, a Casanova. A fucking *playboy*, it seems. Good-looking, popular, an amazing sportsman – there's not much else you could want. And then he abandoned you on the streets to face who knows what at the hands of the Russians.

'So tell me, Ákos, is all that enough to make you hate

250

him so much that you would hire someone to kill four women, taunt him with messages, with snapped blades, and then finally to kill him after you've played with him enough psychologically? Is it you I'm looking for? Did he drive *you* over the edge?'

Ákos's eyes focus on the barrel of the gun. He swallows hard. There's sweat dripping down his forehead. Right now, he's more awake than he's ever been in his booze-fuelled life.

He stutters a response, which Gizi translates: 'I've done nothing. You have my word.'

'I'm not through with you yet, Ákos.' He presses the gun against the old man's temple. *It wouldn't cost much to shut you up forever, József.*

Ákos's eyes look like they're about to explode. He tries to hide it, clearing his throat. 'You don't know what you're talking about.'

'I know more than enough. Have you hired somebody to kill my father?'

'You're speaking rubbish. I've done nothing.'

'Who is Ferenc?'

'I don't know.'

'So what did you mean when you said, *It wouldn't cost much to shut you up forever, József*?'

'I have never said that.'

'You said it to your son.'

'You have absolutely no idea what –'

Michael doesn't let him finish. He brings the gun down over Ákos's head and cracks it against the top of the armchair. The old man's head twists to the side to lurch out of the way, his eyes pulsating at the danger. 'Tell me what you meant when you said it! Have you hired someone?'

Ákos tries to stand up, suddenly roaring some words, but Michael's not having any of it. He resists Ákos's attempt and, with a short, sharp tap, hits the gun against Ákos's forehead. The old man falls back.

'I want to know the truth!'

'Michael!'

'Remember what I told you, Gizi! Now, enough! You're going to tell me everything, or you're going to get *very hurt*.'

'You motherfucker, you hit me.' He lifts his hand to his head, scooping up a small amount of blood.

Michael lunges at him, even though they're only centimetres apart, and presses him into the armchair. 'Tell me!' He smells the old man's stale, anxious breath, recognises the sound of a pounding heart, knows he's getting close.

Ákos nods his head, a hand still pressing on the minor wound, giving up as quickly as his fiery temper sparked up. 'Just let me get a towel.'

Michael shakes his head. He looks around and then moves swiftly to the kitchen sink from which he grabs a tea towel and tosses it to Ákos. He makes his way back, stands over his uncle.

'Okay, I said it, and I meant it. There was a time, when I was younger, when I would have done anything to get rid of him, after the way he destroyed my fencing career and then…'

'I know about 1956. I know he left you here.'

He stares into Michael's eyes. 'Then you understand more than I need to tell you. I *hated* him.' A long pause. 'But that was then. Now I am just an old man, content in a simple life. We are just a *hello* at Christmas. I assure you, you have my word, I have nothing to do with whatever is happening in England right now.'

'*It wouldn't cost much to shut you up forever, József.*' Tell me what you meant.'

Ákos clears his throat again. 'I need a drink.'

Michael turns to Gizi and nods. She asks Ákos a question and he responds. She goes to the kitchen and opens a cupboard door. From it, she removes a bottle of vodka and brings it to Ákos. He takes it from her, twists the seal open and pours a glassful, his hand shaking. He lifts it slowly, creates a slot in his mouth and ingests the contents of the glass. He closes his eyes, letting it do its magic.

As he speaks, he doesn't open his eyes. 'There was a time, many years ago, when I did something stupid. Your father had returned here after several years away. He'd flaunted his success, the way he'd settled in England and made a real life for himself, and made me feel this small.' He shows the tiniest of gaps between his fingers. 'And then he was involved in a car accident. He was drinking heavily, drove wildly and a woman died. A woman he was no doubt treating like a floozy, like he always did.'

'What?' There's a note of alarm in Michael's voice that he can't hide. 'What are you talking about?'

Ákos opens his eyes. 'He was drunk. He should never have been behind the wheel.'

Michael can't believe it. *Drunk behind the wheel? A woman died?* 'No. What do you mean?'

Ákos leans forwards. 'He picked up a chick. Same as he always did. Only before he had the time to drop her, like he did with all of them, *he killed her*. Drinking,

253

driving and crashing.' Having spat out the words, he refills the glass and drinks again. This time, he keeps his eyes open and stares at the window. 'My parents had always viewed him as *the perfect one*. They had revered him as much as all those stupid people who saw him fence. And when this woman died, my father – he was a naïve man, *so bloody naïve* – went to some friends he still had with government contacts – before World War Two, he was a government minister, we were a privileged family until the Nazis stripped everyone of their titles – and they went to the police. Our father paid for your father to be set free. He paid for your father not to go the trial. All reports about alcohol were kept from the press. People were rewarded handsomely for their good will.'

Michael fights himself. He doesn't want to speak, doesn't want to say what's on his mind, doesn't want to show any uncertainty, doesn't want to make himself look weak when he's got the advantage – or had the advantage.

'That was the tipping point. It pushed me over the edge. I enquired – that is *all I did* – about how I could get rid of him once and for all. How much it would cost. Who might do it.'

'An assassin?'

'That's right. But it was decades ago. This can't have anything to do with that. And I paid nothing. It was merely a couple of conversations until…'

'Until what?' There's no response. Michael moves closer, repeating in a low, deep voice, 'Until what?'

'Until my morals got the better of me and convinced me I was being stupid. That I couldn't be the killer that *Playboy Varga* was. Believe me, there were times when I almost regretted changing my –'

'Playboy Varga? Again. What does that mean?' Benedek said the same thing.'

'That's what the newspapers called him. Because that's exactly what he was.'

Michael wants to get out of here. His head's almost spinning. But he needs to know more. 'Her name,' he mumbles, unsteady on his feet. 'Tell me her name.'

Ákos stares at him for a time, tries to stare him out. 'Her name was Iza Topa.'

Sure he'll faint, Michael stumbles backwards, letting the gun slip from his hand, back, back, back, until he's out of the door, in the corridor, down the stairs and back outside. There he crouches to his knees, leans against the building and presses his arms against it.

He visualises the notebook as if it's directly in front of him. '*I. T.*,' he whispers to himself. Shaking his head: '*I* fucking *T*.'

As if on automatic pilot, he snatches his mobile phone from his pocket. He can't immediately see the screen – his eyes are misty, water blocking the way. As they clear, the words come into focus. On the screen. Another missed call from his father. There's a voicemail.

He doesn't listen to it. Instead, he selects his father's phone number. There's no answer, but the answerphone picks up. Michael knows he should hang up, shouldn't speak when he has lost charge of his emotions, but he can't control himself. 'Who the fuck is Iza Topa? You were drunk that night, weren't you? Drunk and you drove her. What have you done?' He rages, yelling it again: 'What have you done?' And then, close to tears, almost silently: 'What have you done?'

Gizi and István, who had gone in to find out what was

255

happening, come out of the apartment block. 'What the hell was that all about? What were you doing?' She stops as soon as she sees the wreck on the floor.

'Fucker deserved it. This could all still come back to him, somehow. He's far from innocent in all this.'

'He could press charges. You could cost me my job!'

'Don't be overdramatic,' Michael says, not looking up at her, yet daring her to challenge him. 'I judged it right and I made the right decisions.' Now he looks up, makes eye contact: 'I did what I had to do. Now we have some answers.'

'Oh, yes, I see that. And while you're at it, why don't you just pick up the tank from Terror Háza, bring it here to blow a hole through his door, and carry him to the cells in the building's basement.'

A tank. Cells.

A museum.

Gizi lights a cigarette. 'So where do you want to go now?'

Michael's up. 'Hang on.'

'What?'

'Three tanks, István said. Three tanks accompanied the protestors to Parliament Square.' István nods. 'And there they were massacred. Lives were lost. *A Russian tank*. Lives lost. Gizi said earlier, Terror Háza, the House of Terror, *commemorates the lives lost*. And that there's a Russian tank in it.'

'That's right.'

'So Papa Bem pointed us to Parliament Square. And Parliament Square is where lives were lost even though Russian tanks showed them support. So what if that's the next step? What if he wants us there? To where the lost lives are commemorated and where the Russian tank is remembered.'

'Maybe.'

'Look, find out everything you can about Iza Topa. And let's get to Terror Háza.'

Chapter Forty-One

Charting the history of the two brutal regimes that used the building to incarcerate, torture and murder, Terror Háza Múzeum, which haunts Andrassy Avenue in Pest, was first used by the Hungarian Nazis during World War Two and later by the communist secret police. In 1945, when it was taken over by the communist political police including the ÁVO, a maze of cells was created in its basement where interrogation of political prisoners took place. During the Revolution of 1956, all evidence of the evils committed here was destroyed before the secret police fled.

Michael and Gizi enter. She approaches a member of the museum's staff, who nods keenly in response to her words. Gizi signals to Michael that they can enter.

The Soviet tank fills the internal central courtyard. Gizi leads Michael to the balcony from where it's possible to peer down at the tank. 'It's huge,' Michael says.

Gizi doesn't answer.

They scan the courtyard.

'There,' Michael says, pointing towards the tank.

The staff member guides them through a staff-only side door and down three sets of stairs. They emerge through double doors at the bottom and encounter the tank, larger before them now than it was possible to imagine it could be.

Michael leaps onto the front end of the tank. He dangles for a moment and then manages to pull himself all the way up.

A brown envelope, padded, sits on top of it. One word on the front: *Varga*.

Michael squeezes it, feels for the metal he expects to be inside it, but it's soft. Standing atop the tank, he opens the envelope and peers inside. Paper. Folded. He removes it.

A word and three numbers.

Plot 301.

He drops down. 'Any ideas?' he says, holding it out to Gizi.

She nods her head without hesitation. 'Let's get to the car.'

Chapter Forty-Two

Gizi pulls up to the gate and inserts payment. Michael sits in the passenger seat. István sits behind him where he'd remained while the discovery was made at Terror Háza Múzeum. The barrier opens.

Új köztemető, or the New Public Cemetery, is about twenty minutes from the centre of Budapest. It contains over three million graves and, covering an area of over 2km², is one of Europe's largest memorials to the dead. 'This is a confusing place to drive,' Gizi explains. 'There are so many graves in so many directions.'

'I no come here often,' István says. 'But I think I help find okay.'

They immediately pass two large buildings with what seem like towers in the centre of them. As soon as they're in, they have four route options. Trees tower over all the roads, their overgrown branches eliminating the view of the sky. Bushes and overgrown weeds cover much of the grass by the sides of the roads. The instantaneous sense is of oppression.

Gizi explains, 'The cemetery contains Plot 301, which is where many of the martyrs of the Revolution are buried.'

Prime Minister Imre Nagy was executed on June 16th 1958 and his body was dumped in an unmarked grave. He died a national hero. Before he was removed from his role as prime minister, he was permitted to make a final statement in which he said: 'I have twice tried to save the image of communism in the Danubian valley. If my life is needed to prove that not all communists are enemies of the people, I gladly make the sacrifice. I know there will one day be another Nagy trial, which will rehabilitate me. I also know I will have a reburial'. He was right, but it wasn't until 1989, after the fall of communism in Hungary, that his and others' remains were disinterred and buried in a memorial: Plot 301.

They pass several parked cars and hundreds upon hundreds of graves. Simple road signs, white arrows on blue backgrounds, attempt to guide drivers. On the left side of the road are what look like filing-cabinet-style drawers.

'What are they?' Michael asks.

'They're where urns are kept,' Gizi explains. 'For the ashes. They're much more meaningful than they look.'

By the time they drive deeper into the cemetery, most of the grass disappears and in its place is dried mud and dust. It seems like it doesn't rain this far in.

To get to Plot 301, it's necessary to pass through the main area of the cemetery and then drive through a wooded area in which there are many randomly located unmarked graves. It's surprisingly eerie. En route, occasional crosses stick out of the ground, often deep amid the trees, barely visible from the road.

Plot 301 is a long way from the main cemetery space. They emerge, suddenly as the space opens up, along a narrow road through some trees. Plot 301 is before them. Hundreds of square off-white graves laid flat on grass, names of the dead written on most. Hundreds of unmarked short wooden poles held upright in the grass.

'Where is Imre Nagy's grave?' Michael asks as they get out of the car. It's all he can think of.

'Here,' says István, his arm extended, his feet leading the way.

They walk along the gap between gravestones and reach a paved area. Two larger gravestones, also off-white but rectangular, sit raised off the ground.

The former prime minister's name is printed is gold. And directly beneath his name, a brown padded envelope.

Written on it, one word again: *Varga*.

Michael picks it up, feels it for the piece of snapped metal, again finds nothing, just softness. He opens it without hesitation.

Inside there's more paper. Folded. He removes it and opens up an aged newspaper, dated 1971. He can't read the words, but he recognises a word in the headline and, as he scans the text, he recognises his father's name mentioned several times. Written over the article in red ink are three familiar characters: *65C*. 'What does this say?' he says, handing the article to Gizi.

He notices her eyes widen and hears her breath exhale. 'What? What is it?'

'The headline,' she says. 'It says *Playboy Varga*.'

'Does everybody know what the fuck is going on but us? The article – what does it say?'

She reads, nods her head. 'It's about the accident. It says your father was involved in a car crash. Like Ákos said. Iza Topa was killed. Your father was arrested. Was held for three months. He was acquitted before the trial. A lorry driver was found to be to blame. He had stopped just below the peak of a steep hill, a blind spot, and hadn't put out any kind of warning sign.'

'And drinking and driving? Does it say anything about him drinking?'

'No,' she says, still scanning. 'No, nothing.' A few moments, then: 'Shit, no.'

'What?'

'Here,' she says, her finger pointing at a paragraph of text. 'It mentions her family and her boyfriend at the time. His name was Jakob Puskás.'

'Shit.'

'Yes, shit. And the red ink. The numbers and letter. I don't know why I didn't see it before. We're here – it's so obvious. Come.' And she's running to the car before Michael has the chance to say anything else to her. István follows.

She slams the car into reverse and turns around. They quickly reach the main part of the cemetery again and she tries to work out which road to take, asking István, and he responds.

Michael sees the numbers and letter as they reach an intersection. There's a concrete stump. It sticks out of the ground by the side of the road at the turning. It's straight-edged and square, and its base is wider than its peak. It's a marker, indicating a row of graves. *102B*. Numbers and a letter.

'Grave row markers,' he says. '*65C*.'

'That's right. Each row is numbered and sub-divided by a letter. I don't know why I didn't think of that earlier.'

'Where will it be?'

'65C must be an old grave. Easily twenty years before these ones. A few more minutes.'

The accelerator is floored again, the wheels spin, gravel spits into the air.

She brakes hard when they reach row 65.

'This way,' she calls, and she says something to István.

He stays in the car.

Gizi leads the way. They jog along the row, scanning the names on the graves. 65 is a long row, full of dozens and dozens of graves. They pass section A, then section B. Their heads turn from left to right, search, left, right, search, as they move along and enter section C.

'Here.' Gizi spots it first. It's a black grave, on the ground again but with no headstone, with gold lettering that's heavily worn. As they reach the grave, they see the name, despite the worn lettering: *Iza Topa*. The date, her age, a few words.

'Mother of God.'

Michael's eyes almost fall out. 'What is *that*?' His hand lifts as if to point, but its weight is suddenly too much for him. It drops. 'What the fuck is happening here?'

They both lean towards the grave, so close they almost lie on it.

Underneath Iza's name, written in white chalk, there's another name. And a date.

Today's date.

'Jesus.'

Chapter Forty-Three

Three words: 'Michael, call me.'

József left a message for Michael, reluctantly, not long after they'd finished speaking about Ákos. He'd wanted to say more. He *should* have said more. But the conversation had chilled him. He was full of anger but also concern. And he was still shaken up by last night's incident in Finchley Road.

He finished a half-bottle of whisky that he'd pulled out of the cabinet in the lounge. Even though it was early, even though he was preoccupied, he found himself feeling tired, so he decided to try to nap. He double-checked the front and back doors were locked. He could see the two police officers in a car out front. Satisfied that all was secure, he made his way up the stairs.

He took a shower – his second of the young day – allowing the water to revive him, or at least hoping that would be its effect. He stood under the powerful rays of the water, willing its goodness to pierce through him.

After almost twenty minutes under the water, and feeling relatively awake, he decided to collect a bottle of whisky in case he couldn't sleep.

When sleep didn't come, he poured himself a glassful. He did this every ten minutes, well into the afternoon, and soon came to the decision that he would continue pouring and drinking until he either fell asleep or passed out.

They were dancing. She was drinking. He was drinking. She was laughing. She was gorgeous. Her skin energised him. So soft. He ran his hand up and down her arm. He placed his hand on the small of her back. She moved well, responded to the rhythm of the music. He was a good dancer. Their bodies blended. The music was lively. She was drinking. He was drinking. He had hold of her and then he let go. She spun. Then he brought her close to him. Their legs moved the whole time, didn't stop. She was smiling. She was laughing. He was smiling and laughing. Yes, she was gorgeous. The things he said and did, the same things as always, they convinced her to let herself go. She was going to be his for the rest of the night. She was drinking. He was drinking.

After the dancing and drinking, they were driving. She had her hand on his leg. She was still laughing. He was still laughing, cracking jokes, showing off his biting wit. The alcohol made her love it, or his personality did. The same as always.

He didn't see it. Couldn't see it. The lorry. He turned the steering wheel. Slammed on the brakes. The car swerved. Clipped the lorry. Spun and rolled and rolled.

Outside, on the road, he was holding her in his arms. Her face was covered in blood.

He was sitting in the chair in József's bedroom, a shadow in front of the drawn curtains. Smoke was rising in front of his face, from a hand in which he held a cigarette. As he inhaled, its tip lit up. It lit up his face, but barely. Cast a shadow, full of shadow. A few features.

Could it be? *Him?* How could it be him, here?

It was so bright in the room, like those headlights yesterday, but he didn't open his eyes. Too tired. Exhausted. Drunk. And then it was dark.

The phone rang. He didn't pick it up. Couldn't move

his arms in the right direction. His head was heavy, his body weighted down. He'd drunk too much.

The answerphone picked up the call. He heard Michael's voice, but recognised only sounds, not words. He didn't know what his son was saying.

His head was heavy, his body completely weighted down. He'd drunk too much. But so much he couldn't move, couldn't open his eyes? Drowsy, swaying. Sick. He managed to fight an eye open. The white cloth over his mouth. That smell, what was it?

Him. Then, on the piste; now, right here. Earlier, in the chair; and now, standing over him. His hand was holding the cloth over József's mouth. Pressing hard. Trying to push his head through the pillow.

And that was when József realised it was really happening, that he wasn't dreaming. The nightmare was over.

He grabbed the arms that were pressing the cloth against his face, tried to hold his breath, battled to survive, but whatever had been poured on the cloth had already entered his system, had started its work, was making him fade, and it had the alcohol as its partner. And then he needed to breathe, couldn't not.

For a moment, he felt so light he was almost content. He thought of fencing. He thought of Michael. He thought of the loves he'd lost. He'd taught so many students, had had a son.

Non omnis moriar. It's true: not all of me will die. Regardless of what will happen to me.

One final intake of air, so necessary, so unavoidable, and he was history. The darkness became complete.

Chapter Forty-Four

Having left István in the car, and now hammering on the door, Gizi shouts, 'Police!'

No answer. Just that bloody dog still barking.

After yet more pounding on the door, to no avail, Michael asks, 'Break it down?'

Gizi turns to him, perspiration on her forehead. She nods, speaks in Hungarian to the two bulky uniformed officers who were watching the building, and steps aside.

They throw a heavy metal battering device at the door. Two times, then it gives. The door springs back, inviting. The dog charges, unwelcoming. An Alsatian. Angry. Scared. Rage and saliva spewing from its mouth. The hair on its back stands on edge, there's ferocity in its eyes.

'Easy boy,' Michael says, attempting to reach for its coat, give it a pet. It snaps at his hand. Michael jumps back.

Gizi tries. She murmurs some sweet Hungarian notes.

The neighbour, the one from earlier, the old lady, opens her door. When the dog sees her, it charges in her direction. She shrieks, tries to shut the door, create a barricade, but it's too late. The dog's inside.

'Shut that fucking door!' Michael bellows, pushing the elderly woman inside her apartment and pulling her door shut.

'Michael!' Gizi shouts some Hungarian over the top of his instructions, perhaps an apology, but probably isn't heard by the old lady.

She leads the way into the apartment, the only one of

the pair armed, gun drawn. She exudes power, confidence. Michael's impressed by how she moves. He follows closely behind. One of the uniformed officers, also with gun drawn, joins them, the other staying in the doorway.

They're in a narrow hallway. The kitchen is a few steps in, to the left. Gun pointing straight ahead, Gizi enters it. Nothing.

Further down and also to the left: bedroom number one. A single bed. A wardrobe. Empty.

The living room is at the end of the corridor. Part of it can be seen from where they are. One end of a dining table is in view.

But first, bedroom number two. The door is closed. Gizi presses down sharply on the handle and barges the door with her shoulder. It swings open and they're in the room. She drops the gun to her side. Her body slackens. There's not as much air in her lungs as before. 'Check the living room,' she whispers.

Michael and the other officer do so. Also empty.

Michael returns to the bedroom, to find Gizi standing over the body.

'It's too late,' she says. 'The name and date on the grave didn't lie.'

Jakob Puskás is lying on the bed, face up. His hands are by his sides, palms up. His head leans on a pillow, eyes up. They're wide open. Horror-struck. In his stomach, there's a blade. It pins him into the bed. The handle and guard stand victoriously in the air. The bed's light-blue sheets have changed colour, are covered in blood, a lake around him.

On the wall, scraped into the wallpaper above Jakob's head, is *196D*.

'Oh God, no. What now?'
'We have to go back.'

Chapter Forty-Five

Leaving the uniformed officers at the apartment, Gizi and Michael jump back into the car. Gizi lights the engine.

'Cemetery again, István. 196D.'

'No,' István gasps. The car doesn't move. Both Michael and Gizi spin round in their seats to face him. 'No, Michael, no. I sorry. Oh, I sorry. Why I no say before? Why I no say sooner?'

'What? What are you talking about?'

'Your father, he tell me no say anything about Playboy Varga and newspaper articles. But I no remember girl name. I no remember Iza Topa before. I sorry. I can't. He make me promise. Is your father. I do anything for him.'

'You fool!'

'And now 196D.' He's panic-stricken. '196D. Oh, no. What they do to family? What this mean?'

'What?' Gizi snaps in Hungarian. 'What are you talking about?'

'196D is grave of József parents.'

'My grandparents?'

'Yes. Yes, yes.' He's struggling to breathe. Starts wheezing. 'I should stop this sooner. I should say. Now what? Now who? What they do to grave? To family? I no see. Sorry. Please. I no see.'

At his wish, Gizi pulls over at the nearest metro station. They leave István and his repeated apologies. 'God speed,' he says to the departing car. 'God speed.' And the old man's tears start falling.

271

With siren blazing and car swerving in and out of traffic, they manage to arrive back at the cemetery in a little less than fifteen minutes.

Through the barrier, straight ahead past the candle and flower stalls. They pass several turnings and keep heading straight.

'Whatever we find,' she says, 'remember one thing: we are getting close.'

'I know. But this can't be part of the plan, whoever's plan it is. Surely. This guy can't be reacting to us so quickly. Ferenc, if that's what his name is, how is he always able to stay one step ahead of us?'

The intersection. The third option.

'Keep your eyes peeled,' Michael says.

Gizi drives slowly. They look in all directions as the car crawls, hopeful to spot anything out of place. Someone. Ferenc, ideally. All the while, they keep their eyes on the grave row numbers.

'There.'

196D.

Gizi parks the car on the side of the road. They get out, still searching, scanning, Michael starting to feel desperate, wanting to find someone lurking in the shadows so that this can all be ended. Also feeling desperate about what they're going to discover.

No more bodies. Please.

Gizi's gun is drawn. They look at each grave in turn. Both sides. It's a typically long row. Flowers, candles, some lit, some extinguished, most graves well tended, some a few decades old and seemingly untouched since then. Graves freshly cleaned, maybe polished, others neglected, covered in dust, moss, lettering worn, some of the lettering invisible to the point of namelessness. Wreaths. Benches. More dead grass.

Names. Old people. Young. Even tiny children.

'Here, I think,' Gizi says. 'Yes, here! It's tucked away over here.'

They move through some trees. The grave, which is rectangular and lies flat on the ground, looks centuries old. It's hard to believe it's been here for only thirty years old. The names of Michael's grandparents on the upright headstone have been worn away. The final few letters, *RGA*, can be made out. Moss has built up on the stone in various places. On the ground around the grave, the grass is dead.

Scanning the grave, Michael doesn't see anything unusual. He rotates on the spot, tries to locate something unusual in the area surrounding it.

His mind wanders. He thinks about the funerals his father will no doubt soon have to attend. And then he thinks about Rachel Bradshaw. He'll be at her funeral, standing in a church and then around a grave with her family and friends, everyone mourning, no one understanding why. He doesn't understand why and, even when he gets to the truth, he still won't understand why Rachel was taken.

He returns to the present and still can't see anything. 'It has to be something. We aren't here for no reason.'

Graves nearby are several feet away, so Michael slowly circles the grave. As he walks behind the headstone, which rises about half a metre high, he stops. Winded from a punch to the stomach. He falls to his knees.

Gizi leaps towards him, tries to catch him. Can't avert his fall. 'Michael, what –'

She doesn't need to say any more. She's reached his side. She has a clear view.

He kneels, she stands. To an onlooker, they're paying their respects.

They remain silent. No words, just minds overflowing.

Michael's chest tightens. He can't breathe. Tries to cough, to clear himself. Can't, or won't. 'No,' he whispers, finally, shaking his head, squeezing his eyes shut. His voice cracks, it's hoarse. 'No.'

Written on the back of the headstone in white chalk, with a red and green wreath placed on the ground beneath the lettering, is an inscription that tells the rest of the story:

> *József Varga*
> *3. 4. 1937 – 9. 10. 2003*

Then one line of text in Hungarian.

Michael swallows, finally breaks through, strained yet somehow emotionless. 'What does it say?'

He hears Gizi sigh, doesn't look at her. 'It says, "Today it ends only with you."'

They remain here, Michael on his knees until they go numb and Gizi standing, hunched. After a time, he slowly rises. 'I've got to get back. God, I've got to call him.'

Michael pulls his mobile phone from his pocket. He sees the symbol for voicemail, remembers the missed call from his father, the voicemail that he didn't listen to. He dials to retrieve it.

'Michael, call me.'

Three words that make his skin crawl. He dials his father's number. It rings. And it rings and it rings and...

He closes his eyes, slowly shakes his head. 'No, come on,' he says softly. 'Not like this.'

Answerphone.

Michael, call me.

He hangs up, tries again. 'Fucking no.'

Answerphone.

Michael, call me.

This time, he speaks. 'It's Michael. It's the ninth of October. If you get this message, go straight to the police station. Ask for Detective Constable Sally Davison. Don't go with anyone but her. She'll know why you're there.' A pause. 'Get there straightaway.' Then a longer pause. 'I am so sorry.'

He turns to Gizi, defeated, sunken. 'I see it now. This was the plan all along. Maybe he wanted me to know, to fully understand. But he wanted me out of the way. I've fucked this all up. I've given him the opportunity.'

'We don't know anything yet,' she reassures him, placing her hand on his arm, stroking it. 'Let's get to the airport. Forget your things at the hotel. I'll send them to you.' His eyes are glazed over. 'Hey, snap out of it! There could still be time. This could still be part of the game. You could still end it. Get onto that detective in England and let's get the hell out of here.'

They run back to her car. Michael's on the phone to Sally Davison, explaining what's going on, barely able to contain the explosive emotions within. Asking her to check out his father's address, to find him, to save him from certain death, for Michael now believes it's certain. And what of the officers who are supposed to be watching the house?

Gizi accelerates. The steering wheel's pulling to the

left, the ground's unsteady. Something's wrong with the car. 'No,' she says, braking.

Michael hangs up, gets out. 'Fuck.'

'What is it?'

'How the hell…' He scans the area.

Gizi gets out and comes round to the passenger side of the car. The tyre, it's punctured. In it, a snapped fencing blade. 'No.'

'Where are you, you cocksucker?' Michael shouts, hitting the car roof with his fist. He turns, looks around, stands on the interior trim and tries to spot Ferenc. 'He must be here.' He drops to the ground, peers down at the tyre. 'I'm getting sick of this shit!'

'Me too.' Gizi's bent low, inspecting the damage. 'I could try to drive through it until it gives in completely. We really don't have time to change it or call for another car.'

'Okay, let's move.' Michael stops suddenly. His vision veers towards one line of graves. Then another. And another. He knows Ferenc is here, watching. So he shouts, 'I will find you!'

It's an unsteady ride, the car wrestling against Gizi's instructions. She's struggling to make the twenty-minute journey to the airport. The wheel's clearly completely deflated after almost ten minutes of driving.

'There,' she says, pointing at a police car that's being filled up at a petrol station. She pulls the car over to the curb, or rather lets it drag them to the side, and puts on her warning lights. 'We'll get a ride.'

They run to the police officer who's standing at the petrol pump. Gizi speaks to him with urgency. He stops filling up and, within moments and without paying, they're on their way, the siren screeching in the air.

While in the backseat, Michael writes down his phone numbers, email address and home address for Gizi. 'As soon as I know what's going on, I'll call you. And please, call me if anything happens here. If you find out anything.'

'I will,' she assures him.

Gizi's mobile phone vibrates. She answers it and speaks fast. Then to Michael: 'It's Tibor. He's arranged tonight's meeting, but he says there's something that can't wait.'

'What is it?'

'Someone's there he says we need to meet.'

'Can you get to the club as soon as you've dropped me at the airport?'

'Absolutely.' She speaks to Tibor again, even faster. After hanging up, she turns to Michael. 'Okay, I'll call you as soon as I find out what's going on. Then I'll stay there until everyone arrives for the meeting. I'll get one of our artists to meet me there. Maybe we can get an impression of Ferenc to show people. I remember what he looks like well enough.'

'Great.'

But Gizi's on the phone again, speaking more words that Michael can't understand. When the call ends, she explains, 'An artist will meet me there.'

'Please can you thank István for me for everything he's done? Tell him I understand his actions, however foolish. My father is a persuasive man. You don't just say no to him. I'll call him myself when I'm back, but you'll be able to convey it more appropriately in Hungarian.'

'I will. Don't worry.'

Because of the siren blazing, cars are diving out of their way and they arrive at the airport in no time. Michael and Gizi run in and go to the British Airways and Malev reservations counters respectively. They're only metres apart, so they can communicate to find out which is the soonest option.

'One's just left,' she calls. 'Ten minutes ago. Next one's in two hours' time.'

'Ninety minutes. BA wins.' Michael buys a ticket. No luggage.

At the security entrance, Gizi wishes him luck.

'Thank you for everything,' he says, slightly out of breath, handing her his hotel room key. 'You know, after all this I might come back for a holiday. See the sights for a different purpose. Maybe you won't need to send my things to me. I might be able to collect them from you in person. And maybe I could take you out for dinner.'

'That would be nice,' she says, smiling. She's standing close to him. 'I'd like that.'

'Me too,' he says. 'Then you can meet the real me.' He takes her by both shoulders. 'But I meant what I said yesterday. You *are* beautiful.'

She lowers her eyes. Her face is so close to his.

With his fingers, he softly encourages her chin to rise. Their eyes meet. 'Beautiful,' he whispers. And he kisses her. Just a soft pressing of the lips, a brief coming together. Her lips taste sweet, even though he only feels them for a fraction of a moment.

'Until we meet again,' he says, and then he disappears into the security area. And then he thinks of Sally Davison and his head feels even more fucked up than usual. He really doesn't know how to be with women.

Michael fills the time waiting for the plane by getting something to eat, although he can barely swallow. He sits in a coffee shop with a stale sandwich in front of him on the table, mostly staring at it, occasionally biting, though what he's chewing on seems to have the texture of a brick.

He starts to picture dangerous things, his conscious allowing visions of Jakob Puskás's dead body to adopt his father's face. The blade inserted in the stomach. The vacant eyes, the raw horror, or is it shock, or disgust, or recognition of what's to come? Metal into skin, life seeping away. Is that how one appears, the look one adopts, when faced with certain death? Michael has never thought about it before, has faced death countless times, but now that it's closer to home, is personal, is as intimate a connection as it could ever be, he can't stop trying to relate to it. He and death, at this very moment, are tied together.

He rings his father's phone number again. Still no answer. So he calls Sally Davison. 'Anything?'

'No. I'm there now and there's no one home. The uniformed officers are still outside. They say they've seen nothing unusual. I'll hang around. Hopefully he'll turn up. Michael, what's going on?'

'I think today's the day they plan for him to die.'

'My God.'

'I'll be on a plane in less than an hour. I should be back in about four hours. Please find a way in – break down the door if you have to. And please don't leave the house till I'm back.'

'You sure you want me in there?'

A body on the bed. A blade inserted. His father's

lifeless form. He wants to say, *No, that's for me to see, no one else, if that's what's there waiting for me*, but he needs to know his father is safe, or dead; he needs to know whether he can save his father, or not. 'Break down every door, smash every window if you have to. Just find a way in.'

Another call to his father. Hoping against hope. *Michael, call me.* But it's a waste of time. Another failure.

He tries to read a newspaper. Fails.

Then the gate opens. Not long after, boarding is called. His seat is near the front of the plane. It's a busy flight, full of noise. Lots of young children, babies and toddlers. The crying, shouting, shrieking, together with thoughts that he can't escape, predominately that's he's lost this bout, that he's not been able to solve and salvage this thing, that he hasn't lived up to his father's expectations, and his own as a detective, make his head spin.

Chapter Forty-Six

Gizi directs the police officer in the car to race to Spartacus Fencing Club. Traffic's heavy as rush hour begins, but the siren makes vehicles move like the parting of the seas.

When the car approaches its destination, she spots Tibor standing at the top of the steps outside Spartacus's front entrance. There's a man, aged about forty, with short brown hair, slim, standing next to him.

The car stops and Gizi gets out. Tibor shakes her hand. They speak in Hungarian. 'No Michael?'

'He's had to fly back to England. An emergency. But I'll deal with things this end.'

'Very well. This is Lóránt Pusztay.' He and Gizi shake hands. She introduces herself. 'It's very important you speak. But inside.' Tibor ushers them in.

Out of the cold, they go into the office. Gizi and Lóránt sit on stools. Tibor remains standing. He offers Gizi a drink. 'No, thank you,' she says. 'So what can you tell me, Mr Pusztay?'

Lóránt Pusztay has a light voice, a tone higher than it should be. As he speaks, his thick eyebrows move up and down and his forehead creases and uncreases. 'I was here yesterday when Michael Varga visited. I wanted to come here to meet him. I know of József Varga by reputation. I've been a fencer my whole life. Since I was ten years old, and now I'm forty-two. You probably don't remember because you saw so many people last night, but I spoke with Michael. Only briefly, though. I didn't have much to say because I didn't know his father, but I wanted to say how much I admire all his father has achieved. I imagine that's what a lot of people wanted to say.

'Anyway, Spartacus isn't my normal club. I still fence a bit and I teach just outside of the city. While I was here last night, I recognised someone from my competition days. I thought nothing of it – this is a great fencing club, after all. Then, today, I received Tibor's message. The one about wanting to see everyone today because you want to ask questions about a stranger who was here last night. Well, I am a stranger, so I was concerned that the message was about me. I called Tibor, explained who I am, and he explained it was actually about the man with the shoulder-length curly black hair.'

'Ferenc?'

'Yes.'

'Do you know him?'

'That's the thing: he is the person I recognised from my competition days. I have fenced him before.'

Gizi's heartbeat quickens. 'Are you sure it was him?'

'The first time I met him, we were fifteen. It was the under-sixteen championships. I was one match from the final and then someone knocked me out of the semifinal. I was fencing the best in my life that day. My opponent in the semifinal used all kinds of delay tactics to throw me off the good start I made to our match, and then I lost. You see, I lost my concentration and then I lost my nerve. It was my first big disappointment in fencing, so I remember it well. And I remember very well that Ferenc was the one who did it and beat me.'

Gizi's nodding. She's excited, but she realises this is nothing but a long shot. She calms herself. 'But you've just said you were fifteen. So young. How can you possibly know it was him?'

'If that was all, then maybe I couldn't be absolutely positive. But then nine years later I met him again, this time in the final of the same tournament's senior final. I remembered him from the time before. Just like I remember him from last night. It was the same man and it *is* the same man. He beat me in the final, was just too good by that time, and I was so angry. I was angry because I should have beaten him the first time. If I'd won the first time, when I should have, the second time wouldn't have hurt so much. The first time I was better, the second time he was. I remember the feeling of loss still today.'

'Where was this tournament?'

'Lake Balaton.'

Lake Balaton, which is also known as The Balaton due to its sheer size, is the largest lake in Central Europe, and is situated in the Transdanubian region of the country.

'Is his name Ferenc?'

Lóránt shrugs his shoulders. 'I'm sorry, I don't remember.'

Gizi spins on the stool towards Tibor. 'Do you know who runs this tournament?'

'Of course.'

'Would there be any way to get a copy of the list of participants in… Do you remember which years, Mr Pucztay?'

'1979 and then 1988.'

'So could you try to get for me the names of everyone who entered in these years? In 1979, the novice tournament, and then in 1988, the senior.'

'I will ask,' Tibor says. He turns and picks up the

telephone that's on his desk. 'I will ask.'

Part Three: Halt

England

Chapter Forty-Seven

The flight takes longer than its three hours – at least, that's the way it seems. Michael tries to read the in-flight magazine. Fails. Tries to eat the meal that's provided. Fails. Tries to snooze. Succeeds, but wishes he'd failed. The images are even stronger in sleep. Mountains of blood. Broken blades everywhere. Dead faces, but he can't make out their features. He knows they're his father, though. There are lots of his father everywhere. They're all speaking to him, taunting him, telling him he should have done better, that he can't live up to his father's expectations as a fencer and, likewise, can't live up to his expectations as a cop, whose sole responsibility has been to find out who's tearing – perhaps now torn – their lives apart.

He has a snapped blade in his hand. Runs his thumb over its end. It's sharp. He presses it against his throat. He can end it. This should be easy. He won't have to find out what's happened in England. Can escape right now. It can all be over, here in this aeroplane seat. He presses the blade into his skin. It pierces, draws blood. *Got to keep going.* Pushes hard, further. It's inside now, connects with something hard. Might be bone. Could be the Adam's apple. There's a crack and the blade goes through it. He's gurgling, his throat is spewing blood, reams of the stuff, and the blade's twisting around in there, up and down, in and out, and blood is erupting from him, erupting from his throat, covering the chair in front, the head of the person in front, his clothing, the floor, blood's everywhere, blood and blood, filling the plane, piling high like an overflowing bath.

He awakes with a start. He's soaked: there's sweat under his arms, on his forehead, the back of his neck, his spine.

Pull yourself together, he thinks.

He goes into the toilet, cleans himself up. He speaks to himself, motivates his core. As a detective, he knows he can live up to expectations: he's not failed before and he doesn't intend to fail now.

When he comes out, he asks a stewardess for some water. Normally, he'd notice her good looks, but not now. Utter focus on what's to come. He's given a plastic cup filled with water and returns to his seat.

He holds the cup close to his mouth. *This isn't how it's going to be. I will not fucking fail.* He squeezes his eyes closed, then opens them. He's determined. He believes it. He sees with clarity. He has to. All the training, it has to come into play. *This is it. This is not going to end any other way than the way I decide it's going to end.*

And it ends today. It ends only with you.

As soon as the plane is parked at the gate, Michael switches on his mobile phone and dials his father's number. The same result as before. Then he calls Sally Davison. 'I've arrived. Anything?'

'No, nothing. The house is empty. I'm parked outside. The officers are guarding the front and back doors.'

'I'll be there in an hour.'

'Michael?'

'What's up?'

'Your father's bed. It was messy. He had clearly been in it. And on the floor by it, a rag with what smells like

288

chloroform on it.'

Running. With no luggage to pick up, Michael gets through security and out of the airport in about fifteen minutes. He takes a taxi, which will be expensive but he hopes the quickest option. Throughout the journey, he looks out of the window, but he sees nothing.

And then here it is: his father's house. He knocks on the window of Sally's car. She goes to kiss him, on the lips, but he turns and kisses her on the cheek. It's an awkward moment. He's on automatic pilot, doesn't know what's he's doing.

'Thanks. I'll take it from here.'

She's unsure how to react to his aloofness. Finally, she says, 'You sure there's nothing I can do to help?'

'Not until I find my father, no. I'll be okay. Off you go. These guys can stand by the doors until someone comes and fixes the locks. There's nothing but boredom here.'

He waits for her to drive away, then he turns towards the house. He peers up at it. It feels so much larger than usual, like it might swallow him, like it's on a hill, Bates Motel- style, and there's someone in the window who he can't see watching him.

Only there's not and it's not. It's just his father's house, the same as always, right in front of him, the house in which he grew up, the house in which his mother died, and it's empty.

The life within it was dragged from it, drugged, hours ago.

At the front door, he greets the police officer and then takes the key from his pocket, then remembers he doesn't need it. He presses the door, edges it open. On the floor in front of him lies his father's fencing blade. *Protection*, he thinks. His father's no longer; his now. He picks it up and, instinctively, holding it in an attacking position, makes his way to the left and into the living room. It's empty.

He goes into all the rooms, regardless of what Sally told him. And he finds nothing except the rumpled sheets on his father's bed. He stares down at them, wondering how his father felt when he was sucked from the bed and then the house. Could the man have felt fear? He wonders if that's possible.

From the bathroom window, he peers down into the back garden. It's not large, it's overgrown and it's empty, except there's a shed at the back of it in front of a fence.

He runs down the stairs and asks the officer, 'The shed – has it been checked?'

'Don't think so.'

He charges through the house and exits by a door in the kitchen. He approaches the shed with caution but lunges at and thrusts open the door without any hesitation, bringing the blade forwards with an almighty yell. But no, it's empty.

He returns to the house and finds himself in the kitchen. All looks fine, normal, in here as well. An empty bottle of whisky sits on the furthest counter. *So the old man's been drinking. A lot to think about, no doubt.* But then he double takes. Something. There's something there, under the bottle. Something that's not normally under a bottle in the kitchen. Something no one has seen.

A piece of paper.

He goes to it, uses makeshift folds in his sleeves to

pick it up and unfold it.

Two words are written on it, blue ink, capital letters: *SALLE VICTORY.*

Chapter Forty-Eight

The first time Michael had stepped foot in Salle Victory as it stands today was over five years ago, when his father had convinced him to let Salle Worth take part in an inter-club match. It was the first time they'd ever done such a thing. And the last, Michael decided after his team was destroyed.

Now he stands outside again. And, again, there's a fencing blade in his hands. He's shuffling it between his hands. He knows he should call for armed support, but if there's anything inside that's going to make him crumble, his weakness must be for his eyes only. And if there's a fight to be had, it's for him alone to win.

Something tells him that it's not going to be as simple as find a body and then it's all over. Too much of this has played out like a game. He knows that whoever's behind this wants the ending to be big, explosive, memorable. It has to make an impact. The only thing is, Michael is determined that he will make an impact, and the blade in his hand gives him confidence in believing he won't be beaten. He feels at home holding it, even though it's his father's and not his own. Perhaps there's no better blade to be armed with than his father's sabre, after all.

Michael looks at the entrance door. There's a handwritten sign on it that says *Closed*. He knows it's nonsense – the place would either be locked or open – so he knows he's in the right place and at the right time.

Right, let's end it. He turns the handle, pushes the door open. The blade's in his right hand and he's ready to strike with it. His legs are slightly bent – centred balance, an attacking poise. His breathing is regular – *in through the nose, out of the mouth*.

To the left is the reception desk, empty. In front of Michael is a corridor. At the end of it and to the right is the gymnasium. He moves cautiously along it.

He knows the end-moment is coming.

Chapter Forty-Nine

'I can't get a list of participants,' Tibor says, 'but they can send me a copy of the tournament grid.'

'What's that?' Gizi asks.

Tibor turns and unpins a piece of paper from the noticeboard. 'Here.' He hands the paper to her.

On the left side is a column of boxes. The boxes are connected in pairs. In each box, a name is written. Then to the right of each pair is another box and there's a line that joins the pair to the box on the right. The name of the winner of the match named in the pair of boxes is written in the box in the column on the right. And this process continues until the sixteen entrants in the first column of boxes goes down to one name in one box, the winner, on the far right-hand side of the page.

'So we'll get their names that way,' Gizi says. 'It lists the participants.'

'Exactly.'

Lóránt Pucztay has been sitting in silence for the past ten minutes. Now he speaks up. 'What is this all about?'

'Mr Pucztay –'

'Lóránt, please.'

'Mr Pucztay, it's a serious criminal investigation, so I can't give you any details.' He looks deflated, but his eyebrows and forehead continue working. 'But I'll need you to stay. I may need you to see if a name stands out.'

'It would be my pleasure to help.'

She smiles, tries to keep it sweet. 'You already have been helpful.'

Lóránt feels gratified.

The telephone rings and the fax machine lights up. After sounds are made, it starts to spit out a piece of paper. Tibor and Gizi step over to it. The paper's moving slowly; it only increases the trepidation, nerves and anticipation that Gizi's already enduring.

Finally, a beeping sound is heard, and the message has arrived intact. Tibor tears the paper from the machine and hands it to her. She places it on the desk, leans over it and uses her finger to trace from the top box on the left down to the bottom one. She moves her hand slowly, deliberately. She mimes each name she encounters.

The sixth name. She mimes two names she's heard spoken aloud in recent days. 'No,' she says.

Chapter Fifty

Michael goes up a set of stairs that is accessible just before the gymnasium is arrived at. It leads to a viewing area: three rows of tiered seating. He creeps up the steps, aware that in the silence his footsteps are creating an echo. He wants his appearance to be sudden, so he slips off his shoes.

After the last step is a set of double doors. The balcony edge, a wall, is directly in front of it. The tiered seating is to the left. He presses his body up against the glass door. From here he can see the first row of seating. Nothing.

Pushing the door open slowly, he remains on the ground and crawls in as soon as there's enough space to squeeze through. He can't stand – he knows he'll be visible to the gymnasium below if he does. He crawls along each of the three rows of seating, checking that no one's hiding or been hidden on the ground between them. Nothing.

He isn't able to feel the mobile phone that's vibrating in his pocket.

He lowers himself back down the six steps and comes to the balcony wall. He places his hands on top of it and cautiously pulls his body up until his eyes can peer over the top of it. Then, unseen, he looks down onto the gymnasium floor below. When his eyes connect with what's there waiting for him, his head darts back and he sinks to the floor.

Chapter Fifty-One

The phone rings again. It switches to the fax machine.

'That one,' Tibor says, pointing to the desk, 'is from 1979.'

Gizi doesn't speak. She hasn't even blinked. She's on her mobile phone, ringing Michael. But he's not answering.

Tibor tears off the next sheet. 'This one's 1988.'

Gizi takes it in her hands. She scans the page, looking for a name and surname.

Voicemail. 'Michael, it's Gizi. I know who –'

Her voice freezes as her eyes freeze on a name and a *different* surname. Goosebumps cover her body from head to foot. She feels like she might fall.

Through frozen lips, she manages, 'Jesus,' and she drops the phone.

Chapter Fifty-Two

The gym's floor is bright blue. Piste markers are laid down all the way along the length of the large space.

Michael needn't creep, he needn't hide. He walks back down the stairs, replacing his shoes on his feet. He turns to the right, walks past the glass window that's used for viewing by those who don't want to climb the stairs, or can't, and walks through the open door on his right.

There's a man in the gymnasium, sitting on his knees some way in the distance, his back to the entrance and to Michael. But Michael recognises the man's hair straight away. Black and curly. Messy.

Michael walks past the window and through the door. Now he's in the gymnasium again. In Salle Victory again. In his father's hallowed space again. *Where it will end.*

The man must know Michael's here, but he doesn't react. He remains on his knees, both hands on his hips.

Michael walks further in, the blade by his side. He senses no threat.

He's probably fifteen metres away from the man when he says by way of introduction, 'Where's my father?'

Slowly, thirty-eight-year-old Ferenc rises to his feet. He turns around. 'You made it,' he says, his English perfect. No trace of an accent whatsoever, sounding like a different man from the one in Budapest.

Michael doesn't back down, doesn't show a trace of fear, hesitation, uncertainty. '*Where is my father?*' he says deliberately.

In the distance, behind Ferenc and completely

298

concealed by his body when he was kneeling, lie two fencing blades. He steps back, twists his body, bends with some difficulty and picks them up. He holds one in each hand and holds them out towards Michael. 'Fencing is such a wondrous sport, don't you think.' It's not a question, so Michael doesn't answer. 'My father taught me that. And he always said to respect the sport. *Treat it with respect.* It's not a game of brutality. It's a *game of brains*, mastery. Like a physical game of chess. Like the game I've been playing with you. When a blade hits someone, it does so with elegance when the hit is accurate, when it's correct. The bend of the blade is an exquisite thing. But when a blade is broken, when it snaps and its sharpness, its true potential, is revealed, it changes the game completely. It can destroy. The blade can kill. Which is exactly what your father did to my father. To his life. He destroyed it. And, in turn, he destroyed my life. Your father, the *playboy*.' He spits out the last word.

'Where is –'

'You know, you didn't really beat me in Hungary. *I let you win.*'

Michael steps forwards with more definition, closes the distance between them; maybe eight metres now.

'I let you win, Michael Varga. You have an ego. You must. You're *his son*. But it's so hard, isn't it? Not being able to match the talent or the success of the father. I understand you, Michael, I really do.'

'You don't know shit.'

'You're wrong. I understand you because I have had exactly the same kind of life as you. The son of a fencing master. *The matre d'arme.* But where you have an emotionless, self-centred, egotistical maniac for a father,

I have one that nurtured my talent and appreciated what I managed to achieve. Yes, not the same as him, but I did my mother proud, or the memory of her. That was all he ever wanted. And all of this, this will do my mother proud. It's all I live for.'

'And how the hell could murder ever please your mother, unless she's some kind of psychotic bitch?'

Ferenc erupts. 'Watch your fucking mouth! Don't you fucking dare!' He laughs to himself. 'This,' he shrugs his shoulders to indicate the room, looks all around, 'all *this* is for her. Don't you see? My mother was an angel. She was a pure woman, *angelic*. She deserved a life of happiness, a wonderful life. She had me. I was so young. And him, that bastard, he took it all away from her. That *fucking playboy* of a man you call your *father*. And then, when she'd been taken, he came to take care of me as if I was his own. He made me his own. He became my father. He nurtured me. He did it for my mother.'

Now Michael sees. He nods. 'Iza.'

Tears well up in Ferenc's eyes. And he nods in agreement. 'Iza. My Iza.'

'That was a long time ago.'

'It wasn't to me.'

'How old could you have even been?'

'One year old. I was a baby. I never even knew her. I don't even remember her. I just have this photo.' He removes a small photograph from his pocket, holds it to his chest.

Snot drips down Ferenc Topa's face. He's crying. Michael senses he'll be able to seize the advantage soon. 'She's only a picture to me. And all the wonderful stories my father told me about her.'

'Father?'

'He *is* my father. He may not have impregnated my mother, but he found a way to become part of the family, to help raise me, to teach me the sport he so loved, to teach me to realise who I needed to hate for the rest of my life.'

'Jakob Puskás?'

He slides the photograph back into his pocket. 'Puskás was nobody. Just a boyfriend. I didn't know him. Not until I killed him.'

'So who then? Who are you talking about?'

'The great man your father ruined. It's all because he flirted, took her, *seduced* her. Drove like a madman and killed her. Snuffed the life right out of her. Well, now I've shown him. Now he knows what it's like to have your life torn apart.'

'You know it won't bring her back.'

'No,' he muses slowly. 'No, it won't. It won't bring her back.' There's silence for a long time. Neither man moves. 'But payback is sweet.' He starts guffawing uncontrollably, like a wild animal or a stupid child. 'Payback is oh so sweet. And don't you now know it.'

'This game of yours has got to come to an end, you know that.'

Ferenc suddenly stops laughing.

'Today, I will end it.'

'Well, yes, you will have the chance,' the Hungarian snaps. '*This* is where it ends. Right here, right now. *With these*.' He hisses the last two words, then he echoes, 'With these.' He places one blade on the ground in front of his feet, takes the other in two hands, lifts it into the air, and brings the blade down sharply against the floor. He

301

manages to create a tiny tear in the metal near the tip. Then he places the loose bit of blade beneath his foot and pulls at it until the tip breaks off. He repeats this with the second blade, then he holds both snapped blades, one in each hand. 'With these.' Wincing, he throws one blade to Michael, who catches it. 'That one,' he says, pointing at the blade Michael has brought in with him. 'Throw it to the wall. Today will be different from last time; this will not be an elegant fencing match. This will be… brutal.'

I will end it now.

Michael walks to the wall and places his father's blade on the floor. When he turns back, Ferenc has moved, heavily limping, and is taking his place at the end of a piste. 'We'll use this one,' he says.

'Where is my father?'

'Kill me and I'll tell you.'

The game hasn't ended, Michael can see.

Ripping fiercely through the air with his voice, Ferenc shouts, 'En garde!' The volume is unexpected. Michael is surprised, but he manages to maintain his composure. Now it's needed more than ever. *In through the nose, out of the mouth.* He hears his father's voice, is sure it's in his head.

Michael walks casually, confidently, wrestling with his own pain, to his end of the piste. This time, Ferenc is wearing a green T-shirt and blue jeans. Michael takes off his jacket and throws it aside, leaving a shirt and trousers as his only protection. With blades in this state, there can be no protection. One hit with enough force and it's straight through skin and any material covering it. Through the heart if the aim's good enough.

Ferenc has adopted his en garde stance, but he can't

302

bend his knees much. Michael does the same, manages to go deeper than his opponent, but the pain is approaching unbearable. There's no salute this time.

'Allez,' shouts Ferenc.

Michael steps forwards, every precise fencing movement in place, despite his body still reeling from the incident on the bridge. Now, more than ever, it's important to keep the technique precise: small movements, cut off the angles of attack.

But Ferenc does the opposite. He charges at Michael like a barbarian, screaming to the point of his voice cracking, little girl shrieks coming through, aggression and pain mixed together, the blade swinging wildly above and around his head. Not the fencer Michael faced in Budapest.

When Ferenc is about a metre from Michael, he brings the blade down, cuts and lunges. His leg colliding with the ground gives him a shock, he slows, Michael defends with a tight parry quarte, deflecting the blade. The bellows continue, though, as Ferenc recovers quickly. Within a second, he's swinging again, more yells, now some Hungarian words. He swings the blade out wide and attempts to bring it against Michael's ankles. Michael jumps into the air to avoid the swiping metal and immediately faces a blade that's coming direct to his chest. This time, he beats it out of the way and pushes Ferenc away with a kick to the stomach. The Hungarian stumbles backwards and falls to the ground.

Michael seizes the advantage and attacks as Ferenc is rising. Three quick steps forwards in succession, a balestra lunge and then a fleche. Ferenc offers his own parry quarte and Michael runs past him. They've swapped sides.

Michael's attack seems to have awoken Ferenc from his stupor, or stupidity, and now he's in as deep an en garde as his ailing body will allow, his blade held steady.

They're close, so close. Beat attacks, counter-attacks, each man sizing up the other, trying to find enough space through which to take the blade or around which to go. Ferenc engages Michael's blade, tries to push it to the side. Comes in with a lunge and disengages as he attacks. He fools Michael, whose parry sixte goes astray, but Michael adds a jump back to the parry, so he manages to avoid the blade that's thrust at him, but only just. Inches, that's all.

More toing and froing. A lot of blade engagement. A lot of beats and near attacks. But neither man's able to gain the advantage; there's too much on the line. Whatever confidence they manage to exude, they understand the danger they're in.

Michael catches Ferenc's blade with a parry octave when he attacks low. Ferenc disengages then brings the blade high up, attempts a cut over to hit Michael on the centre of the head. Michael has only a fraction of a second to lift his blade, parry quinte, and he manages to catch the blade before it slices into his skull. Then he feels Ferenc's foot in his stomach. He envelopes forwards, bent, and Ferenc smashes the side of Michael's face with the blade's guard. Michael's cheek splits open and he goes down. Ferenc stamps on his leg. Michael shouts out in pain and frustration.

Ferenc is hovering above him, looking down, beaming. As Michael manages to get to his knees, he receives a kick in the ribs. He falls back onto the ground. Ferenc allows him the time to try to get up again. As Michael struggles to his knees, Ferenc kicks him in the face, connecting with the chin and jaw. Michael flies back and lands heavily, hitting his head on the ground.

Ferenc laughs. 'A brutal game,' he says. 'I told you, you didn't beat me. You *can't* beat me.' He leans and punches Michael in the ribs as Michael lies on the ground on his side. Michael clutches at his body, releasing the blade. Ferenc kicks it away.

The Hungarian helps Michael up, struggles to do so, clutching at his own hip, Michael's bodyweight almost pulling him to the ground. Michael's eyes are half shut. Both their faces are seeped in sweat, but Michael's is mixed with blood. Ferenc manages to pull Michael to his feet and drives him, keeping hold of his shirt, into the wall. Michael's back collides with the concrete, but Ferenc doesn't let go. He holds him as steadily as he can and punches him in the face. And again. Then in the stomach. Then one more punch.

There's a noise in the gym. A noise not made by either of them. A gasp. Then heavy breathing. Michael barely realises it. Instead, he sinks to the ground.

'It's over,' Ferenc says.

He drags Michael to his feet, presses him against the wall, then takes the blade, in his right hand, all the way back, bow-and-arrow-like. It's aimed at Michael's throat. 'For my mother. *For Iza Topa.*'

Michael is slouched against the wall, with nowhere to go. His hands are fallen to his sides. He's lost.

There's noise. Somewhere else in the gym. Something in the background. Breathing, gasping that sounds like wind blowing.

Ferenc's arm pulls back even further, so far it's

unimaginable an arm could extend that far. It's going to be shot at full force. The blade's likely to go right through Michael's face.

As Michael's arms dangle by his side and as he sways loosely on his feet, ready to fall into a heap, his right hand connects with his trouser pocket. And what's in it. The lapel pin. The one shaped like a fencer that Tibor gave him. It's still there.

With only the slightest sense of what he's doing – and with almost no time left in which to do it – Michael removes the pin from his pocket. Ferenc looks back at his ready blade, in admiration. There's a huge smirk on his face. He's about to bring the blade sluicing into Michael. He turns towards his target to finalise the aim.

The pin clasped in his hand, the sharp, thin blade protruding between his fingers, Michael lifts his arm and presses the pin into Ferenc's eye. He's not able to use much force, but the eye is soft enough for it to pierce with ease. Right into his eyeball.

'No!' It's a distant cry, one Michael doesn't really distinguish.

Ferenc cries out in pain, dropping his blade and doubling over, grabbing his upper face. Still leaning against the wall, Michael lifts his leg as hard as he can, mustering as much force as he can in the condition he's in. His foot connects with Ferenc's face and he topples over. Michael pushes himself off the wall, drops to his knees. He lifts up Ferenc's blade, twists his body halfway to the right and, as Ferenc is back up and stumbling towards him, he spins round, the blade cutting through Ferenc's T-shirt and entering his sternum. He drops forwards. For a moment, his body sits on the blade, inverted. Their eyes meet. The Hungarian's eyes say a lot; Michael's say little but pleading.

'Tell me where he is.'

Ferenc spits in Michael's face.

Michael whispers, 'I beat you.' Then letting go of the blade, he pushes Ferenc's body, which tumbles backwards to the ground. He lies, looking up at the ceiling, the blade perched like a flag marking a point of discovery.

Chapter Fifty-Three

Three more times, Gizi has tried to ring Michael. Each time, he hasn't noticed the vibrations in his jacket pocket.

On the third attempt, she says, 'Michael, I know who it is. Ferenc is Iza Topa's illegitimate son. I've just checked. The newspaper report didn't mention him. No one knew about him. The family must have kept him secret because of the shame it would have brought on them. But I cross-referenced with the birth records. She had a son. But Michael, there's more to it than that. He moved to the Lake Balaton area and, when he was twenty, he legally changed his surname. He changed it to Polcz.'

Chapter Fifty-Four

On his hands and knees, Michael gradually begins to recognise where the other sounds are coming from. The left-hand side. He turns his head. Coming towards him, tears filling his eyes, is a man. Michael doesn't recognise the man. But the man has in front of him Michael's father. József Varga's hands are taped behind his back, his mouth is taped shut, his face is blackened and bruised, and he's being edged towards Michael. He's resisting, which is slowing the man's progress.

'Don't move,' the man says in a strongly accented voice.

Michael doesn't know if the stranger has got a weapon, but he has a hand behind József's back, so Michael complies.

'You killed my boy,' he says. Tears are still streaming down his face, but there are no sobs, no sounds, he appears unmoved in all other ways. 'Now you can watch me kill your father. Watch the great József Varga die. Once and for all. The man who so many years ago destroyed my fencing hopes and then destroyed my life's hopes when he took the woman I loved from me.'

'László.' A man too familiar with tragedy. A man with few white hairs remaining, a face full of lines, a stooping of the shoulders, who life has not treated well. The man who, at the height of his fencing career, József Varga defeated and who subsequently went off the rails. The man who, after Iza Topa died, found a way to hide away and recover from his addictions, who found a way into the heart of her child, who then found a way to fester in that child, teenager, adult, a hatred so deep he would help him do anything to destroy the cause of all their ills. A man who has waited all these years, patiently, for revenge.

With speed befitting a man much younger, to Michael's surprise, László moves fully behind József, his arms a pincer around his adversary's neck, squeezing. For a moment, Michael thinks about lunging forwards to tackle László, but something stops him. It might be the fear that he thinks he spots in his father's eyes, a sight alien, something that comes across like a sickness in a man who has never been ill in his life.

He's showing fear because he's dying, because he knows it.

The air's escaping him, being forced out. László is strangling him. His eyes are bloodshot, his body's writhing, his hands are calling for Michael, but his eyes are telling a different story. They're saying, *Wait*. It's a signal. Like his father's at the end of the piste, guiding him. Michael sees it, understands it. He wants to nod, doesn't. Then the eyes get wider, telling him that this is the moment.

With his last possible breath, József pushes his head forwards, then springs it backwards. It collides with László's face. His nose smashes, blood erupting, sinew destroyed. His grip of József is released. József drops to the floor. Michael, holding the snapped blade like a spear, charges forwards, the blade in his arm wound back, and he flings it forwards, like a javelin Olympian. The blade glides through the air. As László straightens up, his hand holding the mushy cartilage on his face, the blade drives through his neck. It only comes to a stop when the guard hits László's jaw. He remains frozen on the spot for a split second, his eyes wide, locked on Michael, shocked, and then he plummets, landing on his knees. His body topples to the side and he lands on his back.

Michael dashes to his father, tears off the masking tape that's on his face, then breaks the tape that's imprisoning his hands. József gasps for air but quickly manages to steady his breathing.

'Are you all right?'

His father, on the floor, stares up at him. 'I've been better.'

'Don't move. Stay there. I'll call for help.'

Gurgling noises. The sound of the wind coming from László's mouth, or neck. Michael's attention is caught by it. József realises. 'He's still alive?'

Michael nods.

'Help me up.'

'You shouldn't move until a medic –'

Deliberately, without question, and one word at a time: '*Help… me… up.*'

Michael offers a hand, but when it isn't helpful enough, he lifts his father up by the shoulders. József Varga stumbles to his feet, has difficulty remaining there. Suddenly, he's aged, an aged man, not the man Michael knows, and Michael feels sorry for him, for this is a prelude of what, perhaps, is to come as old age takes a firmer hold.

József Varga clears his chest and staggers the few feet to where László lies on the floor, immobile, save his exaggerated breathing. His chest is lifting up and sinking down in short staccato movements, as if there's a miniature creature inside him trying to punch its way out. Or dig.

Bent to one side, József Varga stands over László. One eye is nearly swollen shut; the other is moist. They see each other, properly, for the first time in almost fifty years. József speaks, the softest of sounds coming out. 'Te meghalsz én élni fogok. Ahogyan a pástom, amikor te vesztettél, én győztem. De hidd el nekem, bánt Iza halálának az éjszakája, mindaddig, amig élek. Ahogy te sem, én sem leszek túl rajta. Tele volt élettel és ezt én vettem el tőle. Mindez az én hibám. Megértelek és nem hibáztatlak. Egyáltalán nem tudlak hibáztatni.'

László tries to speak but isn't able to. But he does manage to speak with his eyes. Michael sees it and, although he doesn't understand a word his father has said, the clarity he gets from László's helpless, pitiful eyes couldn't be clearer. József sees it too and nods.

Still in Hungarian: 'Egész életemben bánni fogom, hogy nem kértem tőled bocsánatot. Így most kérlek, bocsáss meg.' Then to himself: 'A lifetime of regrets.'

László, through immense pain, nods slowly.

'Aludj jól testvérem.'

József lifts his leg, places it on the side of the blade, underneath the guard, closes his eyes, as does László, and he presses down with the full force of his bodyweight so that the blade careers sideways down to the ground. László's neck is cut open, his larynx crushed. His eyes remain closed. József falls to his knees, his eyes remaining shut.

'Sleep well, my brother,' he repeats. Tears from his open eyes fall to the ground. He sobs. Sobs like a baby, uncontrollably. He is a different person, one Michael has never met. Michael feels helpless, wants to hug the man who's on his knees only feet away, wants to kiss his head, wants to tell him it's okay, but he can't. Because the man in front of him is József Varga.

Regardless, the pity is immense. Michael lowers himself to his knees next to his father, pats him softly, repeatedly, on the back. 'It's okay,' he manages to say, quietly. Soothing, he hopes. 'It's okay.' And he repeats it, how many times he'll never know.

József Varga's sobbing doesn't subside. Not for a long time.

Chapter Fifty-Five

There was a knock at the door. A shadow approached from the inside. Opened it.

József Varga appeared in the doorway. Michael Varga was on the doorstep. 'Good to see you,' father said to son. He stepped aside and Michael came in.

'How are you keeping? The eye looks better?' It had almost healed.

'I'll live.' He led Michael to the dining room.

Lamp lit, complete darkness outside. In the middle of the table sat a whisky bottle, two glasses by its side. 'Drink?'

Michael asked, 'Is the Pope Catholic?'

József motioned for Michael to take a seat. He did so at one end of the table, placing his wallet and some papers to one side. József poured them a glass each, took Michael his, and went to sit down at the other end of the table.

The two men sat facing each other, a glass in front of each pair of hands. A moment of silence.

'Well,' József said. 'Cheers.'

'Egészségedre.'

'Egészségedre.'

They savoured the taste for a moment. József closed his eyes, the same eyes Michael saw closed a week ago, under very different circumstances.

'Good day?'

'Not bad. Just been with Ricky. Julianne finally agreed to let me see him on my own. Must be all those nice things the press have been writing about me.' *I must make an effort with Ricky. I will make an effort. It won't be like this.*

'Well, they say every cloud…'

'Indeed.'

'What are those?' József asked, indicating the papers on the table.

'Airline ticket. When I leave here, I'm going back to Budapest. A week off. I've got some catching up to do.'

'A lady?'

Michael thought about Gizi. And then about Sally. Conflicted; he was always that way. 'Maybe.'

József laughed. 'Like father, like son.'

Michael shrugged. 'Maybe.'

'So…'

'Everything's sorted. Everything's fine.'

'Thank you.'

'No need to thank me. I said I'd sort everything.'

'Not for that.' József Varga, who was just starting to look like himself again, decided to act in a way quite unlike himself. In fact, he'd been waiting to act like this for the past seven days. 'For helping me. And then for saving me. I have a life left to live because of you.'

'You're my father.'

'And I'm glad I am.'

Another moment. Michael felt some sort of recognition come from his father. It was almost pleasing. 'Me too.' He raised the glass in the air. 'To you.'

'No, Michael.' The glass raised in the air. 'To you. Egészségedre.'

'Cheers.'

They both polished off the whisky in their glasses.

'Just one thing,' Michael said. He wanted to ask, hadn't known until this very moment if he'd be able to muster the words. 'Before you… Before he died, what did you say to him?'

József put his elbows on the table, made a cup of his hands and placed his chin in it. He closed his eyes again, this time leaving them shut. 'In short,' he explained, 'I told him I was sorry, that I have regretted the night Iza died every day of my life. That, like him, I have never got over it. You see, she was so full of life, and I took it away from her. I acknowledged to him that it was *my* fault. And I told him I don't blame him. I can't blame him, even now. And I apologised.'

'You think he loved her?'

'He must have known her well if he was so able to become part of her son's life and, in that case, he must have had feelings for her. We'll never know now, but this couldn't have only been about fencing.'

Michael lifted his eyebrows. 'Really?'

József's eyes focused on the air that filled the space between him and his son. 'I think. Surely.' And he said no more for a time. 'I *am* sorry, Michael, more than you could ever know. You know that?'

Michael nodded his head.

'I truly am.'

Michael nodded again. His nod said *good*, but he didn't. He glanced at his watch. 'Okay, I must be going. Got to get that flight.'

Both men stood up and moved. They met next to the middle of the table. József offered his hand. Michael took it. They shook, firmly. And not a quick handshake. Then Michael drew his father into a hug, patted him on the back. Not a long hug, not a close hug, but a more definite one than they'd shared for a long, long time, and with more meaning. With feeling. József Varga patted back.

'Safe flight,' he said, and they came apart.

'Thanks.' Michael moved towards the front door.

'Just one thing, Michael.' Michael stopped as he put his hand on the door handle and turned around. 'Remember to behave when you're out there.'

Michael thought about answering but didn't.

'And don't be a playboy.'

Acknowledgements

My thanks to the 60,000 readers who gave an unknown writer a chance and, as a consequence, made my last offering, *The Missing*, a bestseller. Writing it was a challenging and very often frustrating journey and, therefore, it is even more gratifying that so many readers chose it and enjoyed it. You ultimately made it a delightful journey.

Sincere thanks also to the numerous authors who have read and supported my fiction writing over the past few years: Sophie Hannah, Matt Hilton, James Becker, Patrick Lennon, Thomas Perry, Karen Campbell, Robert Ellis, Cathy Kelly, Glenn Cooper, C.M. Palov, Elly Griffiths, Quentin Bates, Scott Phillips, Damien Lewis and Adrian Magson.

Sins of the Father, like *The Missing*, endured a long journey of rewrites to reach you in its current, much more appealing shape. Particular thanks here must go to my agent, Sonia Land, whose guidance and high standards have made me a better writer and the books better than I ever thought possible. Thanks also go to her wonderful team at Sheil Land Associates.

A special thank you to Tomek Walicki of Salle Boston Fencing Club and Jonathan Weekes for allowing and arranging the photography that resulted in this novel's front cover.

About the Author

After studying literature, linguistics and Spanish at university, Karl Vadaszffy trained as an English teacher and actor. He has edited magazines, taught English as a foreign language in Poland and taught English, Media Studies and Drama in secondary schools in England.

Working in schools in Hertfordshire, UK, he became Head of Year when he was only 25 and a Head of English at 26. He is currently the Head of English, Drama and Media Studies at an Ofsted outstanding-rated Catholic school in Hertfordshire.

Karl currently juggles his teaching responsibilities with work as a freelance journalist. His articles regularly appear in ten industry-leading magazines that cover the automotive, aerospace, technology and travel sectors. His articles are read by over 12,000 subscribers in print, and more online. While in a previous teaching role, Karl established The Astley Cooper School's author visits programme, which saw a number of authors, many internationally bestselling, visit the school to give talks, sign books and host workshops. These included Frederick Forsyth, Jodi Picoult, Sophie Hannah, Peter James, Darren Shan, Joanne Harris, Michael Marshall, Deborah Moggach and Elizabeth Buchan. The programme ran for three successful years until he left the school. Karl was a competitive fencer for seven years. Fencing is in his blood; his father was Hungarian Foil Champion and three-time British Epee Champion, coached the under-21s British Olympic foil team and was the personal coach of Bruce Dickinson, lead singer of Iron Maiden, for almost thirty years. He also coached actors, including Ralph Fiennes and Robson Green, to prepare them for screen roles.

Similarly, Karl's passion for drama was inherited from his father, who also trained as an actor. Zsolt Vadaszffy trained at RADA before having a successful film and television career in the 1960s, working with actors such as Michael Caine, Sean Connery, Anthony Hopkins and Alec Guinness. Karl followed in his father's footsteps by training at the London Centre for Theatre Studies.

Visit Karl's website: karlvad.com or follow him on Twitter: @KarlVad